TRADED

rebecca brooke

Copyright © 2015 by Rebecca Brooke

Cover Design by Sommer Stein of Perfect Pear Creative

Editing by Ryn Hughes of Delphi Rose

All rights reserved. No part of this book may be reproduced or transmitted in any form or by any means, electronic or mechanical, including photocopying, recording, or by any information storage and retrieval system, without permission in writing.

This is a work of fiction. Names, characters, places, and incidents are the product of the author's imagination or are used factiously, and any resemblance to any actual person, living or dead, events, or locales is entirely coincidental.

The author acknowledges the trademarked status and trademark owners of various products referenced in this work of fiction, which have been used without permission. The publication/use of these trademarks is not authorized, associated with, or sponsored by the trademark owner.

All rights reserved.

DEDICATION

To anyone who has ever thought they couldn't do better. You can. Don't be afraid to go after your dreams.

TABLE OF CONTENTS

Chapter 1
Chapter 2
Chapter 3
Chapter 4
Chapter 5
Chapter 6
Chapter 7
Chapter 8
Chapter 9
Chapter 10
Chapter 11
Chapter 12
Chapter 13
Chapter 14
Chapter 15
Chapter 16
Chapter 17
Chapter 18
Chapter 19
Chapter 20
Chapter 21
Chapter 22
Chapter 23
Chapter 24
Chapter 25
Chapter 26
Chapter 27

Chapter 28
Chapter 29
Chapter 30
Epilogue
Acknowledgments
Other Books
About the Author

She stood in the storm, and when the wind did not blow her away, she adjusted her sails.

~Elizabeth Edwards

CHAPTER 1

Elena

"What the fuck you looking at?"

The acid in his voice made me drop my eyes to the floor.

I should have made something else for dinner.

"I'm sorry, would you like me to make you something else?" I said, my voice barely above a whisper so I didn't hurt his ears.

"No," he snapped. "Since you can't make a decent dinner, I'm going to skip to dessert. Hurry up and get your ass in the bedroom so I don't miss the game."

Afraid to disappoint him again, I jumped from the table and began unbuttoning my top as I made my way down the hall. The bedroom was dark, with only minimal light coming from the kitchen and the hall—exactly the way Dominic preferred. He said it was the only way he could enjoy himself. If he had to look at me it ruined his fantasies of having a gorgeous woman beneath him. He also didn't appreciate me talking or touching him.

Letting my uniform dress and underwear drop to the floor, I took my normal position on the bed—lying on my back, arms at my side, legs spread as wide as they could go—and waited for Dominic to join me. After a few minutes he came through the door, shedding his clothes on the way. He grabbed the lube off the table next to the bed and gave himself a few quick strokes before climbing on top of me. With one painful thrust he entered me and I bit the inside of my cheek to hide my wince. Anything to help him enjoy the experience.

Over and over he thrust into me, groaning the closer he came to reaching his climax. Grunting, he pulsed inside and pulled out, letting his come dribble down my legs and onto the sheets before he rolled off me, picked up his boxers and pulled them on.

"I need to go watch the game. Make sure you wash the sheets before bed." And out of the room he went.

Taking deep breaths, I tried to hold back the tears, all the while reminding myself that Dominic took care of me. He was the man of the house. I had to do everything in my power to keep him happy. I couldn't afford, physically or emotionally, to lose him. Once I had myself under control, I stood, wiping myself with the sheets and looking for something to throw on to start the laundry. Folded neatly on the table at the end of the bed was a pair of shorts and a T-shirt. Pulling on the clothes, I stripped the bed and walked back down the hall as the sounds of the baseball game flowed into the kitchen from the living room.

I didn't want to disturb him by doing the dishes, so I quietly grabbed the laundry detergent and keys to the basement and left the apartment. The sheets would take about half an hour, enough time to get a quick shower and get back. Starting the machine, I went back upstairs. Dominic was standing in the kitchen, in front of the fridge.

"How many times do I need to tell you that no one wants to see your pasty white legs? Put on a pair of pants, for all of our sakes." Shaking his head, he grabbed a beer and went back to the game.

"I forgot, I'm sorry. I'll change after my shower."

The minute he left the room, I sprinted to the bathroom, shutting the door and leaning against it, my body sliding to the floor. My eyes burned. If I just followed his directions then there would be no reason to get upset when he said things to me. I wiped furiously at my face and pulled myself off the floor, showering in record time.

Remembering what Dominic said, I put on a pair of yoga pants and a T-shirt to head back down to the laundry, throwing the sheets in the dryer, then coming back upstairs to clean up the kitchen. Collecting the plates of chicken, I carried them to the trashcan and began scraping them off.

TRADED

"Would you keep it down in there? I'm trying to hear the TV," Dominic yelled. "Can't do anything quiet, can you?"

"Sorry. I didn't mean to be so loud. I'll do my best to be quieter."

I finished cleaning up, tiptoeing around, trying to make as little noise as possible. I'd just finished when the timer I'd set for the sheets went off and I hurried down to the basement. There was very little time left in the game. Dominic would want to go right to bed when it finished. He worked long hours and deserved to get as much sleep as he could. His job provided for us.

As quickly as I could, I made the bed. Cheering sounds reached me in the bedroom and I knew that meant the game was over. My hands shook waiting for Dominic to come in the bedroom. Would he approve of the job I'd done? Quietly, I sat on the end of the bed and waited for him, wanting to make sure there wasn't anything else I could do for him before he went to sleep.

Dominic walked through the door, his eyes zeroing in on the bed. "The sheets are wrinkled. You'll need to iron them tomorrow. Right now, I'm too tired."

My heart sank. I'd tried so hard to get it right that time. Standing, I stepped toward the door and nodded. "I'll take care of it as soon as I get home from work," I said, my voice shaky.

He pulled the sheets back and crawled into bed. "Did you make my lunch yet?"

My eyes dropped to the floor. "Not yet. I wanted to make sure the sheets were ready when you came to bed."

He turned on his side, his back to me.

"I'm going to do it right now, while you sleep."

"Good. And none of that shit you tried to feed me for dinner."

I watched him lying in bed, wishing that for once he wanted me with him. "No, of course not."

Stepping out of the room, I shut out the lights and closed the door, moving quietly to the kitchen, giving him time to fall asleep before I went to bed, otherwise I would disturb him with all of my tossing and turning. I made him a sandwich for lunch and packed his cooler. That way, he could grab it on his way out the door in the morning and he wouldn't be late to the office. I gave the room one last scan; satisfied everything had been done to Dominic's standards.

The clock on the oven flashed. It was after eleven; he should be asleep. Flipping off the lights and TV, I snuck into the bedroom, silently changing into pajamas and setting the alarm on my phone for four in the morning. Slowly and carefully, I climbed into bed. Dominic should have already set his alarm for eight, but I would double-check it in the morning before I left for work. With the long days at the diner, then coming home to take care of the household, the eighteen hour days caught up to me quickly. Once my head hit the pillow, it didn't take long for me to fall into a deep sleep.

৩৩৩

TRADED

It felt like I'd only just closed my eyes when the vibration of my phone pulled me from sleep. The sun hadn't yet risen but if I didn't get up right away, I'd be late getting into work and with so many customers coming in early, grabbing breakfast before their day started, I couldn't afford to be late. Creeping out of bed so as not to wake up Dominic, I took a clean uniform from the closet and tiptoed, in the dark, to the bathroom, waiting until the door was closed to turn on the light.

I was dressed and ready to walk out the door in less than twenty minutes, which gave me a little more than ten minutes to walk to work. Thankfully, the diner was only a few blocks away and I could make it there in five on foot if I didn't dawdle, so I used the extra time to double-check Dominic's lunch and coffee.

When I was sure everything was ready, I grabbed my purse and stepped out the door.

The humidity had risen throughout the night, something I hadn't noticed with the air conditioning on but now, even at this early hour, the heat felt almost overpowering. Fanning myself with my hand, I made the trip quickly and clocked in for the day.

"Morning, Elena," Gretchen called from behind the counter.

"Morning. Let me put my purse in the back and I'll be right there."

She walked over to take an order and I stepped out to hang my purse on the hook in the back. Grabbing an apron and tying it around my waist, I loaded my notepad and pen into the front pocket, hurrying behind the counter.

"Who's not taken care of yet?"

Gretchen pointed to the row of customers. "Everyone up here, but there's a table in the back I think might be ready to order."

We didn't have a hostess to help us, and since we were the only two who did the early morning breakfast shift during the week, we took whatever tables needed help and split the tips down the middle. It was easier than figuring out who should take what table. Once I'd taken and entered the order from the back table, I went back to wait with Gretchen, who'd already served their drinks.

"Did you give him any money last night?"

I sighed. "No. Dominic stayed home last night."

"Yeah and let me guess—treated you like shit the whole time," she snapped.

Gretchen and I were never going to see eye to eye on this. It was an old argument. She didn't understand that I needed Dominic. He loved me. My eyes began to blur. Turning my face away, I tried to hide the tears.

"Oh, Elena." Gretchen dropped the empty cup and pulled me into a hug. "I'm sorry. I didn't mean to make you cry. I wish you could see how wonderful you are, and that you deserve so much better than him."

Stepping out of her embrace, I shook my head and wiped at my face. "No. He's the only man who has ever, or will ever want me. I'm not pretty like you. I'm just so plain."

Gretchen had long blonde hair and crystal green eyes, not to mention a new date every weekend. I'd had one boyfriend in high school, and I'd married him.

Her hands landed on my shoulders. "You're not, but until you see that, you're stuck with him. Please don't give him any money to gamble again."

I let the subject drop. It wasn't worth the argument. I knew full well if Dominic asked me for money, I'd give it to him. What Gretchen didn't realize was that with every suggestion, he was only trying to improve my appearance, or the way people looked at me. All of it was to help me. Dominic would never do anything to hurt me.

CHAPTER 2

Elena

After our disagreement, the shift went quickly; odd, considering it was my twelve-hour day. Gretchen apologized later, which I accepted, and at clock out time, I waved a quick good-bye on my way out of the door. She lifted her chin in response, knowing I couldn't stop because I needed to get home and get dinner ready for Dominic. It wouldn't do to have Dominic come home from work and be disappointed in me. Speed walking down the block, I made it home quickly, thankful I'd thought to marinate the chicken last night before I went to bed. Paired with a side dish and a vegetable, it made for the perfect dish, and would definitely be done in time.

I was just setting the table when Dominic walked through the door. "Fucking chicken, again," he said, his tone cutting. "It better not taste like shit."

TRADED

He dumped his stuff by the door and sat down at the table. I cast a sideways glance, making a mental note to tidy it all away once I finished cleaning up from dinner. We ate in silence, Dominic spending the entire time on his phone. At least he liked it. He finished everything on his plate. Dropping his fork, he stood.

"Finally, something edible. Now that you've shown, after all this time, you can cook, make sure it all tastes good."

He left the kitchen and I set to work. My goal was to make sure the kitchen was spotless by the time he came back out to watch TV and, hearing the squeak of the showerhead, I knew I had about ten minutes. In that time, I wiped off the table and loaded the dishwasher. Dominic came out dressed ready to go out. His dark brown hair was wet, making it match the color of his eyes. At five foot nine, he had about six inches on me. He watched me and for one small moment I hoped the points I'd earned at dinner were enough for him to take me with him.

"Where are your tips?"

Dropping my shoulders, I reached into the pocket of my uniform and pulled out the sixty dollars I'd earned, handing it over to him. Whether Gretchen liked it or not, we were married and whatever was mine was his.

He grabbed the money from my hand and counted it. "This is it? Jesus, you can't even earn a decent amount delivering food to tables." He shoved his phone and the money into his pocket. "It'll have to do. Make sure my lunch is made for tomorrow."

Without another word, he walked out the door. My throat burned in an attempt to hold back the tears. I did as he said and made his lunch, followed by a quick shower. Dominic was out, meaning I didn't need to wait for him to fall asleep, so I went to bed early. Exhausted, I climbed under the sheets and let sleep take me.

The bed dipped down, letting me know that Dominic had made it home from his night out. A quick peek at the clock told me it was after three in the morning. I had about another hour before the alarm went off. I attempted to go back to sleep, but Dominic's constant tossing and turning kept me awake. Eventually, the alarm sounded on my phone and I got up for the day.

Whether or not Dominic had gone to sleep or not, I didn't know, but by the time I got home from my shift, he was gone. And I'd finished early. Gretchen was off for the day and I saw no reason to hang around and talk.

A few hours later, dinner was on the table and ready but Dominic still wasn't home. I called his phone. No answer. Knowing it would be bad manners to start eating without him I waited. And waited.

Over an hour later, he showed up.

"Elena, where the fuck are you?" he yelled, slamming the front door.

"In the kitchen, waiting for you." I didn't want him to think I'd started without him, or done nothing all day. I sat stoically at the table, hoping he would notice how clean the living room was on his way through.

He came storming into the kitchen. "Go get changed into something . . . nicer. Not sure you have anything, but try. And pack an overnight bag."

Excitement flooded my body to the point where my hands shook. Listening and following Dominic's instructions had finally paid off. He was taking me out. Digging through my closet I found an older dress that would be perfect, no matter where we went. Who cared about dinner? I'd deal with the mess later.

I hurried to pack my bag, not giving him the chance to change his mind. When I stepped out in the hall, he raked me over with his eyes.

"I guess that'll have to do. Let's go."

Taking my arm he led me out to the car.

"Where are we going?" I was practically bouncing in my seat with excitement.

"Don't worry about it. You'll see when we get there," he snapped.

The almost imperceptible shaking of Dominic's hands caught my attention. He was nervous, something I'd never seen from him—even when we'd woken up married after a long night in Vegas. How much had changed since then.

We pulled into the lot of the baseball stadium. Excitement tore through me. Baseball was Dominic's favorite sport and the fact he invited me to come see the game with him meant so much.

"You brought me to a game." It was hard to keep the glee from my tone but I tried. I didn't want him to change his mind or regret his decision, thinking I couldn't behave.

"Just shut your mouth and do as I say." He got out of the car and waited at the front for me to get out. I opened the door. "Grab your bag."

I wanted to ask what I needed an overnight bag for but I'd already upset him enough. Quietly, I climbed from the car and followed him to the Will Call, where he checked in and strode to the elevators. Gripping the handles of my bag, I walked quickly to keep up, following him as we made a right down a hall where there was no access to seating. In front of us were about ten doors.

The club box section? How had he afforded this?

At the next to last door, Dominic knocked and waited. The silence was heavy, and I got a feeling in my gut that told me this evening wasn't going to turn out the way I'd thought. I chanced a glance at Dominic using just my eyes, careful to keep my head lowered to the floor. His skin was void of all color. It sounded a stupid thing to say, but it was true. More often than not, his cheeks were reddened from alcohol, so to see him like this made me even more nervous. His hands fidgeted at his sides, and he bounced up and down on the balls of his feet. There was a noise on the other side of the door and he froze. After a few seconds, the door swung open to reveal a guy you'd expect to see sitting outside a club checking IDs, bouncing the idiots who didn't belong. His gray T-shirt was extremely tight, stretched across muscles so large I knew the guy either took steroids or lived in a gym.

"Don't stand there and hold the door open. Come in or leave."

TRADED

My attention was drawn to a man, sitting alone in the middle of the room. I drew in a deep breath and my lungs burned. It was like the air in here was different – thinner. Goose bumps erupted all over my body, even though the temperature was no different. I told myself I was being silly, but I'd always had the innate ability to sense danger. It was something that had likely saved me a few times with Dominic. I was always able to tell when his mood was worse than normal, ensuring I was even more careful. And with the feeling that had made its way from burning lungs to the base of my spine and was currently wrapping around my chest, making it difficult to breathe, I knew without a doubt that the man was no saint.

Dominic pushed me from behind, forcing me into the room. I looked back at him but he said nothing to explain what was going on. He grabbed my arm and pulled me forward.

"I hope the bag she's carrying means you brought my fucking money," the guy in the chair said and for the first time, I got a good look at him. His hair was a deep honey blond, the thin black-framed glasses perched on his nose contrasting nicely with his green eyes; shrewd eyes, trained on my husband.

Dominic raised his hands. "Ashton, hear me out for a moment."

"I'll take that as a sign you don't have the rest of my money yet," the man drawled, his words slow and drawn out.

The hair on the back of my neck prickled and I felt a presence behind me. Taking a quick peek over my shoulder, I saw that the huge, scary guy from earlier now stood directly behind Dominic. His eyes were narrowed, his muscular arms crossed over his chest.

"Give him a chance to explain, Brock," Ashton said, lifting a glass of amber liquid to his lips. "I don't think the asshole is stupid enough to come here without my money and not have another plan. Did you, Dominic?"

"No . . . ah, no . . . of course not. I do have something to offer you." Dominic's voice shook with every word. My gut screamed at me that something was very wrong. I folded my hands behind my back; afraid Dominic would see and reprimand me.

What money could this guy possibly be talking about? I knew we had credit card debt, but exactly how much, I didn't know. Dominic took care of all of the bills. Said he didn't want me to make mistakes.

I stumbled as Dominic pushed me from behind, my shoes catching on the carpet beneath my feet. "I've brought a trade."

Ashton laughed, but nothing about the sound felt friendly. "A *trade?* What could you possibly have to give me that I don't already have, or can't get with the money you owe me?"

"My wife."

My head snapped in Dominic's direction. I couldn't have heard him right. There was no way he'd trade me. I might make a few mistakes here and there, but I was a good wife. I took care of all of his needs and desires—or at least I tried to. I wasn't as skinny as he would like, or as pretty, but I tried to make up for it in other areas.

TRADED

Ashton removed his glasses and rubbed his eyes with his thumb and forefinger. "Your wife. Are you fucking kidding me?" He looked back up, replacing his glasses.

There I stood, in front of a man I had never met, watching my husband for guidance about what the heck was happening.

"Don't be dense, Elena. Turn around so he can see you. This is a matter of life or death. You *need* to save me," Dominic hissed.

Searching his eyes, I could see the fear, so I made a slow circle around, unsure of what else to do.

"What the fuck, Dominic? You come in here, owing me two hundred thousand dollars, and you want me to take your wife in lieu of payment?"

Two hundred thousand.

Everything in my stomach wanted to come back up. How were we ever going to pay back that kind of money? My chest constricted. It felt like I couldn't breathe.

"Yes and no. I'm offering a trade." He shoved me forward. "Elena will be yours to do with as you please for the next three months. After that my debt will be paid. Plus, I gave you fifty grand yesterday."

"That's splitting hairs and you fucking know it. Shit, that's only a quarter of what you owe."

"I know, but I have no way to get you the money. It would take me forever to pay you off. I figure this is easier and faster. She's not very bright, but she'll do anything you want her to in the bedroom. I have her trained. You don't even have to take care of her. Get what you want and go to bed."

The hot sting of tears burned my eyes. My husband, whom I tried to please above all others, wanted to trade me to pay off his debts. The rational part of me had a feeling that if I didn't go along with it, something really bad would happen to Dominic. I alone had the power to stop it.

And I would.

CHAPTER 3

Ashton

What the fuck?

All I wanted was to enjoy the game in peace in quiet. Instead, I'd entered the fucking twilight zone. I knew the moment I lent the asshole the money it was going to be problem. Never once in a million years did I believe he'd try and trade his wife to pay off that debt. Who the fuck does that?

My first reaction was to tell the dumb fuck to get the hell out of my face and give him twenty-four hours to come up with the rest. Then I saw the way he treated his wife. I might not have been the most upstanding citizen but that didn't mean I didn't have my own set of morals; one being that you never treated a woman the way Tolley just had. I couldn't even call him a man.

In my business, I often skirted the edges of right and wrong. It was the way things were. Yes, I'd been known to use violence as a means of getting what I wanted, but it was only ever as a last resort. The way this woman flinched when he spoke, like she'd been lashed with a whip, made it clear that this was not an isolated incident.

I looked her over. She was pretty, and had the potential to be a knockout if treated right. Her hair was a deep shade of brown, the harsh lighting catching the red highlights, and her eyes were the deepest chocolate color, but she was thin, a little too thin in my opinion. Tolley, on the other hand, looked like he could stand to lose about twenty pounds.

There was no rhyme or reason as to why the words left my lips. I didn't need another person to take care of, especially someone as meek as she appeared to be, but the sight of tears rolling down her face was somewhat compelling. Someone had to save the poor woman.

"Here's the deal. She'll stay with me for the next three months." I heard her gasp, but continued. "During that time, *you're* going to find a way to come up with another hundred thousand dollars. If not, I come after you."

"Deal."

The words left the bastard's lips before I'd even finished. Fuck, the guy was unbelievable. What kind of man was he to give her up so easily? The woman tried to control her tears, but her shoulders continued to shake with sobs even as Dominic walked over to her.

"You better do whatever he says so he doesn't come after me. If he wants you to spread your legs every hour on the hour, you'll do it."

Blood roared through my ears listening to him talk to his wife that way. I waited for her to stand up to him, to say something, but she simply nodded, not a word leaving her mouth. Enough was enough.

"Dominic, get the fuck out of my sight before I let Brock here have a shot at you."

His eyes widened and he scrambled for the door, leaving one very scared woman in his wake. Brock watched him leave, then turned back to me. "What now?" he mouthed.

I waved my hand at him, giving him the signal to take a break, and seconds later the door closed quietly behind him. I walked over to the woman who had become my responsibility for the next three months.

How the fuck do I get myself into this shit?

Her eyes were downcast. I reached for the bag in her hand and the second my fingers brushed hers, she flinched. "Let me have your bag, then we'll get you something to eat."

Thankfully, we were in a club box and had a chef catering to our every whim, otherwise the poor girl would be stuck with ballpark food. Good, yes, but she'd had a rough enough day. She let the bag go and I set it on the ground next to the chair I'd been sitting in. I pulled another chair close. I didn't want her to think her only choice was to stand until we left.

I would have taken her home right then if I didn't have another client to meet with. It wasn't often that I dealt with two in one night, but I wanted more time in the restaurants and doubling up here made that easier. Besides, I had some arrangements to make. She didn't move, and remained rooted to the spot.

"Elena, wasn't it? Come and sit down."

When she still didn't move, I rested my hands lightly on her shoulders and waited to see her reaction. She flinched but didn't push my hands away and I guided her over to the second chair.

I didn't blame her for not trusting me. Even though I could only surmise as to what she'd been through, the grass on my side of the fence was no greener; of that I was certain. As much as I'd tried to steer clear of this life, it had claimed me—at least for the moment, and staying alive in this life meant becoming someone I didn't like. When I thought back on the things I'd had to do to make it, it made my stomach roll. And that was coming from someone who grew up the way I had, knowing the things I did. I was not a good guy. She was right to be wary. I would never hurt a woman, but she didn't know that. She was surviving the only way she knew how.

Just like me.

"Are you hungry?"

Finally she looked up, her big brown eyes haunted and shimmering. She shook her head. "No, thank you."

For most women, I would see that as them throwing a fit because they hadn't got their own way but from the small glimpse I'd had of the way Tolley treated Elena, I knew this was instinctive. She would respond to orders and directions. After tonight, we'd work on getting over that, but for now though I was willing to give in. It reminded me of the way my uncle had treated my aunt, at least until my dad got hold of him. No motherfucker was going to treat his sister that way. Dad raised my brother and I to respect women. He said men who didn't would get theirs. Seeing Uncle Dave in his wheelchair, a permanent fixture, was enough to convince me of this fact.

"Elena, I'm guessing this is not what you expected when you came here tonight. Hell, this isn't what I expected, but you need to eat. You're here for the next three months. You can't starve yourself until Dominic comes back for you."

"If you want me to eat, I'll eat."

Once again, she made it clear if I said jump, she'd answer how high. That shit was going to end, starting tomorrow. "I'll get you the menu."

"Menu?" For half a second she looked interested in something besides her own misery.

"Yes, menu. This is my personal club box. We have a chef to prepare meals outside of the normal ballpark food."

"I'll have whatever you're having."

I shook my head. "No. You'll pick what *you* want to eat."

The menu sat on the table next to my scotch. The fifth I'd poured was definitely not going to be enough. I handed her the menu and walked over to the bar. I didn't need a bartender to pour me a scotch on the rocks. The ballpark made sure to keep my favorite, Glen Livet, on hand. Pulling out the bottle, I watched Elena scan the menu like she wasn't sure what she was looking at.

"Would you like something to drink?" I gestured to the bar when she looked my way. "You name it, I have it."

"Oh, Dominic says I shouldn't drink. It makes me crazy."

"Well, Dominic's not here, and I don't think one drink is going to make you go wild and start dancing on tables. In fact, I'm pretty sure it'll help calm your nerves."

"If you think I should."

Permission again. *What the fuck did he do to her?* "I do. If you don't normally drink, how about a glass of wine?"

"Okay."

I grabbed a bottle of white wine from the cooler and poured a glass. Handing it to her, I looked at the menu in her lap. "Did you decide what you want to eat?"

"Whatever you're going to have is fine."

Elena's eyes hadn't moved from the floor since her piece of shit husband left. She was subservient and submissive; two things I liked from a woman, but only in the bedroom.

"Elena, when was the last time you ordered your own meal?"

Her head lifted. Her eyes were dazed. "Dominic doesn't take me to restaurants. He says I don't look nice enough to take out."

Fuck, it kept getting worse. While the dress she wore didn't fit her very well, she had an appealing face. First thing in the morning, I was going to get her set up with some new clothes, and some other appointments. I had a feeling the poor woman had never been pampered a day in her life. It struck me that the reason she sat before me was because her husband owed me money, yet I thought nothing of spending some on her.

I covered her hand with mine, but Elena snatched hers away and I sighed, pulling back.

"I'm not sure what your husband told you, but you are beautiful. And you can pick anything you want for dinner." Knowing that giving her permission might only get us so far, I picked up the menu and began to offer suggestions. "Do you prefer meat or fish?"

"I've never had fish that wasn't flounder."

"You've never had salmon?"

She shook her head.

"Okay then. Let's have you try something new. I'll have them send up a chicken dish as well, in case you don't like it."

"You don't have to do that. Whatever you get will be fine."

"Elena, it's not a problem. You've had a challenging day. Now take a sip of your wine. I'll order dinner."

I watched her bring the glass to her full lips. For a moment she stared at the liquid, tipping it up to take her first sip. Satisfied, I walked over to the phone that connected me directly with the concierge and placed our order.

She watched me place the order, her eyes growing bigger as I listed enough food for five people.

"Of course, Mr. Hawes. We'll have everything up there as soon as we can."

"Thank you, Robert."

Hanging up the phone, I returned to my seat and watched Elena for a few moments. She looked uncomfortable, awkwardly perched on the edge of the chair. I wanted to find a way to get her to relax. *So much for a peaceful night of baseball.*

"You didn't need to order all that food."

"Well, Brock and I need to eat too."

"Brock?" Her head snapped up, looking all around the room.

"Yes, Brock. He's imposing but I promise he won't hurt you."

"That's not what you told Dominic."

A little more forceful. Maybe there was hope for her after all. "Yes, but I couldn't listen to him spew more shit. Idiot has verbal diarrhea."

She looked out the front window and down onto the field. "He just wants me to be the best wife I can. I'm not very good at it."

"Don't think like that. Not many women would go along with what happened here tonight, but we can talk about that tomorrow. Have you ever seen a baseball game before?"

A small tear escaped from the corner of her eye. "Never."

"Then please, for tonight, sit back and enjoy. We can worry about everything else tomorrow."

She didn't say anything, but she did lean back in her seat, the glass of wine gripped tightly in her hand. Whatever her husband had put her through, there was a strong woman underneath. My guess: she'd hidden that person for so long that she'd forgotten how to stand up for herself.

When dinner arrived, her eyes rounded as the waiter pushed in the cart with the food. Her focus solely on that, she missed Brock returning to the box. He quietly took a seat at the bar, behind where she sat and once the waiter had placed our food on the tables in front of us, he took Brock his steak.

TRADED

Elena picked up her fork and speared a piece of salmon. Just like the wine earlier, she examined it before putting it in her mouth. It became evident that she liked it when she immediately went back for another bite. I barely tasted my steak. Watching her eat fascinated me.

"That was delicious." She dabbed at the corners of her mouth, placing her napkin on her plate.

"I'm glad you liked it."

There was another knock at the door. Taking two drops in one night was dangerous, but I was tired of giving up nights in the restaurant.

Derrick Reynolds walked in. Unlike Dominic, he had a confident swagger and a smirk on his face. The first thing I noticed was lack of bag. I dealt in cash. I'm not sure what he was thinking.

Leaning my arms on the chair, I regarded him, waiting for him to begin. He didn't speak, just crossed his arms over his chest.

That's the way it was going to be. Fine.

"Do you want to explain to me why, when you owe me one hundred and fifteen thousand dollars, you come here empty handed?"

He shrugged. "Why should I pay you back it's not like you're going to do anything about it?" He nodded towards Brock. "You need him to deal with your problems, and I'm pretty sure the two of us could work out a deal."

From the corner of my eye, I saw Elena stiffen in her chair. Brock moved, but I shook my head and he stopped.

"See what I mean. You need muscle to take care of shit for you." He called over his shoulder. "What do you say man, I give you half of what I owe in cash to let me walk away."

In a flash I was out of my seat, my fist connecting with Reynolds' face. He went down. I grabbed his wrist, rolling him over, wrenching his arm up around his back.

"Make no mistake, you piece of shit, I don't need *anyone* to deal with my problems. I can handle them all on my own. Brock is for when I don't want to handle them. But tonight, for you, I'll make a special exception."

His free hand sat flat on the floor, where he attempted to get enough purchase to throw me off. Taking advantage, I picked my foot up and slammed the heel of my shoe into the back of his hand. Bones crunched and the fucker shouted, only to have Brock shove a handkerchief in his mouth.

A gasp sounded behind me, but I ignored it.

I bent down to where he was lying. "Listen very closely. You are going to get out of my sight and work on getting me my money. You be back here in a week with one hundred and thirty thousand dollars, or a broken hand will be the least of your worries. Do I make myself clear?"

He nodded.

"Now Brock will escort you out and explain a few more things."

Standing, I turned to see Elena, eyes wide, her shaking hand covering her mouth. I thought about comforting her, but the reality was this was her life for the next three months. Not that I'd bring her with me again.

TRADED

Silence descended once again when she turned back to the game. Leaning back in the chair, I continued to watch her and as the end of the game grew closer, I saw signs of nervousness. At first, her knee bounced slightly, swiftly followed by her clenching the stem of her wine glass, her knuckles turning white with the force. I leaned across, gently taking the glass away so she wouldn't accidentally cut herself.

When the final out was made, Elena's eyes darted around the room like she was looking for an escape. When Brock spoke, she jumped in her chair.

"Mr. Hawes, I've already had the car brought around for you."

"Thank you, Brock. We're ready to go."

Elena reached for her bag, which obviously didn't have enough clothes for a week, much less three months, but Brock beat her to it.

"Let me, Mrs. Tolley."

She looked surprised that he knew her name.

I interjected. "I've dealt with your husband for many years. This just happens to be the first time he couldn't pay me back."

She sighed and it was a somber, resigned sound. "I guess that's why he always wanted my tip money."

I escorted her from the room and down the hall, toward the elevators. "Tip money?"

"Yeah, I'm a waitress in a diner downtown." She stopped dead in her tracks. "How am I going to get to work tomorrow?"

"You let me worry about that."

If anyone needed a break from working, it was Elena and for as long as she was in my care, I'd make sure she got it.

"But how can I help Dominic pay off the debt if I don't work?"

I turned her to face me. "Remember one thing, Elena. While it would give me great pleasure to send Brock over to your house right now to have a little chat with Dominic, I won't, for your sake. This is Dominic's debt, and it is his to pay off. You are already doing your part by staying with me."

"Um . . . o—okay." Defeat colored her tone and it was clear she thought that she should do more.

Dumb fuck.

Forget letting Brock beat his ass; I wanted him for myself. Then again, any man who treated a woman as badly as Tolley obviously treated Elena, deserved worse than that. I'd have to call Dad tomorrow and explain the whole mess, but I had no doubt he'd understand my decision. Placing my hand on the small of her back, I guided her toward the door where my car, a 2014 Bentley Flying Spur, was waiting for us at the curb.

Brock opened the rear door, gesturing for Elena to enter the car first. I followed, taking the seat next her. Brock placed her bag into the trunk and took the front passenger seat. The car pulled away, but Elena refused to look at me the entire ride to my house. The reason became all too evident after Lewis dropped us off.

TRADED

Standing in the foyer with her bag in my hand, I offered to show her to her room and her body locked tight, her eyes like saucers.

"How long do I have before you want me naked?"

I spun around to face her. "Excuse me."

Her cheeks were flushed bright pink, her eyes to the floor. "Naked. Dominic said to have sex with you."

Slipping my fingers under her chin, I lifted her eyes to mine. "Elena, you are not going to pay off the debt by fucking me because Dominic told you to. Any woman in my bed is there willingly. Do you understand?"

She nodded, but the second I moved my hand her eyes were on the floor again. There were a lot of things I'd been forced to do since taking over this side of the business for my dad—things I'd wanted no part of. I'd hoped to never be part of it, but that didn't matter anymore. I was in too deep.

But fucking a woman to cancel out a debt? That was line I would never cross, no matter the circumstances.

With a sigh, I made my way up the stairs to the guest bedroom. Swinging the door open, I flipped on the light and gestured inside.

"This will be your room. Make yourself at home." I set the bag on the chair next to the door. "I'll leave you alone to get settled and I'll see you in the morning. We have a lot we need to talk about."

I stepped to the side, allowing her to walk by me. Just as our bodies drew level, I heard her say quietly, "Thank you for dinner," and then she walked into the room without another word, closing the door behind her.

I needed a drink. And a plan.

The first thing I needed to do was get in touch with my assistant and get everything set for tomorrow. I might have been in charge of the loans for my dad, but I still had businesses of my own to attend to. Heading back down to the den, I pulled my phone from my pocket and dialed Joanne, who promised to have everything set up and sent to me in the morning. She didn't press for more information. I paid her enough to not ask any questions.

Once most of the phone calls were out of the way—I still had to call Dad, but that could wait until the morning—I kicked my shoes off and sat on the couch with another glass of scotch. A clear head while I processed the whole mess would probably be preferable, but I needed liquor to help me understand the last three hours.

And what the fuck I was going to do about all of it.

CHAPTER 4

Elena

The second the door closed behind me I fell into the chair, on top of my bag. How the hell had I ended up in this situation? *Dominic is supposed to take care of me*, I thought, *but how can that be when his idea of doing that is to send me to live with another man, telling him he can have sex with me anytime he wants?*

Tears burned the back of my eyes and I went straight for the bed, burying my head in the soft pillow. I had no idea where *Ashton*, that was what Dominic called him, had gone, much less where his bedroom was. I didn't want him to hear me cry. Especially not after I'd offered myself to him like Dominic told me to, and he'd turned me down. Without that, I didn't have a clue how to help Dominic pay off the debt. I knew I wasn't pretty, but Dominic usually took me anyway. He said it was the least I could do.

Then to see Ashton break that other man's hand, I was terrified. Yet, Ashton had made no move to do any harm to me.

Once I let the tears go there was no stopping them. It had been years since I cried that hard. Each day, I'd learned more and more about what made Dominic happy, meaning less mistakes, fewer reasons for him to correct me. My body convulsed with the force of the sobs. My throat burned. Eventually the weight of it all was too much, and the tears pulled me into sleep.

For the first time in as long as I could remember, I was woken by a bright light. My eyes burned as I cracked them open, finding sunlight streaming through my window. I sat up, trying to get my bearings. I knew where I was, but it was shocking to not have an alarm wake me.

Rubbing at my swollen eyes, I remembered the fit I'd thrown the night before and resolved to shake off my feelings. My husband had asked me to do something, and I was going to do it. Forcing myself from the bed, I found my bag where I'd left it the night before. The room was filled with heavy oak furniture, the kind that dominated a room. The carpet was thick and plush, my feet sinking into it the moment my feet hit the ground. Walking in farther, I notice the en-suite bathroom. The luxury continued there, with extra robes and towels hung in the room, and a variety of toiletries on the counter.

Pulling out the things I needed, I decided that a shower would help me to start afresh. The double showerhead made for the most relaxing twenty minutes of my life and lifted my spirits somewhat; at least, until I realized I couldn't hide in my room all day.

Opening the door, I followed the path Ashton had taken last night, bringing me out at the main foyer. The house left me with a feeling similar to how Jack must have felt in the Giant's house after climbing the beanstalk. Everything was so much bigger than I was used to. So much . . . *more*. Vaulted ceilings sat high above where anyone could touch without a ladder. Winding staircases led to the second floor. The heavy drapes that adorned the double-height windows probably cost more than my entire wardrobe. The whole environment was incredibly daunting.

The smell of freshly ground coffee filtered in from a hall to the right. Following its comforting scent, I found the door to the kitchen and pushed it open to find Ashton sitting at a table, reading the paper. I stopped in the doorway, unsure what to say or do.

"Good morning, Elena." Ashton lowered the paper.

"Good morning," I said, my voice squeaking at the end.

He stared at me for a moment and when I didn't move, he said, "You can sit down and have breakfast. Unlike your husband, I don't expect you to wait on me while you're here."

"Umm . . . okay."

How did I explain to him that Dominic didn't expect me to wait on him; that it was my job as his wife to take care of his needs?

I pulled out the chair in front of me and took a seat, folding my hands in my lap. I sat there, staring at the table.

"Elena, are you hungry?"

I shrugged. "I guess I could eat."

"Elena, look at me."

Lifting my head, I saw that Ashton's gaze hadn't moved from me. His proximity allowed me, in a moment of boldness, to take him in. His blond hair and green eyes were only the beginning, all of his features melding together to create the type of man who haunted women's dreams. Unfortunately for women like me, men like Ashton were a pipe dream. I needed to follow the rules. Dominic was the only man willing to take care of me, and he wouldn't do that if I let him down. I needed to make myself useful.

"What would you like for breakfast?"

I stood from my chair and walked to the middle of the room. "I can make you something, if you point me in the right—"

"Stop."

Oh God, what did I do wrong already?

Ashton came over and led me back to my chair. "You are my guest. I'll make you something."

"But—"

"No buts. I understand Dominic expected certain things of you, and we'll talk about that later. For now, you need to understand that I am *nothing* like your husband. Now tell me what you like to eat for breakfast so I can make it for you."

"I . . . umm . . . I usually eat pancakes at the diner."

"Pancakes it is then."

Ashton began collecting ingredients from different cupboards, pulling out everything needed to make pancakes. Unlike the "just add water" kind I usually bought from the store, he was making them from scratch. While the pan heated, he brought over a cup of coffee.

"I wasn't sure how you liked it. Pancakes will be done in a few minutes."

The coffee smelled delicious. Taking hold of the cup, I took my first sip. It was unlike anything I'd ever tasted before, the flavor rich and sweet. Ashton had made it just right.

"Thank you. This is delicious."

"I'm glad you like it."

My knee started to shake under the table. Not many people went out of their way to be nice to me, except Gretchen. Many times, she'd tried to talk me into leaving Dominic, and while I understood that she was just trying to help, she didn't get it. She didn't see what Dominic did for me. He helped me. He wasn't the easiest of people to get along with, but that was just his way. It had crossed my mind to get her to spend some time with him, show her the other side of him, but when I mentioned it he'd said, "If you have time to have friends over then you're obviously slacking," so I'd let it drop. In truth, Gretchen hadn't seemed all that enthusiastic either, so it had likely been for the best.

Ashton came back to the table with two plates stacked high with pancakes and sausage. Definitely more food than I could, or should, eat at one time.

"Oh my God, that's so much food."

"Sorry. I'm used to making big portions. Eat as much you want, leave what you don't."

He dug into his pancakes while I picked up my fork slowly, my mind focused on his apology and the ease with which he delivered it. Sorry wasn't a word I heard very often, especially from a man's mouth. I didn't know what to do with it.

"Is everything okay?"

I looked up to find him watching me. "I'm not used to people apologizing to me."

Ashton dropped his fork to his plate and leaned back in his chair. "I guess we need to have our talk now, before we eat."

I swallowed hard. "Our talk?"

He rested his elbows on the chair and steepled his fingers in front of his mouth. He sighed. "About the next three months."

My stomach became queasy, and I set down my thus far unused fork.

"Elena, I'm not sure how to say this so I'm just going to put it out there. Your husband is a world class asshole." My mouth dropped open in shock, but that didn't stop Ashton from continuing. "I've seen men like him before. Ones who aren't good enough to keep a woman like you, yet they manipulate you into believing that they are the only one who will ever want you. Let me tell you, it's all bullshit. Every word he says to you is complete shit. No decent man would ever consider giving their wife up to save their own ass; much less, tell her to be another man's fucktoy. That's not okay and I will not treat you that way. I agreed to the deal in hopes of getting you out of his clutches long enough for you to see that you deserve better than a fucker who makes you feel lower than the dog shit he scraped off the bottom of his shoe."

That was a lot of information to take in. My eyes burned with the effort of holding back the tears, but Ashton words rang loud in my head, every word cutting deeper than the one before. Could he be right? It did hurt to know that Dominic was willing to leave me with a stranger, to not care if I slept with another man. The tears fell in earnest as my shoulders shook.

"Please don't cry. I don't want to see you upset, but you deserve to see how a real man treats a woman." He reached over and covered my hand with his. "Let me help you."

He handed me a tissue to wipe my eyes and I swiped at my tears, desperately trying to find my self-control. There couldn't be any truth to his words.

"My husband loves me."

He shook his head. "If your husband loved you, you wouldn't be here right now. You'd be home having breakfast with him. Let me ask you a question—when was the last time Dominic did anything for you?"

"He takes care of me, works to pay our rent."

"Prick hasn't taken care of you a day in his life. But that's not what I asked." The look he gave me was unnerving, like he could see down to my soul.

"He married me and stays with me when no one else would ever want me." I gestured down at myself, pointing out the obvious.

"That man has you completely brainwashed." He sat back and pointed at my plate. "Finish your breakfast and I'll show you what I mean about doing something for you."

My stomach rolled at the thought of putting anything in it, but I wouldn't disobey Ashton and risk something happening to Dominic because of my behavior. Taking ahold of my fork, I picked at my pancakes until I couldn't fit any more in my stomach. Ashton finished his own breakfast and stood from the table, holding a hand out to me.

"Come on. I want to show you how women should be treated by their husbands."

"You don't have to take me anywhere. I'm sure you have to work—wait . . . do you go to work?" My face heated. *I just asked a loan shark if he had a job.*

He laughed. "Yes, I work, and, no, it's not all collecting debts for my dad. I own three different restaurants downtown, but I took today off to get you settled. I can deal with the books tomorrow."

"Don't worry about me. I can hang out in my room. I won't get in your way. I just need to make one quick phone call and then I'll disappear. I left my phone at the apartment, if you wouldn't mind letting me use one of yours?"

"You can use my phone, but these are the things I'm talking about. This is your home for the next three months. You don't need to stay in your room, or hide from me."

"I don't? I thought you'd want me out of your way as much as possible?"

"No. I want you to enjoy your time here and realize there is another way to live. Now let's get you a phone."

He waved his hand, which was still outstretched, and I took it, silently following him down the hall to his study.

"I figured you might want some privacy. I'll be in the living room when you're done."

"Thank you."

TRADED

The second the door closed behind him, I picked up the phone and dialed Gretchen's cell."

"Hello?" she answered, her voice unsure.

"Gretchen? It's me."

"Oh my God." Her scream was so loud I had to pull the phone away from my ear. "Elena, are you all right? They said you quit. No one could tell me anything. I didn't know how to find you."

Her concern ate at me and I felt the tears slip down my face. "Oh, Gretchen, I'm helping Dominic pay off a debt he owes."

"What did that fucker do now?"

Telling her seemed like more trouble than it might be worth. I couldn't have her interfere, but she was my friend and deserved the truth. "He made a deal with the loan shark he owes money to."

"And what's the deal?" I could tell by the tone of her voice that her brows were narrowed down over her eyes.

"I . . . umm . . . I have to stay with the loan shark for the next three months," I rushed out, fumbling over my words.

"Are you fucking kidding me?" she yelled. "That's it. I'm calling the police."

"No!" I panicked. "Please, Gretchen, I need to do this."

"So he trades you like that chick off *Indecent Proposal* and you think that's okay?"

"It's not like that. Ashton doesn't expect me to sleep with him. And if I don't stay, they'll do awful things to Dominic."

"Asshole deserves it," she mumbled.

"Please, Gretchen, you have to promise me you won't say anything. If you're my friend, you'll do this for me."

"This pisses me off." She paused. "I won't say anything—as long as you promise me that if this guy tries to hurt you in any way you'll call and I'll come get you."

"I promise. Thank you. Look I have to go. Ashton wants to show me something. I'll call you later."

"'Bye, Elena. I hope you know what you're doing."

"I do."

"Be safe."

The call disconnected. I was just about holding it together, nearly succumbing to the tears, when there was soft knock at the door.

"Elena, is everything okay?" Ashton called.

Putting on a brave face, I stood and opened the door. "I'm fine."

"Good," he said softly. "Now, let's go. I have a surprise for you."

I was hesitant to say the least. The last time someone surprised me, I'd ended up tied to a stranger for three months. I'd had enough *surprises* to last me a lifetime. But it didn't seem like I had much of a choice.

Ashton led us through the house until we reached a door.

A garage.

He grabbed a set of keys off the hook by the door and opened the passenger side of a sports car for me. I climbed in and waited.

Ashton backed out of the garage and down the drive. I was so nervous my hands were shaking and I gripped the sides of my seat, my fingers biting into the soft, supple leather. "What kind of car is this?"

He glanced at me out of the corner of his eye. "It's an Aston Martin DB9."

"It's beautiful."

"Thank you."

I twisted my hands around in my lap. "Where are we going?"

He smirked. "You don't like surprises?"

"Not after the last one. I thought Dominic was taking me out to dinner. He told me to pack a bag. He hadn't had to correct me very much lately. I thought he might be rewarding me. Not once did I expect to be traded for his debt."

I couldn't believe I just admitted all of that to a stranger; a man I'd only met the day before. Dominic didn't like me to talk to other men, so I wasn't normally that comfortable around them, particularly in such close proximity. Yet, for some reason, I found Ashton easy to open up to.

"I'm sorry I didn't think about it that way. I'm taking you to a spa. Figured you'd never had the chance to be pampered."

"A spa day? You don't have to do that. We already owe you enough money."

"I'll say it again, Elena." His voice was firm. "Your *husband* owes me the money, not you. Besides, this is something I'm doing for you. Did you pack much in that bag of yours?"

I looked out the window, embarrassed at not being prepared. "Just what I have on, plus the dress from yesterday."

"That's what I thought."

"Yeah, I'll need to use your washing machine tonight after you go to bed, if that's okay?"

"No."

My eyes opened wide as I turned my face to him. "What do you mean? What am I going to wear?"

"I'm having a personal shopper meet you at the spa. She'll take your measurements and have clothes sent over to the house for you to try on later."

"Ashton, please, you can't keep spending money. I won't be able to pay it off."

"I don't expect you to pay it off. These things are for you, nothing to do with the money Dominic owes."

The car came to a stop outside what looked to be a residential address, the tall pillars on either side of the heavy wooden door giving it a grandiose feel. Reading the name on the brass plaque to the left of the door, I realized where Ashton had brought me. I'd read about it in magazines at the diner. Celebrities had been spotted here. It was one of the most expensive places in the city.

"Here?" My voice was incredulous. This was too much.

"Yes, here. Come on, I'll walk you in."

On legs that felt like jelly, I climbed out of the car and followed Ashton inside. My shoes clicked against the marble floor of the foyer, and pictures of models sporting different hairstyles lined the walls. At the counter stood a woman, dressed in a tan business suit, her long hair hanging loose. Soft music filled the air.

TRADED

"Hello, we have an appointment scheduled for Elena."

"Let me check," the receptionist said. "Ah, yes, here we are. Full session?"

"That's correct."

I noticed the way the girl's eyes focused on Ashton every time she thought he wasn't looking. It wasn't hard to see why she was staring, with his neatly styled blonde hair, and green eyes hidden behind his glasses, Ashton was absolutely gorgeous. Wait. "What's a full session?"

Ashton smiled at me. "It means the works. You'll get all of the services today."

"All of them?" I knew I was just repeating what he said, but I needed to make sure I'd heard him correctly.

"Yes. Now promise me something."

"What's that?"

It was hard not to smile back at him when he was being so sweet. Last night he scared me when he'd hurt the other man and he could have used me, done what he wanted then discarded me, but he hadn't. Instead, he'd put me in a beautiful room, told me to go to bed and get some sleep, and now he was sending me to get pampered for the day.

"Promise me you're not going to worry about any of the bullshit with Dominic. Relax and enjoy yourself."

"I'll try." I faced the receptionist. "Okay, I'm ready." My heart raced, but it was hard to keep the grin off my face.

"Great," she said, her bubbly personality shining through. "My name's Lisa, and I'll show you around before getting you ready for your first appointment."

Ashton leaned forward, his mouth dropping down to my ear. "Lewis will be here to pick you up later. Remember, relax."

I nodded and clasped my hands together to keep them from shaking and said, "Thank you. I'll see you later."

Following Lisa back through the door, I embarked on my first day of being pampered. Why would Ashton set this all up? Did he want me to sleep with him? No, that was stupid. I'd tried last night and he turned me down. There had to be a reason, but until I figured it out, I'd been brought here to be pampered.

Might as well enjoy it.

CHAPTER 5

Ashton

Seeing the look on Elena's face, I knew I'd made the right decision in getting everything set up the night before. The way things were, Elena couldn't see her worth, but I intended to change that. It would have to happen slowly, though. Her low self-esteem, no doubt ingrained by her husband, had been given years to take root. Changing the way she saw herself was going to take time. I needed to do it slowly.

First things first, I had to stop by my dad's house and let him know what had happened. He'd be looking for the money sooner or later. I figured a face-to-face explanation was the way to go.

The drive to his place gave me an opportunity to plan what to say. While I preferred a house outside the chaos of downtown, Dad liked living right in the middle of things. Fucking stupid, if you asked me. With all the pies my father had his fingers in, surrounding himself with law enforcement was asking for trouble.

So far, Dad was off grid as far as the police were concerned. To the community, he was nothing more than a local businessman, and that was by design. He was clever. Regardless of their suspicions, the cops could walk into any one of the four car dealerships he owned tomorrow and demand to see his books and wouldn't find anything. It helped that he had a forensic accountant on his team. Tired of working for the government, he helped disguise any wrongdoing, keeping it away from prying eyes. My father paid him handsomely to make every transaction look clean.

My brother, Miller, was not so invisible. Sports betting was harder to hide. He'd had a few run ins with the police, but lucky for him, he had a few politicians in his pocket and having them owe him favors helped to make any potential problems disappear. Miller got smarter after one instance. He went to ground for a while and came back having created a system that eliminated the need to use the back room of a bar to place the bets. Lately, he'd also been helping Dad at one of the dealerships. I couldn't deny the business was a great cover. It didn't do too badly either.

Someday I hoped to get out of my dad's business, but I wouldn't have what I did without him. Growing up, all I wanted was to be a chef in my own restaurant, but reality came knocking not long after I finished culinary school. Dad was insistent in handing over the collection business to me. He promised I wouldn't have to deal with the people who didn't pay—he'd take care of

TRADED

that—I just needed to collect the payments. That eventually turned into a few of my dad's men joining me, and what was supposed to be a thing on the side became my responsibility; my *job*. It wasn't something I'd taken on lightly, but Dad made up for it by giving me the money to buy the restaurant. I used the profits from the first to buy the next two. I'd realized my dream, but it came with conditions.

After he'd paid for the restaurant and culinary school, I didn't feel like I could walk away from my obligations. Someday, I hoped that would change. But that someday wasn't now.

When I pulled up into the valet of my parents building, I saw my brother getting into his car. "Miller," I called before he shut the door.

"Ashton, hey." He stepped out of his car and pulled me in to clap me on the back. "What are you doing here?"

"Just business."

We both knew that you never talked in the open. It was a surefire way to get your ass thrown in jail.

"Oh, things not going well?"

My jaw went tight and he read it. "Explain later, yeah?"

He opened his mouth then promptly shut it again. My brother happened to be one of the few people who knew me well enough to understand that my silence meant something seriously fucked up had happened. But being as smart as he was, he also knew when to leave it alone.

"All right, man. You know whatever it is, I'll help."

"I know."

"Just call."

"I will. Later."

Walking through the front door, I noticed the lobby full of people going about their lives, oblivious to anything but themselves. The elevator doors opened and I climbed in, pressing the button for the penthouse but the doors remained open. It took me a moment but then I remembered. The key. Every single time, I forgot the damn thing. I slipped the keycard out from my wallet, pushed it into the slot, and the doors closed, the elevator rapidly making the climb to the top floor.

The doors opened to reveal my parents' front door. Without bothering to knock, I let myself in.

"Mom? Dad?"

Mom came out of the kitchen wearing an apron covered in flour and her trademark smile. "Ashton, what are you doing here?"

I bent and kissed her on the cheek as she wrapped me in a hug. "I needed to talk to Dad."

She stepped back and put her hands on her hips. "Never to see me. Let me guess—*business*."

I laughed. As much as she might grumble, my mom knew how things worked. It was, after all, Dad's business that kept her in the life she loved. That didn't mean she didn't like to pull our legs about it, though. "Yes, business, but I need to talk to you too. I just need to talk to Dad first."

She beamed. "I can deal with that. He's in the office. I'll be in the kitchen when you're done."

"Thanks, Mom."

TRADED

Despite being able to afford to hire staff, my mom did all the cooking. She refused to hire anyone to work in *her* kitchen. Growing up, she taught me how to make different foods and she was the one who'd inspired me to go to culinary school. That was why I had to speak to my dad first. I knew I'd end up helping her in there for at least an hour before I left.

The office door was open, but I still knocked before going in. Most of the time, I didn't want to know what my father was dealing with, the less I knew the better, so it was always safest to err on the side of caution.

"Dad?"

"Ashton. Come on in." He closed a file and leaned his arms on the top of his desk. "What's up?"

Normally I would have closed the door, but Mom was going to find out all about what happened anyway so there was little point. "We have a problem."

His eyes narrowed. "A non-payment? You know how to handle those." He waved me off, opening the folder and dismissing the whole conversation.

"It's more than that." I took a seat and waited for him to pay attention.

He looked up. "Jesus Christ, Ashton. Fuckin' handle it already. I've got enough of my own shit to deal with."

Sometimes the only way to truly get my father's attention was to shock the shit out of him. "Dominic Tolley, he couldn't come up with the cash. Offered to trade his wife to wipe out the debt."

Dad's head snapped up. "What the fuck did you just say to me?"

"The bastard offered me his wife for three months and made it clear she was to fuck me every night to pay off his debt."

Dad knifed up, the force of his hands slamming against the desk causing his pen to jump and roll onto the floor. He left it where it was. "Motherfucker! I hope you had Brock follow his ass home and take care of him."

"No."

The muscles in his neck strained, the blue veins covering his skin like rivers on a map. "You sent her home with him, right?" My eyes dropped to my shoes and he growled. "Tell me you didn't, Ashton. Tell me you didn't take the girl in lieu of payment." I lifted my chin and he got his answer. "Jesus, fuck."

"I made him a deal," I said. "I get Elena for three months, and he pays back half of what he owes."

"Half? Are you crazy? Does she have a golden pussy or something? She must have. There must be a good reason for this . . . *insanity*."

By this point my dad had rounded the table, grabbing handfuls of my shirt, pulling me flush against him, his face millimeters from mine as he shouted his displeasure. My fists clenched at my sides. At six-one I was a big bastard, but Dad was bigger. He could take me without breaking sweat. Even so, my voice was tight when I looked him straight in the eye and replied, "He abuses her, Dad," the volume dropping slightly when I continued. "I don't know to what extent but she won't even look me in the fucking eyes when I talk to her. Can't make a decision on her own. Swear to Christ, she jumped six fuckin' feet in the air when I touched her hand. I have no intention of touching her, but I couldn't let her leave with him. If I shot him down and let Brock rough him up a little, imagine what that would have meant for her." I paused before saying quietly, "You of all people *know* what that would have meant."

Understanding washed through his features and he lowered me to the ground, releasing my shirt from his grip, smoothing out the crumpled material. "She's staying with you?"

"Yes." I made the split-second decision to share my plan with him. "I've only got three months to repair what he broke. It'll be tough but I'll be damned if I don't give it a try."

Dad leaned back against his desk, his heavy sigh audible in the otherwise silent room. "I don't understand why you didn't kill the bastard."

"Trust me, I thought about it, but you know as well as I do it wouldn't do any good. Just like Aunt Veronica, she'd end up with some other loser to bully her. I can break the cycle. Show her she's strong enough to leave him on her own. I just need the next three months." I paused. "*Then* I can send Brock in."

Dad nodded. "Interesting plan. Three months isn't long, though. It took at least a year to repair what that cocksucker broke in Ronnie."

Leaning back in the chair, I crossed my ankle over the top of my knee, my foot twitching as I thought out loud. "I'm starting with simple things, like having her make her own choices. She wouldn't even choose from the menu at the ballpark last night. And today I sent her to the spa."

He nodded. "Makes sense. Show her how she should be treated," he murmured to himself.

"Exactly. I'm also hoping Mom can make a big dinner sometime next week and invite Aunt Veronica. I think a talk with her would do Elena good.

"I think that's an excellent idea." He clasped me on the shoulder and gave a squeeze. Then his voice lowered. "I'm proud of the way you handled that. I know you don't always agree with the things we do, but no woman should ever be treated that way by a man."

"No she shouldn't. It'll make us short, but I think it's worth it."

"It is. And half is better than nothing. I'll call Ronnie tonight after you talk with Mom."

"Thanks, Dad." I stood. "I'm gonna get going. I know I'll end up spending some time cooking before I leave."

"Most likely." He laughed and waved me away, returning to work on whatever he'd been dealing with before I walked in. That was my dad's way: if you had an issue you talked it out. Things might get heated, but they'd also get resolved, then everyone moved on. Some might disagree with this approach, but it worked for us.

Back tracking to the kitchen, I found Mom, whisk in hand, mixing eggs. "Hey, Mom."

Unlike many women involved in our lifestyle, Mom knew aspect of my dad's business. She didn't want to be kept in the dark, but she also had rules; rules that my father obeyed to the letter. He loved her too much to chance her walking away. Dad's business was never allowed in the house. Obviously we had discussions, but only ever in his office. None of the men who worked for my father were allowed anywhere near where we lived. Mom wanted has to have as normal a life as possible. Another rule was that neither Miller nor myself were to have anything to do with the business until after we'd finished college. Finally, and most importantly, if either of us were ever investigated by any kind of law enforcement, it was Dad's job to fix it—even if that meant taking the blame himself. Her sons were never going to jail for the family business, according to my mom.

"Done with Dad already?"

I watched on as she flicked her wrist rapidly, the eggs frothing in the bowl as she closed a cupboard door with a nudge of her hip, her eyes never leaving mine. I paused a moment before answering, "Yeah, but it involves you too."

"Talk."

It wasn't just my dad who was direct.

"Well, it has to do with a client of mine who is abusive to his wife."

She stopped mixing, her eyes heated, her mouth tight. "Whatever you need it's yours."

Funny how different my parents' immediate reactions were. Then again, I was only giving mom part of the story. She didn't need all of the details, and I knew for a fact, she wouldn't want them. "She's staying with me for the next three months. I want to help her, Mom. I want to show her what an ass—"

"Don't you dare finish that sentence, Ashton Joseph."

At thirty-two I was still being reprimanded by my mother for using foul language. What the hell? I rolled my eyes, and continued. "Anyway, I was hoping we could have a big dinner here with Aunt Veronica. Maybe they could sit and talk, help Elena see the light?"

"I think that's a wonderful idea. Do you want to do it next Saturday? Give her time to get down here."

"That's perfect, Mom. Thank you."

She smiled and it lit up her whole face. She might be fifty-seven and I might be her son, but I couldn't deny that my mom was a beautiful woman—even more so when she smiled. "You're welcome. Now help me by measuring six cups of flour into the mixer."

"You know it'll work better if you sift it."

She pointed the whisk at me. "My kitchen, my rules. Now pour."

I did as she said, chuckling to myself as I dumped the flour into the mixing bowl. My dad might run one of the largest money laundering rings in the city, but there was no question who was in charge of the household. I'd even seen Dad cower at a pissed off Mom.

For the next two hours, I helped her bake. It was soothing. When I looked at my watch, the face covered in flour, I realized Elena would be back soon. I wanted to be there when Lewis dropped her off. I also needed to get some paperwork done for the restaurants.

I said goodbye to Mom and left for my office. I checked in with each restaurant manager and collected my paperwork before heading home to wait.

Absorbed in the profit numbers for last month, I almost didn't hear the soft knock on the door. Knowing how engrossed I got when dealing with the financials, I'd left it open, and when I looked up I almost swallowed my tongue.

I'd known from the moment I saw her that Elena was pretty, but the woman who stood before me was a goddess. Her hair fell in silken waves around her face. Her make up was light, which was great because she didn't need it. She wore a timid smile that told me she was happy and that, in turn, made me happy. Add to that the fact that every glorious curve of her body was on display in a short green dress, and there was no wonder my dick was hard in seconds, needing to be free of the confines of my jeans.

My mouth opened and shut a few times before I finally managed to say, "Holy shit, Elena. You look fantastic."

CHAPTER 6

Elena

His wide eyes and gaping mouth were a sight I hadn't seen directed at me in a long time. Dominic used to look at me that way before we were married, before he realized that I needed work and help being a good wife. Ashton's eyes were filled with honesty, admiration, and if I wasn't very much mistaken, *lust*.

I shook the thought from my head. No way any man, especially one who looked like Ashton, could think I was worthy of a second glance; much less the "I want to eat you up expression" he wore. I watched carefully as he stepped around his desk, moving across the room to stand in front of me. Suddenly I felt like Little Red Riding Hood being stalked by the Big Bad Wolf. My gaze dropped to the floor.

"Look at me, Elena."

TRADED

My eyes moved to his and I waited to be reprimanded. I shouldn't have gone to the spa. I should have offered to make dinner.

Damn it, Elena.

But as ashamed as I felt, I'd be lying to myself if I didn't admit to thoroughly enjoying my day. I couldn't remember the last time someone else cut my hair, much less, added highlights. Dominic thought it was an unnecessary expense. Frivolous, he called it. Then to add a massage, manicure, pedicure, and personal shopper on top of it all? I sighed at the memory, knowing it had been one of the best days of my life.

"Why do you always look at the floor?"

My attention snapped back to Ashton and I replied, "I'm afraid you're going to yell at me."

"Yell at you for what?"

"I don't know, wasting the day when I should have been cleaning or making you lunch and dinner." My heart rate was thundering, galloping like a whipped horse as I began wringing my hands.

There was nothing for a beat, then Ashton took ahold of my fingers and pulled them apart, holding them firmly in his own. "I told you earlier, I don't expect you to take care of me. Somehow, someway, I'm going to teach you how wrong that line of thinking is. Now, did you enjoy your day?"

"Yes, thank you." The urge to look away was almost overpowering but I fought it. Doing what Ashton said was my goal.

"What was your favorite part?"

What if I picked the wrong thing? My hands began to sweat, which succeeded only in reminding me that he was still holding them. There was no chance he wouldn't notice it. "I really liked the shopping."

He smiled and let go of one of my hands, lifting the other above my head, causing me to twirl around where I stood. "I can tell. This dress looks fantastic on you."

Could the desire I'd seen in his eyes have been directed at me? After only a day away from home my world was upended, and I had no idea which way was up. My hands began to shake. I was so far out of my comfort zone, I didn't know where to begin. He was a man, like Dominic, but their thoughts were polar opposites.

Which of them is right?

As if sensing my increasing nervousness, Ashton changed the subject. "I want to show you around the house, but I just need ten minutes to finish up some paperwork."

"That's okay, I can head on up to my room." I tugged at my hands. He still hadn't let me go.

"Are you going to hide, or for another reason?"

His tone, coupled with the tilt of his chin and his assessing eyes, made it clear he wouldn't let me go if he didn't like my answer, but for once, that didn't scare me. What the difference was I couldn't say, but I answered honestly. "I want to put the new clothes away and change before dinner."

He took a step forward and lifted my hand to his mouth, touching his lips against my skin. "*Your* new clothes, Elena, and I think that's an excellent idea. But keep the dress on. You look great in it."

Heat rushed to my face and I nodded, taking my hand from his as soon as he let me, and scurrying out the door. In the safety of my room, I took deep gulping breaths. No man had ever had an effect like that on my body. Every part of me felt like flames were burning paths down every nerve ending in my body. Then I remembered what brought me here in the first place. Dominic was my husband. I loved him. I'd sworn to love and obey him until death and I'd meant it. So why, for just one moment, did it feel like everything with him was wrong.

A knock against wood interrupted my thoughts, the hinges creaking as the door opened slowly. Ashton stood in the doorway, leaning against the jamb, his eyes on the bags at the foot of the bed. I hadn't managed to put anything away. My face flushed.

"Ready for the tour?"

I nodded, not trusting my tongue to work correctly. Being near him sent my heart into overdrive and made me breathless.

"Then let's go."

It turned out the house was even bigger than I'd imagined. All the bedrooms were on the second floor and each had its own bath. The first floor had everything from a pool to a game room, a small library to a kitchen bigger than my whole apartment. Thoughts of ways to spend my days rushed through my head before I had a chance to push them aside like I normally would.

"Your home is beautiful."

Ashton smiled. "Thank you. For the next few months it's your home as well. Every room in this house is for your use. You don't need to spend the whole time hiding in your bedroom." He winked and I felt a flutter deep in my stomach. I might have lied and said I would do that, but that wouldn't help Dominic. Then again, he *had* just handed me over.

"I'll try not to, but unless I'm cooking or cleaning, I really don't know what to do with myself."

"I'm sure you'll figure it out." He placed his hand at the small of my back, leading me toward the kitchen and dining room. The touch was intimate and unfamiliar but he left no room for me to question it. "Let's have dinner."

The guilt for not contributing to dinner overwhelmed me, yet I kept silent. My stomach clenched, waiting for permission. Ashton had already made it very clear that I didn't need to cook for him and I didn't want to risk upsetting him by going over old ground. When we reached the dining room, I saw the table was set and covered with food. Ashton led me to a seat and pulled out the chair for me. Again, I wasn't used to such a gesture. Dominic usually just sat down and began eating.

"What would you like to drink?"

"I'll have whatever you're having."

My response was immediate. Instinctive. He stepped next to my chair and placing his finger under my chin, he lifted my gaze to his. "Starting now, you need to start making your own decisions."

TRADED

My eyes slid closed and my voice wavered. "I'm not sure I know how. Can't you just decide? Dominic always decides for me."

"That's part of the problem. I'm going to teach you how to make your own choices."

His direct way of talking gave me the courage to ask, "Why is it wrong that Dominic helps me make decisions? He's teaching me how to be a good wife."

There was a slight paused before Ashton answered, and when he did, I noted a tone to his voice that I recognized all too well. He was unhappy. "That's the second time I've heard that from you. He's not *teaching* you, Elena, he's *controlling* you—there's a big difference. As long as he has control, you'll stay with him, no matter how badly he treats you."

"He doesn't treat me badly," I whispered, doing so because a lot of what Ashton had just said made sense, and that in turn was making me question a lot of things; things that I didn't have time to process right then.

"Oh really? How many times have you cried because of things he said or did the last time you saw him?"

Stunned into silence, I sat there. Dominic made me cry at least three times a day—most days it was more. I didn't really enjoy crying or hearing him insult me, but I knew it would continue to happen until I learned. I blinked up at Ashton, staring, unsure how to respond.

"I think you just answered my question. Now I'll ask again, what would you like to drink?"

I knew Ashton wouldn't let it go until I made a decision so I said quietly, "Can I have a glass of red wine?" It felt good to decide for myself, especially when he didn't reprimand me for making the wrong choice.

"That I can do." He smiled and walked to a side table with glasses and different bottles on top and poured two glasses, bringing one to me before taking his own seat, directly opposite me. We passed the dishes back and forth, filling our plates. It all looked so delicious.

"Everything looks wonderful," I said, unfolding my napkin across my lap.

"Thank you. Julia made it."

"Julia?"

He smiled. "My housekeeper. I cook for myself most nights, but every once in a while, if I'm busy, she'll do it. And tonight I wanted to have time to talk instead of cooking."

"Talk about what?"

"Anything you want."

Ashton handed over the tray of chicken. Taking a piece, I then finished filling my plate. The room fell silent and I felt the familiar flush of embarrassment as I fumbled for something to say before admitting, "Dominic and I don't really talk."

"Let me guess, he doesn't want to do anything but eat and then do something else."

I winced when he said "something else." My sex life was not something I wanted to talk about. Maybe that wasn't what he was referring to, but that's where my mind went. With each passing moment his gaze intensified, his eyes darkening, becoming heated. Under his watchful eye a feeling unfurled in my stomach. It wasn't unwelcome—quite the opposite—but acknowledging that him looking as me was having a physical effect on me . . .

Shame washed over me. Ashton must have noticed because his face went soft. He opened his mouth to say something but I got in first.

"Usually there was a game on he wanted to see. He always ate quickly so he wouldn't miss it."

"Did you watch the games with him?"

"No, I had to clean up dinner, get laundry done, make his lunch."

"So you were his slave."

I gasped. "No! He's my husband, it's my job to take care of him."

His brows drew together. "But you worked at the diner, didn't you?"

"Well, yes. I needed to help pay the bills."

"Yeah, he was definitely spending his paycheck on the bills—that's why he borrowed money from me in the first place. Jesus, Elena, this isn't the 1950s. You have a job outside the home; it isn't your *job* to take care of him as well. What he's doing to you—it's abuse."

"Dominic's never laid a hand on me," I scoffed.

"He may not beat you, but it doesn't always require fists to hurt someone."

Ashton let the comment hang in the air and took a bite of his chicken. We ate in silence, the cold atmosphere creeping through the room a sharp contrast to our earlier light conversation, and all the while I sat and contemplated what he'd said. A voice in the back of my head, one I hadn't heard in a long time, started screaming at me that Ashton was right. What Dominic had done, and continued to do to me had nothing to do with love. It was twisted and wrong.

The voice had grown quiet over the years. When we were first married, I wanted to please my new husband, so it was easy to push those thoughts aside; convince myself that I was fulfilling my role. I had to be a good wife, and I couldn't do that if I let that voice cloud my judgment. But now the voice was back, and with Ashton compounding the very sentiments I'd worked so hard to evade, it was getting harder and harder to ignore.

"Elena?"

I looked up. Ashton was finished, but all I'd managed to do was push the food around my plate. He set his wine glass down and leaned back in his chair.

"Want to talk about it?"

It felt wrong, like speaking to Ashton would be betraying Dominic, so I continued to pick at my food, this time forcing myself to eat some of the meal. Out of the corner of my eye, I noticed Ashton waiting. Something told me he wouldn't let it go. Could it really be considered a betrayal when Dominic put me in this situation in the first place?

"Why don't you take a drink and finish eating. Then we'll talk."

It may have sounded like a suggestion, but the way in which Ashton delivered this proposal told me he wasn't going to take no for an answer. I lifted the glass to my lips and paused. "Since I met you, it seems like you're always trying to get me to drink."

TRADED

Ashton's eyes widened. "Did you just say something snarky?"

Where did that come from? "I'm so sorry. I didn't mean to." My hands began to shake so badly I almost dropped the glass.

Ashton rounded the table quickly to take it from me, setting it on the table before saying softly, "Elena, relax. I like it. It's what you should be doing all the time. It's called standing up for yourself."

I stared at the glass, not wanting to meet his eyes. "That's not how I should behave."

"This shit again." He handed me back the glass with a frown. "Drink up."

To avoid spilling the drink, I slowly brought it to my lips, taking my first sip of the tart red wine, feeling myself start to settle as my stomach warmed from the alcohol. I couldn't even blame my brazenness on the wine. The thought that I could have ruined everything with one comment had left me feeling panicked—up until Ashton had reassured me. Not being used to speaking my mind, I was shocked that he liked it.

Ashton didn't try to engage me in conversation and his silence unnerved me, making it harder to get my food down, even though each bite was more delicious than the last. I should be used to silence at the dinner table, except Ashton hadn't been silent from the moment I met him. When he finally spoke up, I almost sighed in relief.

"Tell me, how did you and Dominic meet?"

"We were high school sweethearts. He was the captain of the football team."

"What did you do?"

"Me? I was in the choir and band." I remember thinking how lucky I was that a guy as popular as Dominic wanted to go out with me. He was the captain. He could have had anyone.

Ashton leaned back and crossed his arms over his chest. "When did you get married?"

"After we both finished college—"

"Wait. You have a college degree?" he said, and the surprise in his voice hurt my feelings a little.

"I do. I majored in musical theater."

He shook his head. "Then what the hell are you doing working in a diner?"

I shrugged. "Dominic thought it would be a waste of time for me to go to auditions when I could have a full time job with a steady income."

"Fucker wouldn't even let you follow your dream."

His voice was low enough that I knew I wasn't supposed to have heard what he said. But I did and I sank back in my seat, wanting to defend my husband, but not wishing to upset Ashton any further. "He was right. We needed the money."

He looked over at me, sighed and reached across the table, taking one of my hands and giving it a gentle squeeze, his thumb running lightly back and forth over my knuckles. "Not at the expense of your dream. I know for a fact he's been gambling a long time. My guess—he wanted you to have a job to help pay for his extracurricular activities."

I shook my head emphatically. "He wouldn't do that to me."

TRADED

"Yes he would, Elena, and he did. Don't kid yourself."

That hurt worse than I thought it would. The idea that Dominic would make me give up my dream so he could gamble. My stomach was in knots. "I don't know what to say. We're married. I wanted to do the best I could for him, especially since we didn't plan on getting to that point so young."

He tilted his head to the side. "What do you mean?"

I flinched. "Our wedding wasn't exactly intentional."

Ashton released my hand and leaned forward, his elbows on the table, his hands clasped and resting against his mouth.

"Explain."

I took a deep breath and began . . .

My head feels as if there's a jacking hammer drilling into my brain. Maybe the surprise trip to Vegas for my graduation wasn't such a good idea. Opening my eyes slowly, afraid of the light on the other side, I see Dominic, sleeping peacefully next to me. Our clothes from last night are scattered all over the room, including the three dresses I put on when deciding what to wear. Dominic had said he didn't like any of them and kept asking me to change. One of them was too tight, he said. It made my butt look big. The other two were too revealing; the first showed too much leg, although it was halfway down my thighs; the second too much cleavage, when only last week I wore it to brunch with Mom.

Shaking my head, I smile to myself. Since we're in Vegas, I can always shop for new clothes. I'll take Dominic shopping—make sure he likes the stuff before I buy it. Running my hands over my face, I know a shower and food will help to clear the fog. Carefully climbing out of bed, I make my way to the bathroom quietly because Dominic doesn't like being woken up in the morning. He'll be nasty for the rest of the day if I disturb him so it's easier to just be quiet until he gets up so we can go to breakfast.

I turn on the water for the shower. Waiting for it to heat, I reach for my toothbrush and almost scream out loud. There, on the third finger of my left hand, sits a solid gold band.

A wedding band.

Running from the bathroom, I pull back the bed sheet to look at Dominic's hand, finding a matching band resting just below his knuckle.

Oh God. What happened last night?

With determination, I search through our clothes and bags, looking for something to explain what's going on. There in the pocket of Dominic's pants is a receipt from the Chapel O' Love *for his and hers wedding bands, and one ceremony. Stapled to the receipt is a piece of flimsy paper: the official Nevada marriage license.*

Holy hell. We got married.

We're married.

It's what I've been hoping for—even if it's happened a little earlier than I expected.

For one brief second I think about waking Dominic up, but he probably won't be happy. It's probably better to let him sleep before I tell him.

TRADED

I get into the shower and once out and dressed, I go back into the main room. Dominic is sitting in one of the tub chairs, the license clutched in his hand, the vein in his temple pulsing wildly.

"What the fuck is this?" He holds the paper up, waving it in front of me. I thought he was going to be unhappy, but this is more. He's angry.

I hold my hands up. "Now, Dominic—"

"Don't Dominic me. You tricked me! You got me drunk last night so you could trap me."

A small laugh escapes my mouth before I can stop it. "I did no such thing. I woke up this morning remembering as little as you do. I had just as much to drink last night."

"Which is why I always tell you not to drink," he snaps.

I drop into the chair next to him, the pain in my heart making my chest ache. "What do you want me to do? We could try and get a divorce? Or maybe an annulment?"

He stands, his tall frame towering over me. "You think this is funny?"

This isn't the first time he's freaked out like this. Eventually he'll calm down, but it still makes me want to hide. He can get mean when he's like this and I don't like it. "No. I'm just not sure what else we can do."

"You wanted this, didn't you," he accuses.

I look away, feeling the tears burn my eyes. "I won't lie, Dominic. I was hoping you'd want to make me your wife, someday."

"Do you even know how to be a wife?"

His sneer is hurtful but I answer quickly, "Not really, but I can try. I'm a quick learner."

He paces the room, back and forth until he comes to a stop in front of the large plate window. He stares out at the skyline for a few moments and I'm afraid he'll turn around and say he wants a divorce. "Fine," he says, rubbing the back of his neck. "We'll stay married—but if this is going to work, you need to learn how to be a good wife."

My heart leaps. Dominic has been my world for so long. Things can only get better now that he's mine and I am his. Maybe he'll be less jealous. Less possessive.

I run up and wrap my arms around him. "I promise, I'll be the best wife ever."

He doesn't kiss me like I expect. Instead, he unwraps my hands and drags me across the room, back toward the bed. "And you can start right now. I'm going to teach you how a wife should act in bed."

The soft brush of a finger across my cheek brought everything back into focus. I hadn't realized I'd been crying until Ashton wiped away my tears. He'd dragged his chair closer to mine while I'd been speaking and was now only inches from me, his legs splayed, cocooning me where I sat. "Don't cry, Elena. That prick doesn't deserve another tear from you."

"I just want to make him happy." My eyes closed, trying to block out the pain.

"That's not what he wants. He wants a slave."

TRADED

"I tried to be everything he wanted me to be. Why isn't that enough?" Holding back the sobs made my chest ache and so I gave in, letting them go. Ashton gently pulled me into his arms and held me while I cried.

Eventually the tears slowed, some semblance of control returning. Leaning away, I brushed furiously at my face. "I'm sorry. I don't know what's wrong with me."

"Don't be sorry. I think you needed that."

He cupped my face, using his thumbs to wipe away the remaining tears, and when our eyes connected, the frames of his glasses making the green of his irises even brighter, I was lost. My heart raced and my breath came in pants, my body reacting to the near perfection that was Ashton Hawes. His eyes slid closed and for one brief moment, I thought he was going to kiss me. My eyes fluttered shut and I waited, surprised and a little disappointed when I heard his groan and the sound of his chair pushing back.

I wasn't beautiful enough for a man like Ashton. The fact that I even considered I might be was enough to bring me close to tears again.

"Stop, Elena. I can see your emotions in your eyes. Don't think for one second you aren't beautiful. You happen to be one of the most gorgeous women I've ever seen. Unfortunately, some asshole with a superiority complex has skewed your view of yourself. Last night I promised not to take you to my bed unless you wanted to be there willingly, and I stand by that. I will not sit here and ravage you when you're upset."

He did say that last night, and while my body may be willing and waiting for a night with Ashton, my mind was at war with itself. Locked in a battle of right and wrong.

"You need to be ready if you want me, Elena, because I don't make love—I fuck. But I can guarantee you that if you make the decision to climb into my bed, I'll show you more pleasure than you've ever known."

Heat raced up my cheeks and for the first time, I felt my panties wet with desire. Ashton pushed me to that point through his words alone. Silence was my only defense.

"Now before I can't keep my promise to keep my hands to myself, let's each get into something more comfortable and we'll watch a movie."

"Okay," I said, practically running from the room.

I needed to get myself under control. Something about Ashton kept drawing me to him, despite my head screaming that it wasn't right to betray Dominic. Yes, he'd given me permission, but I made vows and I'd meant them. Grabbing a new pair of yoga pants and a fitted T-shirt, I took deep calming breaths and resolved that I would watch the movie, but I needed to be prepared while I was down there.

CHAPTER 7

Ashton

Watching Elena leave the room hurt. Physically hurt. My dick was so hard it took every ounce of my self-control to keep my ass in the chair. It would blow my softly-softly approach if I chased after her and chained her to my bed, although, that didn't stop my mind from wandering to how I could show her the way a real man treated a woman. With everything that was said, I was amazed at my ability to keep a cool head with her.

Fuck. I shouldn't have asked her to keep that dress on. The second I looked up and saw her curves on display, clearly defined beneath the material, I'd wanted to clear my desk in one swipe and bend her over the top.

A cold shower—that's what I needed to clear my head. With her history, I had to make sure she was ready for my bed because, like I told her, it wouldn't be sweet. I didn't do sweet. Hot and passionate I could give her. But I didn't make love. Slow and sweet meant a connection. Most women wouldn't be able to handle the realities of my life. So I kept myself disconnected, and it worked.

Thoughts of Elena stayed with me while I went to my room, taking my own advice and changing into something more comfortable. Flipping on the shower in my bathroom, I turned the knob all the way to cold—anything to get my cock back under control. I stepped under the spray and with the icy water clearing my brain, I was able to go over everything Elena had told me at dinner. If my desire to keep her close hadn't overridden everything else, I probably would have climbed in my car and gone to beat the ever-loving fuck out of the prick.

He actually told her the only way he'd stay married to her was if she learned how to be a good wife. My hands clenched into fists at my sides as I resisted the temptation to take my frustration out on the tiles. How a man could treat their wife that way was beyond rational thought. And for her to agree . . .

He must have been slowly breaking down her protective barriers until he burrowed so deep under her skin, she had no idea he'd done it.

Goddamn asshole had known exactly what he was doing. He'd scored a beautiful woman. He could have made the decision to give her the world, but he broke her instead. The worst part was, I'd never in my life wanted a woman so badly. Her body, curved in all the right places, breasts the perfect size for my hands, made me dizzy with desire. All the blood ran from my brain to my dick.

I let the water pound down on me, the ice-cold droplets stinging my heated skin as I tried to think of anything but the sexy vixen down the hall. The one who had no clue how appealing she was, or she'd have ditched her husband a long time ago. *Damn it!* I needed to get my mind away from Dominic, and the idea of Elena *and* Dominic, or I was going to end up killing him. Uncomfortable as it might be, I was just going to have to make do with a lethal case of blue balls.

Work.
Loans.
Sports.

I ran through a list in my head—anything that would clear out the image of Elena in that dress. And her eyes. She was completely oblivious.

Work.
Loans.
Loans!
Shit.

I had to collect a payment in a few nights. Another asshole who'd borrowed more than he could pay back. What in the hell was I supposed to do with Elena? Under no circumstances would I involve her in any more of my business. I had family connections and I couldn't wait to get the hell out. I couldn't have her anywhere near it.

Resolving to keep Elena away from that side of my life, I got out of the shower and I threw on a pair of track pants and a T-shirt, heading downstairs to wait for her to pick a movie. Goose bumps still covered my skin but when I stepped into the den, I wanted to march right back upstairs and add ice to the shower.

So much for clearing my head.

With her back to me, she stared at the shelves of pictures and artwork that lined the walls, her ass encased in a pair of black yoga pants that showed every curved muscle. I clenched my teeth as I surmised that she probably worked out to keep from getting fat, like a good wife would, swallowing against the lump at the back of my throat.

Sensing my presence she turned around, still as shy as she'd been when she knocked on my office door only a few hours earlier, and I watched her tongue dart out to wet her lower lip before she drew it between her teeth and met my gaze. I managed to stifle my groan, thanking the Lord that her shirt was nowhere near as low-cut as her dress had been, but it was still fitted enough to allude to her shape underneath. It would seem Elena didn't have to do a lot to get me worked up but as long as she stayed seated, keeping that ass from view, I could keep from thinking with my other brain.

"I wasn't sure how to work anything in here." She gestured toward the TV.

I laughed, the sound strained as I attempted to get myself under control. "How about I turn it on, while you pick a movie."

She took a seat on the couch, her back straight, hands folded in her lap. Innocent didn't fully describe the scene in front of me.

"No, you're going to pick what we watch tonight." Walking over to the table, I grabbed the remote and pulled up my Netflix account.

"But . . . but—"

"No excuses, Elena. We're going to teach you how to make decisions for yourself."

Her face blanched and for one brief moment I felt bad for pushing her. Then I remembered what it took to break Aunt Veronica out of it. I sat down next to her, my thigh running the length of hers, and showed her how to flick through the choices to find a movie. The slight tremble to her hands told me she was uncomfortable. She flipped through and although I'd expected her pick one of the romantic comedies she passed them all by, and it struck me that even though I would rather gouge my eye out with a spoon than watch one of those films, I would have endured it if she'd made the choice. Then she surprised me. *Rush* was an older movie; one I was willing to bet she hadn't seen. She looked up at me through her long russet lashes.

"Is this okay?"

She thinks this is what I want to watch. "Elena, is this a movie you want to watch, or did you pick something you thought I'd enjoy?"

"I've wanted to see since it came out, but I can pick something else if you'd prefer?"

"Enough." I covered her lips with my finger. Probably not the best move on my part, especially when I felt how soft they were. "I told you to pick, which means I'll watch whatever you chose. Now let's sit back and enjoy the movie."

She slid back on the couch but her back remained ramrod straight, the tension in the room was thicker than the fog after a summer storm.

"Elena?"

"Yes?" She looked over at me.

"You can relax. I won't bite."

I realized I was giving her permission, which went against my plan, but she immediately responded, pulling her knees up to her chest, her shoulders losing most of their tension. She wrapped her arms around her knees, hugging them tightly. It seemed protective, or maybe it was just comfortable. I preferred to think of it as being the latter. She hadn't eaten much at dinner. She had to be hungry. And what went better with a film than snack food. "I'm going to grab something to eat. Would you like something?"

"Umm . . ." She shrugged her shoulders. "Sure."

"Give me a minute." She leaned forward to get the remote but I said, "You can leave it play. I've seen it before."

She grabbed the remote anyway, clicking *pause* before retreating back into the couch, her chin coming to rest on her knees. "I'll wait for you."

"I'll be right back."

I headed for the kitchen, moving quickly through the house. Cursing myself for not thinking of this sooner, I figured that popcorn would be the best choice. It hurt to think that Elena probably hadn't been to the theater in years, and I wondered just how much she'd missed out on. Things that I likely took for granted were a luxury to her. The thought made me uneasy.

Searching through the pantry, I found a box of microwavable popcorn and, tossing it in the microwave to cook, I went to the fridge and grabbed a bottle of beer, soda, and water. If I gave her a selection, she'd have to make her own choice.

I carried everything out to the den on a tray, met by a wide-eyed Elena. "Wow," she said dropping her feet to the ground. She started to get up and I pulled the tray back, away from her reach.

"Sit down and relax. Remember, you're my guest." I set the tray on the ottoman. "I wasn't sure what you'd want to drink, so I brought you some choices."

"Beer with popcorn?"

Her eyebrows scrunched together. It was adorable, and something I never thought I'd like about a woman. But with Elena I did. It was refreshing to see her question things without fear of repercussion. Whatever caused her to let her guard down needed a repeat; then again, maybe she hadn't even realized she'd done it. "Absolutely. Beer goes with almost anything."

She looked skeptical but reached for one of the bottles of amber liquid. Taking my seat, I hit *play* and music filled the room.

As the film progressed, Elena relaxed further, tucking her feet underneath her, shoveling popcorn and beer into her mouth and leaning forward at each climatic part of the film. She was enjoying herself, the smile on her face making her glee evident. It was a good thing I'd seen it before because I watched her more than I watched the screen, all the while doing everything in my power to keep myself from turning it into a teenage night in my parents' house. I couldn't stop thinking about how much I wanted to forget the movie and make out on the couch. As the evening wore on, I edged closer and closer to her, the soft scent of lavender and jasmine permeating my senses, making my head spin. Holy hell, I was screwed.

As the credits rolled, Elena stood and began cleaning up our mess.

"Leave it," I said. "I'll take care of it."

She paused, her eyes bouncing around the room like she didn't know what to do with herself. "Are you sure you don't want my help?"

I had no problem with her helping if it was because she wanted to, but I wouldn't let her do it because she felt like it was her duty. "Elena, I don't want you to feel like you need to clean because that's what you've always done."

Her eyes glistened and she held my gaze for a second before turning to head upstairs. I thought about it for a moment before I placed my hand on her shoulder, the muscles tensing beneath my palm. "I know I said this earlier, but I hope you understand, I don't want to be like your husband. He has no idea how to treat you and you deserve so much better."

"I wish I could believe that." I closed my eyes and inhaled sharply, the hurt in her voice stabbing me through the chest. Spinning her around, I pulled her close until her cheek rested above my heart.

"One of these days, I'll make you believe it."

I held her while she cried, and as much as it pained me to hear, the sound making my own eyes burn, I couldn't help the small part of me that recognized that she was giving this to me. She was beginning to trust me and I needed to be careful. My earlier lust forgotten, my only thought was to comfort her. As her tears dried, she sagged against me and, not thinking, I pressed my lips to the top of her head. She immediately stiffened, as did I.

What the hell am I doing?

Stepping out of my embrace, she wiped at her face and stared at the ground. "I think I should go to bed," she whispered, her voice rough and thick with emotion.

Before I had a chance to apologize, she spun on her heel and darted up the stairs. "Damn it, Ashton," I muttered, knowing that move had cost me valuable ground. I took a moment to give myself a mental foot up the ass, then finished cleaning the mess and went to find myself a drink.

For the second night in the row, I sat in my office with a glass of whiskey in my hand. My phone vibrated on the desk. Who the fuck would be bothering me when I'm off? Picking up the phone, I saw a text.

Dad: Box is available next Thursday.

I knew exactly what that meant. Someone owed my dad money instead of me. Usually they borrowed from me, but a few of our old clients preferred dealing directly with Dad. There were guys who knew the deal; willing to hand over the kind of interest Dad liked to charge. Because of that, he was willing to accommodate them, only asking me to collect the payment when he couldn't be there.

**Me: I'd love to see the game. Thanks.
Dad: Why don't you take Elena?**

Dumbest fucking idea ever.

**Me: Don't think she's really a fan of baseball.
Dad: Maybe you should change her mind?**

What the hell was he up to? Deciding to give him a flippant answer, I took a sip of my drink and text back.

**Me: We'll see. Don't forget to let me know about dinner.
Dad: Next Saturday?**

I'd hoped for something earlier, but I knew he was probably working around Aunt Veronica's schedule. Once she'd come out of her shell and started to go out, she made sure to enjoy all of the things she'd missed out on. Her social calendar was jam-packed now—a stark contrast to when she was married to Dave.

Me: That works.

My mind went back to Elena thoughts running wild through my head: from the look on her face when we arrived at the spa, to her shyness when I asked her to pick the movie. I wondered if she'd always been shy, or if that was something forced upon her by a man who asked her to be something she wasn't, over and over again. Then I remembered how she looked when she knocked on my office door and my dick was hard in seconds. Shit, the woman was driving me to levels of sexual frustration I hadn't experienced since my teenage years.

Swallowing the last of my drink, I marched my ass up the stairs. I tried to walk past, honest, but I came to a stop outside her room. There was no light coming from underneath the door. She was probably already asleep. When I found myself starting to wonder what she might have picked out to wear to bed, I knew it was time to get my ass down the hall.

My dick was still hard as steel, but I knew no cold shower in the world was going to help now. I set the temperature to hot and stripped again. If I kept this up, I was going to be the cleanest motherfucker in the state.

I dropped my clothes to the floor, put my glasses in their normal spot on the sink and climbed into the shower, letting the water cover my skin before taking my dick in my hand and giving it a firm stroke.

The pressure in my balls had been building all night. Grabbing the shower gel off the shelf, I poured some into my hand and gave in to temptation. Wrapping my fingers firmly around my cock, I started with long, slow strokes. Flashes of Elena consumed my thoughts, making my hand move faster, my pulls rough as I pictured her on her knees; her doe-eyes staring back at me, watching what her touch did to me.

Imagining her small, delicate hand in place of mine had me gripping the showerhead for support. I took in a deep breath and swore I could smell lavender. I'd never be able to smell that again without thinking of her. My neck bent, my forehead coming forward to rest against the cool tile, the water beating down against the back of my head, my hips surging forward pushing my dick through my fingers faster.

Feeling the telltale sensation prickling at the base of my spine, I couldn't hold off any longer. After a few more quick thrusts up through my palm I came, grunting my pleasure throughout the bathroom. Feeling drained I collapsed, my body sliding down the shower wall. Boneless and breathless, I wasn't sure I could move. I'd never come so hard and quickly by my own hand in my life.

For a few minutes I sat there. Not long enough for the water to run cold, but enough time to come to my senses and get my function back. One thing I knew for sure: if this kept up, Elena Tolley was going to be the death of me.

I climbed from the shower and toweled off. Too tired to care, I dropped into bed naked, dreaming of all the things I wanted to do to Elena.

CHAPTER 8

Elena

Almost two weeks had passed since Dominic decided to trade me to pay off his debts. In the beginning I thought it was my job as his wife to do whatever he asked of me, but Ashton made it his mission to convince me otherwise. Each day he showed me something new, something I'd thought was off limits to me because I wasn't good enough, because I didn't deserve it. Part of me still wondered if I really did deserve better than Dominic. I certainly wasn't worthy of a man like Ashton. As much attention as he was showing me, I knew it was because he hated what Dominic had done. Ashton was a man who could get any woman he wanted. I couldn't get swept away. He didn't need or want me in the long-term.

That first full night had been awkward. After my two breakdowns, which was completely embarrassing, I never expected him to kiss me on the head. Yes, it might only have been a sign of comfort but then again, I never expected for that one simple kiss to be the catalyst for the rush of feelings that swept through me. It was all so overwhelming. I'd run from the room like an idiot. After that display, there would be no chance of him touching me like that again. Not that I'd thought about a repeat.

Oh, who am I kidding?

Of course I'd thought about a repeat. My mind was littered with thoughts of his lips on mine. Even as a young girl I'd had an active imagination. Could I help that each and every day brought more and more evidence of how incredibly sexy he was?

But with those thoughts came the guilt. Guilt at feeling things I had no right to. Dominic was my husband. It was wrong to be lusting after another man.

Not once during the last two weeks had Ashton mentioned what happened that night— nor did he try to do it again. While I was beginning to think it was wrong of Dominic to treat me the way he did, and wondering if I'd have the courage to demand better when I got home, I soaked up everything Ashton gave me, knowing that the attention I was getting from him was the best I was ever going to get.

And there were things I wouldn't want to give up when I got home. Like always cleaning up after dinner, or missing new movies because Dominic wouldn't want to take me. I was becoming more independent. "Growing a backbone" Ashton called it. Little things like picking my own dinner, or choosing the movie we watched got easier the more I did it. Ashton had even taken me out to dinner at one of his restaurants, introduced me to his employees.

My first thought had been to panic. Dominic had no problem announcing his displeasure at having to dine with me to the whole restaurant. If asked, I'd struggle to remember a time when we hadn't rushed through our meal; Dominic always choosing to sit as far away from me as he could, paying more attention to the waitress than me, and not being shy about it either. It wasn't uncommon of him to flirt with these women, even offer them his number, something that left them confused about who I was, even though I sat opposite him wearing a matching wedding band. I never ordered for myself, and if I didn't like what he'd chosen for me then I knew to stay quiet. Once, not long after we were married, I'd made the mistake of speaking up and his response had been to coat my food in pepper and watch on as he forced me to eat it. I'd managed about four bites before excusing myself to the ladies' room to vomit— another thing I'd been punished for when we got home.

Yet in his own restaurant, surrounded by people whom he trusted and respected, Ashton's eyes had screamed pride. I wasn't used to it. It was foreign to me. Everything in this world was new. By the time our entrees arrived, I was relaxed. This may have also had something to do with the two glasses of wine. The whole evening was thoroughly enjoyable. For the most part, Ashton spoke and I listened, and I learned much about him; all of which I liked.

In the early days, Ashton had stayed at home during the day, popping out to run errands or collect paperwork, but for the most part he stayed at home with me. Obviously, this couldn't continue and he eventually returned to his normal schedule. Being left at home while he went to work didn't freak me out anymore, although I still felt guilty about not contributing to the running of the household. But as many times as I tried to help, Ashton blew me off, claiming I'd done enough work over the last few years and I deserved some time off. Then he showed me the gym in the basement and encouraged me to blow off some steam.

The moment the words left his mouth, I was reminded that I hadn't done any exercise since I left Dominic. Even when I was at home I at least managed a small workout, in terms of a brisk walk to and from work. Add to that the fact I was eating more food—richer food—and I could almost feel the extra weight around my stomach and hips, a cold rush washing through me when I realized that Dominic would notice, and no doubt have something to say about it.

Ashton's reply still danced around my head.

"You do not need to lose weight. That's not why I brought you down here. Stop letting Dominic's idiotic comments affect the way you see yourself. The rest of the world doesn't see you that way."

Tonight we were heading to his parents' house for dinner. The whole thing made me want to throw up, partly because I didn't understand why I was invited. I was a temporary inconvenience for Ashton. Meeting the parents didn't exactly register on the agenda for short-term houseguests.

Standing in the kitchen, downing a drink of water after a run on the treadmill, I heard the garage door open and a minute later, Ashton stepped through the door. Seeing him made me almost swallow my tongue. What I wouldn't give to be the kind of sexy that brought a man like him home to me each night; the kind of sexy that drove men wild enough to think of spending the night with me. I'd long ago accepted that men like Ashton Hawes weren't meant for someone simple and homely like me, but that didn't make the disappointment burn any less each time it reared its ugly head.

"Ready for tonight?"

His question caught me off guard and I pulled the band out of my hair, letting it fall around my shoulders as I tried to buy some time. "Are you *sure* you want me to meet your parents? You have to admit, ours isn't the most conventional situation."

He stepped forward into my space, crossing his arms over his chest, a dark look crossing his face. "Elena, we've been through this. My parents already know the situation. This isn't about you meeting them—it's about you getting the help you need."

"I already know Dominic needs to treat me better, Ashton. You've helped me figure that out."

"Except the only thing you've learned is that he shouldn't treat you as a slave. Are you ready to leave him?"

I shook my head, the urge to drop my eyes to the ground almost too much, but I caught myself just in time. Ashton had taught me that if I wanted to keep people from taking advantage of me, I needed to show that I wasn't afraid. "How can I? He's the only one who wants me."

"He's not."

His voice was firm; his eyes cutting to me, turning molten, raking over my body, and although I wore a simple outfit of a tank and a pair of running shorts, the way he was staring at me, I may as well have been in my underwear. I froze in place. Men didn't look at me that way. He was just trying to be nice.

"Dominic may need work, but I can help him change."

He clenched his jaw. "He's an asshole and you need to understand he doesn't *want* to change."

"And how would you know?" The muscles in my body tensed. I hadn't fought back in years and it felt good. Ashton's eye went wide for a second. He was shocked. Then his jaw relaxed and he reached forward to cup my cheek.

"Good to see you have a backbone, even if I won't agree. Now go get ready. We need to leave soon."

And just like that, he walked away. Ashton was one confusing man. One minute he looked fit to jump me, the next he was angry, then he was walking away.

TRADED

I contemplated his varying moods as I climbed the stairs, going in search of the dress I'd picked out to wear. It was the first time in forever that I'd had more options than I knew what to do with and so choosing had taken some time, and even then I wasn't sure I'd made the right decision. My hands shook as I attempted to apply the make up like the girl at the spa showed me; partly because I wasn't sure if I was doing it right, partly because I was going to dinner at crime boss's house. I had no idea what to expect. I had a feeling that my stereotypical ideas, all from TV, were completely wrong. Which left me feeling lost as to what I'd be walking into.

Taking one last look in the mirror, I examined my outfit once again to make sure it worked for the night. The black sheath dress complimented my figure—according to the personal shopper Ashton sent. With its deep V at the neckline and lace capped sleeves, it was nicer than anything I'd ever owned. I took in my appearance in the full-length mirror, seeing my transformation from top to toe. I left my long hair loose, curling the ends, resisting the temptation to pull it away from my face in my normal ponytail. Even with the nerves about the impending dinner, I felt beautiful.

Satisfied that everything was in its place, I grabbed my black purse and left my room. I turned the corner and waiting at the bottom of the stairs was Ashton, his black suit fitting him perfectly, outlining every muscle in his body. I was so busy staring I almost stumbled down the stairs but, luckily, I caught myself before I went down in a heap.

Damn these heels.

My fingers gripping the handrail tightly, I straightened my spine and did my best to take each step carefully. My mouth was dry. When I reached the bottom stairs, Ashton took my hand and spun me around.

"You're gorgeous."

I felt the heat race to my face. "I'm not, but thank you for saying that."

He pulled me in and lifted my chin to meet his gaze. "I wouldn't lie to you. I'm not the type of man to give empty compliments."

Very true. Since I'd arrived, Ashton hadn't sugarcoated anything. He was honest, almost to a fault.

"Thank you."

He sighed. "Please listen. I'm out of ideas on how to help you."

I laid my hand on his arm. "I don't need help. You've taught me so much since I've been here."

"Not enough, or you'd appreciate how fucking sexy you are."

Stunned I was frozen to my spot. That was the first time anyone had ever called me sexy. I didn't know how to respond.

"Let's go, before we're late."

He took my hand, leading me to the garage and the cars. He turned the key in the ignition and the Aston Martin came to life. I waited until the car started to move before I turned to him, my heart pounding in my chest, unsure whether to ask the question but needing to know the answer at the same time.

"You think I'm sexy?"

TRADED

He slammed his foot on the brake, throwing us forward. Slowly, he turned to face me. "Fuck yes, I think you're sexy."

I twisted my fingers in my lap. "I've never seen myself that way."

His hand moved over the center console to take mine, linking our fingers together, and he lifted his other hand to my face. "I know. I wish you would."

Staring in his eyes, I was lost in the moment when his hand dropped from my face to my neck, his fingers finding their way into my hair. Lowering his head, he brought my lips to his. The first connection and I let myself fall into the kiss. No one had ever kissed me and left me feeling it all the way to my toes. The light taste of cinnamon flooded my senses when his tongue caressed my lips, coaxing me to open. Ignoring the voice in the back of my head screaming that I shouldn't be doing this, I parted my lips and let him in. The glide of his tongue against mine was hesitant, but not in a way that made me think he didn't want this. It made heart want to pound out of my chest. Everything around me fell away. It was just him and me. Ashton and Elena, and their kiss.

This *kiss*.

And as quickly as the kiss began he was gone, his hands falling away to grip the leather of the steering wheel. His knuckles flexed and I could see his skin turning white with the effort.

"I shouldn't have done that. I apologize." And without another word, he sped off toward his parents' place.

Without the noise of the radio to cut through the silence, the air around us filled with a tension you could have cut with a knife. I was shaken to my core. I couldn't speak or think. Everything I'd ever known had just been obliterated by one simple kiss. In all my years with Dominic, I'd never once felt this way. Our kisses had always been fairly chaste, and he hadn't really kissed me at all in the last five years. Usually he told me to get on the bed and lay there. No touching, no feeling. No connection, no tenderness. Nothing *personal*. The kiss with Ashton was very, very personal.

So why did he pull away?

Why did he say he shouldn't have done that?

Did I do something wrong?

Doubts and desire warred within me. From the moment I'd met Ashton, he'd made me question everything. From Dominic's treatment of me, to the views I held of myself. It shouldn't surprise me that tonight was the first time I'd felt desire in forever. Anyone would feel special after what he'd given me over the two weeks I'd been with him. But I didn't want to just be special. I wanted to be special to *him*.

I still hadn't come up with an answer when we arrived at his parents building.

Ashton had warned me earlier in the week that his parents preferred to live in the city instead of the surrounding suburbs. As he pulled the car up alongside the valet, the desire to jump out of the car and run down the street was overwhelming. I wasn't done processing the kiss, or Ashton's withdrawal. I couldn't even begin to process what was about to happen. Not once in my life did I ever think I'd be faced with a crime lord. And to top it off, his son brought me here.

The valet opened the door for me. Taking deep, calming breaths, I exited the car, tamping down any residual nerves as best I could. Regardless of what had just happened, I didn't think Ashton would let anyone hurt me; his family included.

I let Ashton guide me through the doors and into the elevator. He still hadn't said a word to me, but the tension poured off of him in waves. It only got worse when the elevator doors closed us in. The air grew static—like there was electricity dancing all around us. I kept my eyes on the doors, only chancing a look when I thought he wasn't paying attention. The third time, our gazes locked. My body burned. All I wanted was for him to back me into the wall and kiss me like we were in some stupid romance novel.

But this was real life, not some fairytale. The man I wanted more than I should obviously didn't see me the way I saw him.

The bell dinged and the doors opened, breaking the connection for only a second before he placed his hand on the small of my back and guided me out of the elevator, toward voices that came from the other side of what looked to be a front door. My stomach was buzzing with butterflies, which only got worse when Ashton bypassed knocking and pushed the door, revealing a group of people sitting around, drinking and enjoying each other's company.

"Ashton."

An older version of the man beside me stood from the couch, his eyes zeroing in on me as he moved around the furniture to join us in the entryway. "And you must be Elena." He took my hand in his and brought it to his lips.

"That's me."

For the second time in an hour, a blush burned my face. *So much for being self-assured.* Not even a minute in and I was already tongue-tied. "It's nice to meet you . . ." The blush on my face intensified. I couldn't believe I hadn't even thought to ask Ashton his father's name.

He laughed. "Call me Malcolm. Come, let's introduce you to everyone else."

He kept hold of my hand and walked me into the room. Everyone's eyes were on me. Even after all the years I'd spent on stage, center of attention, it still made me nervous to be in a roomful of people. It didn't help that I hadn't been on a stage in at least five years, if not more.

"Elena, this is my son, Miller."

A very attractive man with dark hair reached out his hand to me and let out a low whistle as his fingers tightened around mine. "Holy shit, Ashton, you failed to mention she was fucking gorgeous."

Malcolm smacked Miller upside the back of his head. "Language."

"Sorry, Dad, but look at her."

Miller gestured toward me and, unsure of what to say, I just stood there . . . mute. I was so caught up in what was going on around me that I missed Ashton step up behind me. "What did I tell you?" he whispered, his hot breath on my ear making me want to groan. I suppressed a shudder and focused on Malcolm, who was introducing me to a woman with long blonde hair.

"Elena, this is my sister, Veronica."

The woman smiled and, dispensing with any kind of formality, she stepped forward to wrap me in a hug. "I'm so glad to meet you. I would love to get a chance to talk later."

"Of course." I couldn't imagine what she might want to talk about, but she was Ashton's aunt and as a guest in his family home it would be rude to question her.

She gestured toward the man next to her. "This is my husband, Samuel."

I held my hand out and he clasped it in his own. "It's nice to meet you. Ashton, good to see you again."

Ashton gave his aunt a hug and shook Samuel's hand before asking, "Mom's in the kitchen?"

Malcolm laughed. "Where else did you think she would be?"

Ashton lightly touched my elbow. "Will you be okay here, if I go help Mom finish dinner?"

What was I supposed to say? I knew Ashton loved to cook and his food was fabulous. "Sure."

"She'll be fine," Veronica spoke up. "We don't bite."

Ashton shook his head, his tongue darting out to swipe over his white teeth and flashbacks of that tongue on mine in the car nearly had my knees buckling. "I'll be right through there if you need me." He pointed toward a set of double white doors and waited for me to respond.

"I'll be fine. You go."

"Elena, come sit with me." Veronica turned to Malcolm. "Can you get us each a glass of Chardonnay?"

"Anything for you ladies." Malcolm immediately moved to fetch our drinks. It wasn't hard to see where Ashton had learned his manners. It must be a family trait.

As he waited on us, I realized that Malcolm did not fit any of the molds I'd tried to place him in before we arrived, but while he had been extremely kind to me since we arrived, I had a feeling that under the surface was a man not to be tangled with. He bore the demeanor of a man used to getting what he wanted. He'd protect and defend what was his, no matter the cost.

Not wanting offend Veronica, I took the seat on her other side.

"Samuel, I need you to look over an account for me." I turned at Miller's voice, watching him turn to Malcolm. "Dad, can we use your office?"

"Sure," he called over his shoulder. "Let me finish getting these ladies their drinks and I'll meet you there."

Making his apologies, Samuel stood and followed Miller down another hall, just as Malcolm returned and handed us each a glass. "Thank you," I said, taking hold of the stem, grateful for something to do with my shaking hands. I might have told Ashton I was fine but that didn't mean the nerves hadn't returned in full force.

TRADED

"If you need anything else, just yell."

Malcolm turned and took the same path as his son and brother in law, leaving Veronica and me alone in the room. I took a sip of my wine, struggling to think of anything to say. Luckily, Veronica was not so awkward.

"So, Elena, tell me about yourself."

"There's not much to tell." I took another sip. The dry flavor of the wine definitely appealed to me. I reminded myself to slow down. It wouldn't look good if I got drunk.

"I think there's plenty to tell."

My shoulders hunched. How much did she know? "I guess you talked to Ashton."

She laid her hand on my leg, giving a gentle squeeze as she said softly, "No. I spoke with my brother. He told me what happened at the baseball game when you ended up with Ashton, but I didn't need to know that to read it all over you. It's easy to spot when you've been there yourself."

My gaze snapped to hers and my eyes widened.

"My husband verbally abused me for years."

"Samuel?" My voice came out squeaky and I was aware my eyebrows had made their way up into my hairline.

She laughed. "Oh God, no. That man wouldn't hurt a fly. Samuel is my second husband. My first husband was a raging asshole, but it took me a while to see that."

I shook my head, feeling the need to leap to my husband's defense. "Dominic doesn't mean what he says."

"He does." I flinched at her direct tone, but she ignored it and continued. "He means every word of it because it helps him control you. Every time he puts you down, you believe more of the shit he says. You worry you're not good enough, that he's the best you'll get. And *bam!* you're his slave. Any of this sound familiar?"

She didn't pull any punches. "A little. But I'm not his slave."

"Oh, you're not? Don't feed me lines. You already know all of this is wrong—what's stopping you from admitting it?"

There was no point trying to talk my way out of it. While Veronica may have been in my position at one point, it was clear that she was no longer that woman. I doubted she'd accept anything less than the truth. "He's the only one who wants me."

"Have you seen the way my nephews look at you? One in particular?"

"Ashton's only stuck with me because my husband owes him money and can't pay it."

"That may be how you met, but trust me when I tell you that boy wants more."

"No he doesn't."

Taking piece of hair in my hand, I began to twirl it around my fingers, her words running through my mind, confusing me, but I knew the truth. Ashton didn't want me. He'd near enough said it in the car. I looked away, not crazy about admitting this to a complete stranger, but she needed to understand. "Ashton kissed me tonight, but only for a moment before he pulled away. He said he was sorry, and that he shouldn't have done it."

She groaned. "Please tell me that's not what he said?"

"It is."

"Hmm . . ." She tapped her forefinger on her chin. "Did you say he said *shouldn't have?*"

"Yeah."

"Doesn't want to scare you," she muttered into her glass, her eyes focused on something in the distance.

"But he said he shouldn't—"

"Exactly, *shouldn't have* not *didn't want* to. There's a huge difference, Elena. I know my nephew and there is very little he does without wanting to."

It was an interesting theory, but I remained unconvinced. "Maybe."

"Elena, Ashton called because he wants me to try and help you. He knows what I went through and set up this whole dinner so we could talk."

"He told me he wanted me to learn something tonight."

"Yes, he does. He wants you to understand you don't need to put up with the bullshit—that you're better than that, and deserve to be treated as such."

"You really think I can do better?"

"Of course you can. I thought the same way with David, but he was wrong. Malcolm helped me see that. Now tell me about your husband so I can show you why everything he says is wrong. It's what helped me overcome all of David's garbage."

It took another glass of wine and a good while, during which time I noted that none of the other family returned to the room, but I told Veronica everything about Dominic; including what led to me staying with Ashton. My throat burned as I tried to hold back my emotions, but the tears slipped from my eyes anyway, and the whole time Veronica held my hand, offering me a tissue when it got too much, never pressuring for more information but waiting for me to continue. The experience was cathartic to say the least. With each admission I began to see what I'd been living with; what I'd let myself live with. And in getting everything out in the open, talking about things that I'd pushed down for so long, some I'd forgotten until that moment, I began to realize that Ashton and Veronica were right. I didn't deserve the life I was living with Dominic. I was a good person. He was not. And the biggest realization?

    I was worth more.

CHAPTER 9

Ashton

I left the room knowing that Elena had no idea what she was in for. Miller and Dad had been briefed and I was confident they would get the hint and leave the room, probably with Samuel in tow. Aunt Veronica did not pull any punches when it came to abusive men. Once she'd pushed David from her life and found herself again, she used her time and energy helping women in the same position she'd been in. If anyone could get through to Elena, it was Aunt Veronica.

I pushed through the double doors and found Mom at the stove, wooden spoon in her hand, glasses perched on top of her head. "Hey, sweetheart." She smiled over her shoulder. "What are you doing in here?"

I shrugged off my jacket, tossing over one of the chairs. "Helping you while Aunt Veronica talks to Elena." I lifted the lid on one of the pans, only to have my hand swatted away.

"What the hell?"

"Don't use that language on me." She waved the spoon and I ducked. "No touching. I'm almost done. Go hang out with your brother and father."

"But I can't go out there while they're talking. Besides, I like helping."

"I know, but tonight let me do this. Make sure you're there for that poor girl. Veronica won't go easy on her."

I sighed. "She needs to hear it, Mom."

She put her hand on my arm. "And she'll need someone's shoulder to cry on when she understands how wrong it all is."

I rubbed at my hand and rested my hip against the cupboard, watching her work her magic. The woman really was a genius in the kitchen. The smells coming from whatever it was she was cooking made my mouth water but I kept my distance. I didn't need another knock. We chatted back and forth for a while before I fell silent. My mom stopped what she was doing and stared at me, waiting for me to offload.

"You think Aunt Veronica can work miracles?

My mom was honest to a fault. "No. You're probably going to have to help, but Veronica will make her see the truth. Overcoming it will take time." She pointed to the door with the spoon. "Now go."

Laughing, I placed a kiss on her cheek, moving quickly before she swatted me away, grabbing my coat and throwing it over my shoulder. For a brief second I thought about heading to the living room, then I realized I needed to let Aunt Veronica do what she could. Not wanting to interrupt the conversation, I turned away from the living room and walked toward my father's office.

Miller's voice drifted down the hall. When I opened the door, they were all sitting around, drinking. Dad passed a glass to me the minute the door closed behind me.

"Figure you could use it."

Taking a seat on the couch next to Miller, I took a sip of the whiskey, letting it burn its way down. "Why do you say that?"

He scoffed. "After what Ronnie's going to say and do, you're going to have a crying woman on your hands."

My eyes darted to the door and back. The urge to go out there and listen was almost overpowering, but I fought it back and changed the subject. "Dad, why in the hell did you want me to take Elena to the game with me last Thursday?"

He took a seat at his desk and leaned over the top. "For the same reason you want to run out of here and check on Elena."

"I don't want—"

"For fuck's sake, Ashton, do not blow smoke up my ass. I could tell when you showed up that first day to tell me about her. You want her."

"Hell, *I* want her. She's fucking gorgeous." The vein at my temple throbbed at Miller's words, images of him taking advantage of Elena running through my head.

Oh hell no!

Dad pointed his finger at Miller. "You, knock it off. I know you wouldn't do anything, but right now your brother's thinking about beating your ass into the ground."

Miller held his hands up in surrender. "Dude, can you blame me for noticing her. Holy hell, I've never seen her equal."

I had enough of Miller's mouth and threw a punch to his arm, making him spill his drink on his pants.

"Watch it, asshole."

Dad shook his head. "I warned you, Miller. Now go dry yourself off in the bathroom."

Grumbling, he stood and left the room. With his smart mouth gone, the tension finally flowed from my shoulders. "That still doesn't answer my question. If you want me with her, then why send her with me to see what it is we do? I think she got enough of that when she ended up here with me, and Derrick Reynolds showing up the same night didn't help." I leaned forward, rolling the glass back and forth in my palms.

Dad leaned back in his chair. "No, she saw a small glimpse. If you want her to stay, she needs to know it all. I firmly believe your mother and I have been together for so long because she knew from day one what I did. I've never had to hide anything from her."

"Trust me. She saw enough."

"Did she see a payment that went smoothly?"

Knowing he had me, I chose to ignore his question. I groaned. "Why does everyone assume

TRADED

I want this woman? She's got enough baggage to fill an airplane."

"But you want her anyway," Samuel piped up. He'd been so quiet I'd almost forgotten he was there. "Just like I wanted Veronica."

"Yeah, but Aunt Veronica had been away from David for years before you met her."

He downed the rest of his drink and shook his head. "Didn't mean my experience was any different. I had to work harder to earn her trust. I had to prove I wanted her just the way she is. Only then did I get my shot."

My eyes wandered to the door again.

"Go check on her." Dad pointed toward it. "We'll talk more later."

I was on my feet before he'd even finished his sentence. When I got to the end of the hall, I listened. I didn't know what I was hoping to hear but the room was silent. I rounded the corner and saw the tears streaking down Elena's face and my fists went tight at my sides, an unknown feeling overwhelming me to the point where I could hear the blood rushing in my ears. I stalked across the room, my eyes locked on Aunt Veronica. "What did you say to her?"

"Nothing she didn't need to hear."

Taking Elena's hand I pulled her up from the couch, and without giving her the option to refuse, I led her down the hall to my old room. The décor wasn't that different to when I'd lived there, Mom leaving it as it was in case I ever had reason to stay in the city. Gently, I sat her down on the bed, taking the seat next to her. I cupped her face in my hands, using the pads of my thumbs to wipe away the wet from under her eyes.

"Talk to me."

She sniffed. "Everything I've ever known has been one giant, messed up lie."

"A lie?"

"Yeah, he never loved me, just wanted to use me."

Halle-fucking-lujah.

"That's what I've been trying to tell you."

"I know, but you already hated Dominic. It's just worse now, because maybe Veronica's right—maybe I do deserve better."

"Hell fucking yes you do."

I wasn't sure if it was the right move, but it was the move that felt most right in that moment. Lifting her face, I captured her lips with mine and put everything I needed her to feel into the kiss. Her lips were salty from the tears, but unbelievably soft. Our kiss from earlier had been running through my mind and I'd managed to convince myself that I imagined just how great her lips felt against mine.

I was wrong.

She melted into the kiss and I lost all control, tilting her head with my hands, my tongue diving into her mouth, devouring her. A low moan tore through her throat and the sound was so unexpected that it shot heat straight through me and my dick hardened in seconds, my body screaming for hers. My hands began moving of their own volition, searching, seeking more. They ran up her thighs, feeling the muscles shudder beneath my touch, and just as my fingers hit the silky fabric of her dress, moving it up and out of the way, I caught myself.

This isn't right. It's too fast. Too soon.

Pulling my hand away, my head fell forward, my forehead leaning against hers, both of us breathing heavily.

"You're absolutely fucking gorgeous. You deserve the world on a silver platter. And as much I want nothing more than to show you how good it can be, we can't do this right now."

She leaned back, looking around, scanning the room, returning from wherever she'd gone in her head. I knew how she felt because when I kissed her, everything else ceased to exist.

"Oh my God," she whispered, her hand shooting up to cover her mouth and the panicked look that had so often marred her features when she first came to me returned to her eyes. I couldn't have her going backward. Not when we'd made so much progress. Taking her hand away from her lips I stood up, taking her with me, pulling her body close so that it was flush with mine. I could feel the heat radiating from her. But my family was out there, likely worried about how Elena was doing. They'd give us privacy, yes, but before anything further happened between Elena and me, we needed to have a conversation. And that couldn't happen with anyone else around.

"Let's go have dinner. We can talk about this on the way home."

I kept her hand in mine and led us from the room. The scent of Mom's cooking permeated the house and it smelled delicious, my stomach growling as we made our way back toward the dining room. As soon as we walked in, all eyes were on us. While Dad and Miller pretended to be talking about something else and Samuel flicked through the newspaper, Aunt Veronica watched as I settled Elena into a chair and fetched her glass of wine before wrapping her arm around my bicep, bringing her mouth to my ear.

"Ashton, can I talk to you for one second?"

I pulled my lips between my teeth and bit down. I was afraid to leave Elena alone again. Space to think was dangerous. The more you gave her, the easier she found it to retreat. But I knew Aunt Veronica wouldn't have asked unless it was important. I turned to Elena. "Will you be okay?"

She gave me an uneasy smile. "I'll be fine."

"I'll be back in a minute." I felt bad. After all, this was the second time I'd left her alone since we'd arrived. I let Aunt Veronica lead me from the room. The second we made it to the living room she pointed to a chair.

"Sit."

Suddenly, I felt like one of my dad's customers. My aunt was glaring at me, eyes hard. There was a right and a wrong way to approach her. If I got caught yelling, there was no doubt I'd get my ass kicked. On the other hand, I didn't feel like dealing with her bullshit. It was completely irrational for me to be mad at her. She'd done exactly what I'd asked. But seeing just how upset Elena was, I had a hard time controlling myself. Crossing my arms over my chest I stayed rooted to the spot, watching her, waiting for her to explain what was so important. A brief moment passed in silence.

"What do you want?" My tone was clipped, and although I knew somewhere in the back of my head she didn't deserve it, my mind was on Elena. I wanted this done with, and fast.

"Don't start with me, Ashton. You and I are going to have a little talk about Elena. So sit." She pointed at the couch and then at me and I raised a brow. When, again, she didn't elaborate, I grew frustrated.

"You're being ridiculous. I'm going back in there."

"You'll never get her if you don't listen to me," she called to my back and I stopped in my tracks.

She had me by the balls. If I wanted Elena in my bed, I needed to understand what kept her tied to Tolley, and to do that I had two options: the long way, where I did all the groundwork myself; or the shortcut, where I listened to whatever knowledge Aunt Veronica had to impart and used it to my advantage. I paused for a beat. My dad was right: three months was not a lot of time. Perhaps there was mileage in listening to my aunt. I turned back toward her and lifted my chin.

"You have my attention."

Her eyes darted to the couch and back to me. She was a stubborn character. If I wanted to know, I had to play by her rules. I took a seat on the couch and she sat across from me, wine glass clutched in her hand.

"What have you done with Elena since she came to stay with you?"

Weird question. "Sent her to the spa, took her to dinner—"

"When you took her to dinner, did you mention anything about the way she looked?"

Rolling my eyes, I said, "Yes, I told her she looked gorgeous."

"That's it?"

"Jesus Christ." I started to stand up. "What else am I supposed to say? She looked great, I told her."

"You told her you want her?" she countered, and my head snapped to hers.

"That I what?"

She chuckled and pressed a hand to my leg, pushing my back down onto the couch. She took her time, taking a sip of her wine, and giving my leg a squeeze.

"Well?"

"You're so clueless. Everyone in the house figured it out the moment you walked through the door. You want her, and if you want my help getting her, you'd better keep your ass in that seat and listen."

"You do realize there aren't many people who'd have the balls to talk to me this way, right?"

"Cut the crap, Ashton. I learned from the best. Your think your father is good at the big, bad boss routine? *Hah!* I learned from your grandfather. Now there was a man who took shit from no one. David was lucky Dad passed away before we married. Now stay where you are and don't get up until I tell you to."

TRADED

I leaned back in my seat and waited, my silence speaking volumes, and when she was satisfied that I was staying, she began again.

"Now, you haven't answered my question. Have you told her you want her?"

I sighed and lifted my eyes to the ceiling. "No. If she wants to be in my bed she's got to be there because she wants to—not because it's something to do with her husband's debt."

"For a smart guy, you can be an absolute idiot."

"What?" I growled.

"Earlier tonight, you told her that kissing her was a mistake."

"I did not," I answered quickly.

Her eyebrows rose. "Oh really? That's not what Elena told me."

I shook my head, racking my brain for my exact words. "I think I said . . . shit." My eyes focused on hers. "I said, 'I shouldn't have done that.' That's not what I meant though."

"That doesn't matter, Ashton. You have to remember that for the last five years, she's heard she's unattractive, that no man besides him would ever want her. You pulling away and saying you shouldn't have done that only confirmed to her that her husband spoke the truth."

"Shit. *Fuck!*"

My head throbbed from the discussion. There were so many things I couldn't do, or that I should be doing. It was like a minefield. One thing was for certain: that fucker was going to pay for all he'd done to Elena. "That wasn't my goal."

"I know." She smiled. "You can help her more than you know. I understand your reasoning."

Aunt Veronica didn't understand as much as she thought. If she knew my tastes didn't exactly run in the mainstream, she might understand my caution. Elena had been through so much already, Could I really subject her to the possibility of more damage? Could she handle the things I enjoyed?

"You need to show her she's desirable. I don't know about Elena's husband, but David frequently withdrew affection. Take her places, put your hands on her. Don't just tell her she's beautiful—show her. You want to her to be strong enough to choose to be in your bed, then make her feel like she can stand on her own two feet. She sits around your house all day doing nothing, right?"

"She's worked hard enough."

"And when her three months with you are up, where is she going to go? What will she do?"

"I hadn't thought about that."

In truth, I didn't want to. The time with Elena had been refreshing, not anything like I was used to. She was smart and witty. That wasn't all, I was different around her. The man I always wanted to be. She might be sexy as hell, but she wasn't an empty shell, like so many of the women I met over the years. Our time together already seemed so short. I didn't want to wish it away.

Aunt Veronica watched me, and it would seem that without me even voicing my thoughts, she understood where my mind was going.

TRADED

"Elena will never give Dominic up if she feels she can't stand on her own two feet. She said she met her husband in high school. Do you know what she was studying?"

"She said it was theater."

Aunt Veronica's eyes lit up. "Ah, so you do pay attention to people when you want to. You have to know someone in the theater district. That, or I'd be willing to bet someone owes your dad a favor."

"I know exactly who to call." Alan owed me a few favors. After everything I'd done for him over the years, an audition for Elena wouldn't be a big deal.

She stood up, empty glass in hand, and made her way to the door, holding it open for me but saying in a low voice, "Make the call. I think after that you'll find things fall into place."

I leaned in to kiss her cheek and she wrapped her arms around my waist. For such a tiny woman, she had one hell of a body lock. "Oh, and the next time you kiss that poor girl, please don't tell her it was a mistake."

I smiled against her hair, knowing I'd at least done *something* right. "One step ahead of you."

"Oh I know. Don't think us women can't tell the difference between blushes." She winked. "Now get your ass in gear. It's time to eat."

"Thank you."

She smiled and walked through the door, toward the dining room.

Fuck. What a night? I hung back, taking a moment to process everything I'd just heard and get my head around where I was going to go from here. I went to the side bar and poured a glass of Glen Livet, needing something to settle all of the shit firing around in my brain. The first drops always burned going down. The second sip settled me and helped me to start formulating a plan. Even if I never ended up fucking Elena, at least I could help her get away from that asshole.

"Ashton!"

The call came from the dining room. Knowing my mother, she already had the perfect wine for the meal sitting on the table. I jogged down the hall and found everyone already seated, wine glasses full, eyes on me. Composing my features, I took my seat next to Elena, who looked to be doing a lot better. She took her glass from in front of her and took a sip. I hoped my family hadn't driven her to that, and resolved to find out what they'd discussed in my absence when we were on our way home.

Home. How quickly I'd become to refer to my house as hers too. It wasn't the first time I'd reflected on the speed at which we'd settled into a routine, and I had to admit that it was nice to come home to someone at the end of a long day.

"Is everything okay?" she whispered.

Molten chocolate eyes stared up at me through long, black lashes and her nose crinkled at the top. Even concern was a sexy look on her. I took hold of her hand under the table, threading my fingers through hers and feeling the warmth spreading from where our bodies connected, up through my arm until it came to settle somewhere in my chest.

"Everything is fine. Let's enjoy dinner."

TRADED

Out of the corner of my eye, I noticed Aunt Veronica watching. She didn't look as content as I thought she should have been. Something else was on her mind. Whatever it might be, she kept it to herself and conversation around us began to pick up, most of it centering around Elena.

Mom led the charge; the woman could get a clam to open with a few simple questions. She skipped questions about Elena's husband or the arrangement we were currently in, choosing to ask about her childhood, the things she liked, her favorite memories. I thought for a moment that Elena would be too shy to answer, but she was radiant as she regaled a story about her first audition. She didn't talk much about her parents, but that didn't surprise me. If Dominic was anything like David had been, he likely went out of his way to isolate her from her family. Much easier to bring her to heel without outside interference.

Eventually it was time to say good-night. Aunt Veronica gave Elena a huge hug and made her promise to call if she ever wanted to talk. Elena seemed pleased at this prospect and they traded numbers. Finally, after a few attempts, we were back in the car, on the way home.

"Did you enjoy dinner?" I went for small talk, which I normally sucked at but my options were limited. While I had a plan, I'd yet to implement it and after the kiss in the bedroom, I didn't know what to say without giving her the wrong impression. It wasn't easy to focus. Just the thought of her mouth against mine had me discreetly adjusting my pants, which is harder to do than one might think when you're driving.

Elena said more on the drive home than I had ever heard from her in one go. "Your family is wonderful." She paused, and there was a slight quiver to her voice as she murmured, "It makes me miss my mom and dad."

Just as I suspected.

"When was the last time you saw them?" I kept my eyes on the road, afraid if I saw her crying I'd want to pull her into my arms and end up crashing the fucking car. She was silent for a beat, and I thought she might ignore the question until she spoke up.

"When Dominic and I told them we got married, they weren't very happy about it. Dominic thought it might be better for us to find jobs across the country."

"You didn't talk to them after that?"

Out of the corner of my eye, I saw her fidget in the seat, her fingers moving to curl around her bag, fiddling with the clasp. "Dominic said if they still cared, they'd leave a message at the house. We could never afford to go back."

I heard a sniffle and my hand left the wheel to reach over and take hers, nestled in her lap. "I'm sorry. Maybe you can try again?"

She laughed, but there was no humor to it. I felt a sharp pain in the left hand side of my chest. "Yeah, I'm sure that they would understand all of this." I'd never heard Elena be sarcastic and the tone didn't suit her.

"I didn't mean for you tell them all of this. I bet they miss not hearing from you."

"I don't know. Maybe."

TRADED

The car went silent after that. I was aware that I'd promised to talk to her about the kiss but I let it go and continued driving. When we finally walked into the house, her eyes bounced around the room, looking everywhere but at me. Cupping her face, I lifted her eyes to mine and saw the whites were stretched wide, her irises almost invisible.

"Relax, Elena." I kissed her on the forehead. "Today has been exhausting, and you have a big day tomorrow."

"A big day?"

"You'll see. Now why don't you head up and get some sleep?"

She nodded, but before she could step out of my reach I dipped my head, placing my lips against hers, once again finding myself unable to resist her. When she didn't pull away I became bolder, swiping my tongue across her lips, hoping she'd let me in. She didn't disappoint. I took and she gave, the connection of our mouths sending desire burning through my veins. When the need to breathe overrode everything else I pulled away, panting, and if the rise and fall of her chest was anything to go by, she was as affected by the kiss as me.

Taking her hand in mine, I laced our fingers together, watching her closely as she began to close down before my eyes. "I can only guess why you look like you did something wrong. If you feel like this is cheating, it's not. First, your husband gave you permission, and as wrong as that is, it's still permission. Second, you deserve a million times better than him." I bent down to whisper in her ear. "Third, never doubt that I've wanted you since the first moment I saw you."

Her face softened, but didn't relax. "Thank you for everything, Ashton." She stepped away from me. "I'll see you in the morning."

She practically ran up the stairs and while it was disappointing to watch her leave, if she'd stayed then it would have pushed my control to its limits. I'd never force her to do anything she didn't want to do. If she wanted to go there, we'd do it at her pace. Not that I wouldn't try to persuade her; hope she could handle what I had in store for her. Bearing in mind what I knew of her husband, it wasn't conceited of me to say I could show her pleasure she never imagined, and probably never felt before.

Taking my phone from my pocket, I walked to my room to call Alan and arrange her audition. After that, I needed a long cold shower. I was beginning to feel like a polar bear, but I had to utilize what I could to help to take the edge off, and I most definitely did not need a severe case of blue balls all night. And even though tonight had not ended in the way perhaps I'd hoped, it had been successful in a different way. If I'd figured out anything tonight it was that, however long it took, Elena would be worth the wait.

CHAPTER 10

Elena

My lips tingled, my fingers touching the swollen skin as I climbed the stairs to my room. How Ashton read me so well, I didn't know, but he'd hit the nail on the head: a small part of me *did* feel like I was cheating on Dominic. While I didn't care so much about that, it worried me how easily I could ignore the fact I was married and fall into another man's arms.

Stripping out of the dress, I remembered what Ashton's touch felt like. It was a touch that I'd never once felt before, and likely would never feel again. It wasn't just the attraction either. His arms around me felt warm. Comforting.

As I got ready for bed, I let everything Veronica had said play through my head. To think she'd been in the same situation as me was amazing. She seemed so strong, and I wondered if someday I might, too, have that same strength. The more I thought about it, the more I was starting to see how right she'd been. Dominic didn't deserve me. He just wanted me to look after him.

The way Ashton touched me was so far removed for Dominic's touch that it felt like I was experiencing everything for the first time. For one, he kissed me. Dominic had avoided kissing me for years, simply using my body for his own pleasure. Kissing took too much time, too much effort. Since Dominic knew how much I loved kissing, to do it would mean that he was thinking about my pleasure as well as his own, and that wouldn't even cross his mind. My chest swelled when I thought about Ashton kissing me. For him, it wasn't just about the lips; he caressed my face and my body, making sensations run rife through every nerve ending until I had no choice but to lose myself completely. His kiss wasn't just a kiss. It was an experience; one I would love to repeat. And when he spoke to me he was so kind. From the time I'd spent with him, I knew Ashton was not a man to give throwaway compliments. When he said something he was direct about it, and he meant whatever he said; which is what had made it so easy to believe that he thought our kiss in the car was a mistake.

But he was gentle. If I misunderstood him he didn't get angry or cross. He took the time to explain what he meant, and didn't make me feel stupid. The whole evening had left me feeling bewildered. On one hand, I'd experienced possibly one of the best kisses of my entire life. On the other, I was beginning to realize just how much I'd missed out on during my years with

TRADED

Dominic. And that thought was depressing, to say the least.

I slid beneath the cool sheets and, thoroughly exhausted after the turmoil of the evening, I closed my eyes and welcomed the drowsy feeling that overtook me. It had hurt to talk about Dominic, but I felt better afterward, and that had to be a step in the right direction.

I was just about to drop off when Ashton's words ran through my head. *Tomorrow? Something about a big day tomorrow.* I had no idea what he might be talking about. Too tired to figure it out, I decided to ask him again in the morning and fell asleep, letting dreams of Ashton and all the things I'd hoped he do to me float through my head.

♋♋♋

I leaned into the soft caress. The warmth felt nice against my face as it pulled me from sleep. The action was welcomed. Soothing. Wanting the dream to last, I curled toward the warmth, my lips lifting and a small sigh escaping. A masculine chuckle echoed around the room.

"Elena," he whispered. "Time to wake up."

Letting my eyelids flutter open, the sight in front of me made me want to moan, and it was only by the grace of God that I managed to hold it back.

"Ashton?"

"Wake up, sleepyhead. I told you, you have a big day today."

I moved to sit up and felt the smooth glide of silk against cotton. Ashton's personal shopper had insisted on silk nighties and lace panties; nighties and panties Ashton would surely get an eyeful of if I moved any further. Pulling the covers up over my breasts, I sat back against the pillows and watched as his eyes dropped to the start of the sheet, his tongue darting out to wet his bottom lip.

"What big day?" I asked, trying to draw his attention back to my eyes.

His gaze moved back to my face but his eyes looked lazy and his expression was blank. "What?"

"Big day? Some details might help?"

"Oh, right." He shook his head and looked at me again, his gravelly voice sending a shiver up my spine as he said, "Elena, your body can make any man lose his concentration." His eyes darted down and up again and the shivers moved from my spine to between my legs. I clenched my thighs instinctively. "It's a surprise, but I picked you an outfit and Lewis will be out front in an hour to take you there."

My eyes narrowed. "You won't tell me where I'm going, but you want me to trust you?"

"Yes. I've never given you a reason to doubt me."

His finger lifted my chin, the slight domineering tone of his voice like a spark to the embers burning in my stomach. "Okay. You better not let me down."

He smiled his approval. "Feisty. That's a good thing."

My cheeks had to be bright red. A month ago I would never have considered talking to a man this way. Ashton had changed my life so much.

"Why aren't *you* taking me?"

His eyes clouded. "I have some business I need to take care of, but I'll be back later and I'll take you to dinner."

I was guessing the business had nothing to do with the restaurant so, ignoring my desire to ask any further questions, I went with the other thing on my mind. "Thank you. I'd love to go to dinner again."

Checking his watch, he stood up and buttoned his suit jacket. "I need to go. Remember, enjoy yourself." He leaned in, stealing a quick kiss before standing and walking from the room.

I touched my finger to my lips, feeling the burn from the lingering heat of his mouth on mine. Every time Ashton touched me I turned into a big pile of mush. Something about that man woke up parts of me long since buried. With a sigh, I climbed from the bed on shaky legs, wondering if I'd even be able to stand after a few rounds underneath Ashton.

Where did those thoughts come from?

My brain seemed to be stuck on sex, which was unusual because sex was something I never looked forward to. It hadn't been like that in the beginning. But years of Dominic being selfish had taken their toll. He never took the time to get me ready so intercourse usually hurt, and in the end I felt like a real life blow-up doll. But now? Now my mind couldn't stop conjuring images of Ashton naked, touching every part of me, making me call out his name.

I went into the bathroom to get ready, the fizz of anticipation not the only thing making me giddy. I only had an hour to get ready for who knew what. The outfit in the bathroom left me even more confused. On the counter was a cute pair of jeans, heeled sandals, and a trendy T-shirt. Where could he be sending me that would require such a casual outfit? I stepped into the shower and by the time I'd finished, I still didn't have any ideas.

Makeup became my next dilemma. Deciding to apply something light, I finished getting ready with enough time to have breakfast. Not much went down with the fluttering of my stomach, which only increased when I heard the knock at the door.

The time had come to find out what Ashton had planned.

Collecting my purse and keys, I found Lewis waiting outside an SUV I'd never seen before, the back door open, waiting for me to get in.

I smiled at him. "A different car today?"

He laughed. "Mr. Hawes has the Bentley today."

"And this is?"

"A BMW, Mrs. Tolley."

I stepped into the car. "Thank you, Lewis."

He nodded. "Sit back and enjoy the ride. We'll be there in no time."

I had to ask the question. "How many cars does Ashton own?"

"Four, including the jeep he goes off-roading in."

TRADED

"Interesting." Four cars for one man, compared to our single car for the two of us.

Throughout the rest of the ride I kept my hands clasped in my lap to stop them shaking. My mind wandered here, there, and back again. It started with guesses as to where Ashton might be sending me, which led to memories of the night before and Ashton's lips on mine. Like earlier, each thought made it harder and harder to concentrate on anything else. Such was my focus on reliving our evening tryst that I was startled when Lewis opened the door. I hadn't even noticed the car come to a stop.

"Here we are." He offered his hand to me, helping me out of the car, a nice thing to do since I still wasn't used to walking in heels.

I stepped out and looked around, attempting to get my bearings. Since Dominic and I moved here, I'd spent most of my time working. I'd had very little time to explore the city and so most places were new and unfamiliar. Lewis reached his hand out to me, a cell phone sitting in his palm.

"Mr. Hawes wanted you to have this, in case you needed to get hold of him."

Each time Ashton presented me with another gift, I had a hard time equating him with a loan shark, a person who hurt people when they didn't pay their debts. It was like he was a Jekyll and Hyde character. But as scary as the other side of his character was, I knew Ashton would never harm me. I didn't know *how* I knew. I just did.

Taking the phone I placed it in my bag, not wanting to lose it. "Thank you, Lewis. What time will you be back?"

"I'll be waiting for you, Mrs. Tolley. Inside you'll find Alan Trindall. You have an appointment with him in fifteen minutes. He knows you're coming."

"Okay."

I strung the word out, my confusion more than evident and given that the butterflies that had taken up root in my stomach were now dive-bombing my insides, I was surprised I managed to remain standing.

"I'll be waiting here when you're done."

"Thank you."

Each step was as nerve-racking as the one before it. I had no idea what I would find behind the doors in front of me. Pulling open the tinted glass, I noticed a long white hallway, doors on both sides, and at the end were two sets of double doors. When I reached the first one, the second opened and out stepped a man, his long dark hair pulled back into a low ponytail.

"Elena Tolley?" he asked.

I looked around, trying to figure out what in the world was going on. He smiled and reached out a hand to me. "Alan Trindall. Ashton said you majored in theater."

I took his hand and shook it. "I did. But I don't understand."

"Ashton didn't tell you why you're here?"

Shaking my head, I admitted, "I don't even know where *here* is. Someone drove me."

He chuckled and shook his head, but I remained none the wiser about why he was talking to me. "Man, is he a dipshit. Luckily you're early. Follow me."

TRADED

He started down the hall and I followed as quickly as my legs could carry me. He opened a door about halfway down the hall. Inside there was a piano and crates of sheet music.

"Do you mind telling me what I'm doing here?"

He dug through the crate while he answered. "Ashton set up an audition for you for one of the musicals we're doing. *Sondheim on Sondheim*."

Oh my God!

My hand flew to my mouth. "I don't have anything prepared."

"Now you see why I'm glad you're early. Alto or soprano?"

"Soprano."

Alan pulled out a piece of music and placed in on the piano. Taking a seat on the bench, he played through the first thirty-two bars.

"I know that," I said. "*No One is Alone* from *Into the Woods*."

"Good. Can you sing it?"

"I . . . uh . . . I think so."

He played through the music again. On the second time through, I joined in.

For the next ten minutes, we went through the song over and over again. With each turn I felt my confidence increasing. I couldn't believe Ashton set it up and didn't give me any warning. But this was my dream; something I wanted ever since I was little.

Alan stopped playing and looked at the clock before removing the sheet music and coming over to stand in front of me. Taking my hands, he said, "Do what you just did in here and you'll be fine. I'm not one of the producers, so I'll play accompaniment for you."

"Thank you." My voice trembled slightly. It felt like all I did lately was thank people. I'd never had this many people do things for me. It was a strange feeling, one that was taking some getting used to.

Alan guided me back down the hall toward the double doors. The entire way I took deep breaths, trying to calm my racing heart, and when the doors opened, I thought it might pound right out of my chest. I stepped into the backstage area, telling myself to relax.

Enjoy yourself.

Ashton's words echoed in my ear as the door shut behind me and I walked toward the curtain, ready to face the audition with my head held high.

༄༅༄༅

The red strapless dress fell just above my knee, making me feel sexy as hell. Ashton had called as I was leaving the theater, saying he was running late but for me to be ready for seven and to dress up. After a nice long nap and lunch, I hurried to my room to get ready. At seven o'clock on the nose, my phone beeped with a text from Ashton.

Ashton: Here. Meet me out front.
Me: K

TRADED

Collecting my things, I hurried to the front door, excited to tell him about my day. Despite my initial nerves, I'd managed to pull it together and I was proud of myself for giving it a shot. If anything, getting back out there had reignited my passion for the stage and given me something to be excited about.

He didn't see me at first—he was checking his phone—but as soon as he lifted his chin and saw me coming down the steps, Ashton froze.

"Holy shit."

It was the exact reaction I was hoping for. He'd said a few times that he didn't want an unwilling woman in his bed, and for the longest while I *hadn't* been willing. That's not to say that the thought hadn't crossed my mind; I just wasn't comfortable with it. But since my revelations about Dominic, things had started to change. *I* had begun to change. The moment I finished on stage I felt that long forgotten rush of euphoria and for the first time in a long time, I had my confidence back.

And I had Ashton to thank for all of it.

He told me almost every day I was beautiful, and for the first time I was starting to believe him.

With my mind on Ashton and all he was doing for me, I took extra care getting ready for dinner. My hair was in a loose-braided chignon at the base of my neck, and a swirling, silver cuff necklace and matching earrings completed the look. Seeing as I was wearing them nearly every day, I was more confident in heels, and chose to wear thin-heeled silver sandals that put my height closer to Ashton's broad shoulders. I'd put a lot of thought and effort into my appearance and it was nice to see that it hadn't been wasted.

The first thing he did when he reached me at the bottom of the stairs was to lift my hand to his lips and place a featherlight kiss on my skin, sending shivers right up my arm. I sucked in a breath and he must have heard it because a smirk played at the edges of his lips.

"How was the audition?"

I smacked him in the chest. "You should have told me! I would have been more prepared."

He glanced down at his chest and back at me, a full-blown grin on his face. "You surprise me more and more every day."

Excitement poured through my veins and I did my best not to jump up and down in the middle of the driveway. I could barely contain myself. I was excited to share the news but curious as to how he might react.

"I got the part."

His jaw dropped slightly but then he pounced. Picking me up, he swung me around, his lips connecting with mine in a kiss that I felt all over my body. When he pulled back we were both breathless. "I knew you could do it," he said against my ear, his lips pressing against my temple before he pulled me toward the car, leading me to the passenger door and opening it, helping me climb in.

"You didn't tell him to give me the spot even if I sucked, did you?"

"Hell no. You got that all on your own. When I called Alan it was for the audition only. Everything else you did."

TRADED

The fact that he maintained eye contact told me he wasn't lying. I lay my hand on his arm, feeling the muscles tense as he pulled away from the sidewalk. "I'm sorry, I shouldn't have suggested that. Nothing like this has ever happened to me, that's all. It's an amazing opportunity. Something I've always dreamed about. Thank you for making the dream come true."

"That was you. You need to realize you can stand on your own two feet."

"I'm starting to see that. I haven't signed anything yet, but they did speak briefly about figures. When it's time for me to go home, I won't have to rely on Dominic's income anymore." I tried to hide the disappointment, even though it killed me to say the words out loud.

Home.

Ashton showed no physical response to my statement, and I couldn't deny the sting I felt. Each day, my feelings for Ashton grew. I wasn't ready to describe them yet, but they were there.

During the rest of the car ride, Ashton asked question after question, wanting to hear every detail.

"I can't wait to see you in it." He squeezed my hand.

"You'll have to wait a few weeks. I have to meet the rest of the cast and rehearse before opening night."

"You have to rehearse?"

I couldn't stop the laugh that escaped my lips. "Of course we do. How else do you expect everyone to learn their parts?"

He shrugged. "I guess I never really put much thought into it. But I'm glad I get to take you out to celebrate."

My face hurt from smiling so much. It had been years since I felt this carefree.

And I loved it.

CHAPTER 11

Ashton

Elena was glowing, her radiance shining through her whole personality. The corners of her eyes crinkled as she explained all about the play and it was amazing to see her so animated. So content.

Alan had called me not long after her audition, asking all sorts of questions about her background, but I didn't know she'd got the part until she told me in the driveway. She must have aced it. I hadn't lied when she'd asked whether I told him to give her the part. The assumption that I might have had something to do with that was like a kick in the teeth, but I reminded myself she wasn't used to good fortune falling in her lap.

It felt like I was seeing a whole new side of her—a side that was even more attractive than I'd seen so far. Her confidence turning me on so badly I was thinking about bending her over the hood of the car and fucking her until she screamed my name. The only thing that kept my dick firmly in my pants was the need to have her willingly. If she wanted to try some of the things I enjoyed, she needed to do it on her own terms.

The restaurant I chose happened to have a dance floor. I didn't know if Elena danced but all day I'd been dreaming about her soft sweet body pressed to mine. When I made the reservation this morning, I made sure the table would be private, but close to the dance floor. Owning three restaurants in town had its perks. My restaurants were the place to see and be seen. The money I made far outweighed the money people paid me in interest on the loans, and every other restaurant owner in town was more than willing to accommodate my requests, knowing I'd do the same for them when they needed it.

After we were seated, Elena picked up her menu, studying it like she did every time we went out to eat. I waited, knowing the question was coming.

"I can't decide," she said.

I had a feeling that even before Dominic, she hadn't spent much time in restaurants like the one we were currently in.

"What are your two choices?" I'd figured out pretty quickly that Elena always wanted two things off the menu but couldn't choose between them. The first time I told her to order both, she'd balked at the idea so I'd changed tack and helped her narrow down her choice. If one of the options was what I happened to be ordering, it was easy because we'd order both and share. If not, well, then ordering took a little longer.

TRADED

"I either want the lamb chops or the seared tuna."

"I'm getting the lamb if you want to try some of mine and get the tuna."

"Oh, that sounds perfect." She closed the menu and sat it on the table, her arms drawing together, my eyes captivated by the tops of her breasts, so beautifully displayed above the red strapless dress. Her creamy flesh would taste divine under my tongue.

We placed our order, including a bottle of wine, and our waitress brought two glasses, allowing us to sample the flavor before she poured. She took a sip and set the glass down, watching me. I lifted a brow.

"I forgot to thank you for the phone when I saw you earlier. I've never had a smart phone. The one I left at the apartment was a prepaid cell. I had to limit the number of calls I made so I wouldn't run out of minutes. It was nice to feel connected to the rest of the world—even if it took me ages to figure out how to use the damn thing."

Asshole had a smartphone; I knew that for a fact. He'd texted me multiple times over the years to arrange drop offs and new loans, and the fact that he hadn't allowed her the simple pleasure of contacting friends and family made my blood boil. I took a sip of my wine, using the time to tamp down my anger.

"You're welcome. Now you can get a hold of me anytime. Speaking of the phone, why didn't you text when you got the part?"

Her cheeks turned the same color as her dress.

"I wanted it to be a surprise."

Reaching across the table, I slipped my hand across her upturned one, caressing the inside of her wrist lightly with my fingers. "I like surprises."

She squirmed in her seat and her breathing faltered.

She likes this.

As I continued stroking the soft skin, the warm chocolate of her eyes flared to a bronze. Our eyes met and I dared her to say something—to admit to the effect my touch was having on her—but she said nothing. My eyes zoned in on her lips as she ran her tongue across them, rolling the skin between her teeth, her eyes darting left and right before landing on mine again. As much as it was thrilling to see her like this, I decided to throw her a bone and asked more about the audition, all the while continuing my slow, sensual torture.

We talked more about her opportunity to work in the theater and such was her excitement that sometimes her words became caught in her throat. I refused to stop touching her so she had to use her other hand to sip at her wine; something that pleased me greatly. Eventually the waitress arrived and I had to relinquish Elena's hand so she could eat. I may not have been able to touch her, but that didn't mean I was entirely well behaved. When she offered me a bite of her tuna I accepted, returning the favor with my own dish, only just managing to suppress my growl when her lips slid over the fork, my cock pushing against the zipper of my pants when she moaned her appreciation.

"That is delicious," she said.

TRADED

"You certainly are." I'd intended for the comment to tease her and when she paused for a beat, I wondered whether she was going to respond. "It certainly is," I clarified and a flush colored her cheeks.

Dinner continued in an erotic game. It crossed my mind that she might be doing it on purpose, until I realized that Elena had never been that brazen. It had to be my own need to take her in every way possible that was causing me to look for double entendre. With this in mind, I tried to keep the conversation light. At the end of the meal the waitress returned with the dessert menu, but Elena refused; a gesture I silently thanked her for. If the woman thought the lamb was delicious, I'd hate to see what noises she'd make when tasting one of the chef's crème brulees. I was generally a patient man, but I couldn't take much more before I cleared the table and took her right here. One such benefit of the evening thus far was that I now no longer had to guess at what she looked like when she was enjoying something. The image of her wide eyes and parted lips returned and my cock throbbed.

Standing, I held out my hand to her. She hesitated a moment before placing her hand in mine. I helped her up and led her to the dance floor.

"I'm not a good dancer," she whispered softly.

Bending down, I nipped her ear and feeling her jolt, a smile came to my lips. "I am."

Carefully, I guided her across the dance floor and when I pulled her close to me the scent of lavender invaded my senses. Our bodies touched at every possible place. With her breasts pressed against my chest, the searing heat from her skin seeping through my shirt, my heart began to thunder. She lifted a hand from my waist to rest it gently on my shoulder, looking up at me, making sure it was okay. Fuck, this woman left me in a state of sexual frustration I hadn't experienced since I was a teenager.

With very little coaxing, Elena fell in step with me and we moved gracefully across the floor. I kept my eyes on the dancers around us, thoughts of sliding the zipper of her dress down, revealing the surprise inside, invading all the space in my brain until the desire to see her face was overwhelming. Dropping my eyes, I noticed her flushed cheeks, the rapid beat of the pulse in her neck, her breath coming in shallow pants as her eyes locked on mine. The fire there threw me, and when she made her move, my footsteps faltered.

Her hand on my shoulder slid up, moving behind my neck, curling into my hair, and when she applied the slightest of pressure, I obeyed, bending down to devour her mouth, the taste of red wine lingering on her lips. Wanting more, I deepened the kiss, blatantly ignoring the fact that we were on a very crowded and very public dance floor.

Her fingers flexed then tightened in my hair, holding my mouth against hers. I could feel her heartbeat next to my chest. A soft whimper escaped her throat. By the time she pulled away my head was ready to explode with lust. Her lower body still pressed to mine, the hard length of my shaft pushing into her abdomen, I felt the slightest twitch of her hips and my eyes immediately found hers.

Eyes so dark they could be chestnut stared back at me, reflecting the same lust I felt coiled deep within my stomach. She swallowed hard and opened her mouth to speak. At first nothing came out and I chanted in my head.

Please, please, please.

Somehow, I fought off the urge to reach down and adjust myself. It felt like I'd waited an eternity for her, not simply a few weeks, and the few moments we stood in silence, waiting to hear what she wanted, felt twice as long.

"Take me home."

Her words, though arousing, were not the, "Take me home and have sex with me," I wanted and I wasn't going to jump to conclusions, at least, not with such a vague statement.

"You don't want to dance anymore?"

"No." She took a deep breath. "I want to be your dessert."

You don't get any clearer than that.

Without another word, I tugged her from the floor, stopping by our table to toss more than enough money down to cover our bill and tip, and hurried out to the car.

CHAPTER 12

Elena

Desire like I'd never felt before heated my blood the moment his lips touched mine, and only grew when the taste of him sizzled over my tongue. Throughout dinner my need for him had overtaken every part of me; eclipsing any residual fear I might have had until I hadn't been able to contain myself.

Having been with only one man my entire life, Dominic had pretty much set the bar when it came to sex. Listening to women heatedly discuss their latest conquest and how many times the men made them come made me feel like something might be wrong with me. Not once in my entire life had I enjoyed sex of any kind. To me it was uncomfortable and somewhat degrading. With Dominic, it felt like a duty to be carried out because we were married: no different to unloading the dishwasher, or folding the laundry.

TRADED

Yet there was something about Ashton that made me disregard my prior experiences, wanting to drive him crazy, no matter whether or not I enjoyed it.

We pulled onto the main road and my nerves started to get the better of me. Hands shaking, my knee bounced up and down at the same speed until Ashton's hand curled over my knee. I wanted to moan at the skin-on-skin contact. My body started to hum when his fingers slid up the inside of my thigh, his thumb lightly caressing the sensitive skin there. Shivers traveled through me. I wanted him to move farther up my leg. My core throbbed, pulsing with need. The feeling was unfamiliar but definitely not unwelcome. I clenched my thighs, knowing he'd feel the spasm against his hand. I'd never felt like this before. The whole situation made me feel so wanton. Like I didn't have a care in the world.

Ashton pulled into the drive, jumping out of the car and running around the front to open my door. With a quick jerk, I was yanked from the vehicle and into his arms. His hair was out of place, having been combed through with his fingers, and the button at his neck was undone Seeing this man, usually so put together and controlled, in a state of disarray was rough and sexy and made me want to tear my clothes off. His hands plunged into my hair and pulled me up for a searing kiss. The feel of his mouth on mine had me vibrating with desire.

Without breaking the connection of our lips, he walked me backward until my back hit the hard wood of the front door and he used his hips to pin me there. In that moment, it didn't matter to me that we were on the front porch. My hands fisted in the front of his shirt and a low growl tore up his throat. Ashton pulled back slightly and then dipped. His shoulder hit me at my waist and then my feet were no longer on the ground, and my hands clutched at his shoulders as he moved with great speed through the foyer.

Ashton took the stairs faster than I'd ever seen. Within seconds we were in a bedroom. I wished I could take in everything about my surroundings but as my body slowly trailed down his, the feel of his hard length against my stomach, I realized what we were about to do and my mind seized. I didn't want to stop but I couldn't help all of my insecurities coming back to haunt me in waves.

For a moment I thought about asking him what to do, but that seemed ridiculous. Instead, I took a deep breath and willed myself to relax, letting him take the lead. This was his dance and I planned to follow.

He stepped back, running the tips of his fingers over the top of my exposed breasts. "Do you know how fucking sexy this dress is on you, or how much I want to tear you out of it?" His voice was husky and I felt the sound all over my body.

Everywhere.

"No."

"Then I'll show you." He took his hand away and dug in his pocket. "One, are you on birth control?"

TRADED

Oh shit. I hadn't even thought about that. Guess it was a good thing I continued taking the pills after I stopped staying with Dominic.

"Yes. Dominic didn't want kids."

"That man is fucking idiot." He paused before saying, "We'll use condoms until we can both get tested."

That hurt to hear, but I understood the reason. Dominic had lied to me about many things; why would he have remained faithful?

"Second." The commanding tone of his voice caught my attention, my focus back on him. "Is there anything you don't like about sex?"

Oh God, does he have to be so blunt?

My face flamed, probably the same color as my dress. "Umm . . . I don't really know what I like or don't like." I shrugged like it was no big deal. But it was.

"Elena," he groaned, his eyes lifting to the ceiling. "You are going to be the death of me." When he glanced back down, the lenses of his glasses seemed to make his eyes glow brighter than before. He took a step forward and bent to nip along my ear.

"Does that mean you give me permission to take control?" His whisper was so soft I barely heard it. The kind of low voice that made me quiver in anticipation. Nervous or not, I wanted it. I glanced down for a moment, then looked up. Excitement and nervous anticipation caused my hands to shake.

"I want to hear you say it."

"Yes."

Ashton pounced. Taking hold of my shoulders, he flipped me around and before I could blink, the zipper on my dress had been lowered and it pooled at my feet. The urge to lift my arms to cover my exposed body was overwhelming. My hands twitched, but I held still.

"That's a good girl," he said, lips against my neck and I shivered. Him calling me a good girl was quite possibly the hottest thing I'd ever heard. "I like when you stand up to me and everyone else outside of this room. But in here, I want you to submit every part of your body to me."

"Mmm..."

His tongued traveled the path down my neck. "Can you do that?"

"I can," I said, my voice sounding more confident than I felt.

Submitting to Ashton meant I didn't have to worry. I could learn what I liked.

He could teach me.

His hands reached around me to cup my breasts through the black strapless bra, his thumbs brushing my nipples lightly over the fabric, and all I could think about was what it would feel like if he were to delve beneath the silk.

I didn't have to wait long. One hand dipped into the cup of my bra, the other moving around my back to pop the simple clasp, letting the garment fall to the ground on top of my dress. Then his hands came back around and began again. Every pinch and flick of my nipple sent sensation straight to my core.

Unknown sensations.

Amazing sensations.

TRADED

With a sigh, I dropped my head back onto Ashton's shoulder.

"I take it you like that."

I nodded.

"Turn around."

My feet moved, immediately obeying his command. Both body and mind were on the same page. In here, they would do anything Ashton asked, as long as he continued to stroke my body in a way that set me ablaze. I craved his touch, his taste. I needed more of this. More of *him*.

If I thought his fingers were masterful, they had nothing on his tongue. Gentle flicks turned into hard painful, yet pleasure filled sucks. I groaned, unable to hold it back as passion over took my mind.

"That's it, baby. I wanna hear it all—every moan, every whimper. But if you speak, it's to call my name."

His mouth moved to my other breast, teasing my body into such incoherency I failed to notice him lowering me until my skin hit the cool sheets of the bed, his jacket now missing, the muscles of his arms filling out his dress shirt as he crawled up over me. I reached out to take off his tie.

"No, no, no." His hands gripped my wrists, moving my hands back up above my head. "Tonight, I'm going to show *you* the pleasures of sex." Sitting up he pulled his tie off and took hold of my hands. In the blink of an eye, he'd wrapped the material around my hands and tied them to the headboard. It was tight, but not uncomfortable, and my thighs quivered as my imagination began to run riot.

"Fuck, you look sexy tied to my bed."

Being unable to move instead of unwilling was a new feeling. His finger ran down my chest, between the valley of my breasts, and my hips bucked upward. He smiled and his eyes hooded, growing darker. My tongue darted out to wet my lower lip and the muscles in his jaw clenched. "I think you like being tied up. I can see you breathing harder." His fingers dipped into my panties, sliding between my legs, before he pulled them out. I watched on with wide eyes as he brought his fingers to his mouth, his gaze locked on me as he pulled his fingers between his lips, sucking them clean. Nothing I'd ever seen before could compare to this. My breath caught at the back of my throat, making my heart race. "Fuck. So wet for me."

"Please." I had no idea what I was begging for. I just knew I needed something more.

"Soon."

Ashton slowly peeled off the rest of his clothes, every part of his tightly muscled body on display. He leaned over me and captured my lips, his teeth nipping at me, the sharp pain making me jolt before he laved it with his tongue, soothing the sensitive skin. Once again he trailed his lips down my body, lazily, like he had all the time in the world. Like I wasn't turning to Jell-O beneath him. I was so turned on, I couldn't stop my head from thrashing on the pillow, not wanting to close my eyes for fear of missing him, but needing some respite from the torture just the same. I felt his mouth at the hem of my panties and I opened my eyes, watching him tease them down my legs with his teeth. My muscles tightened, waiting for something.

It was becoming clear Ashton was no amateur. As he paused I could hear my own pants, the sound echoing around the room, taunting me with my own need.

Pant
pant
pant

Ashton's tongue swiped through the wet between my thighs and my back bowed off the bed as if lashed with a whip, pleasure coursing through every part of my body.

"Ashton!"

With every flick, lick, swipe of his tongue the heat within me built. I never thought it possible to feel like this during sex; to feel so completed consumed—devoured.

Ashton didn't give me a second to breathe, pushing my body toward the cliff again, his hand coming up to roll my nipple between his fingers, the acute pain of his perfectly timed pinch making me squirm. I wanted to be closer to his mouth, yet farther away at the same time.

I can't take any more.

Spots danced in my vision, the muscles in my legs trembling. Ashton sat up, a mischievous sparkle in his eyes. His tongue darted out and licked his glistening lips. "You're my new favorite flavor."

"Ashton," I moaned.

"The second best thing about dessert at home is hearing my name on your lips."

He watched me and slowly removed his glasses, tossing them on the table beside the bed.

So I'm not the only one losing control.

His body between my legs, I watched in awe as he slowly rolled the condom down his length, his hand holding his cock tightly as he positioned himself. I knew what was coming. I knew Ashton wouldn't want to hurt me, but I braced anyway.

The heat of him pressed against me, his hips falling forward as he slowly slid into me. But there was no pain—only an all-consuming feeling so wonderful, if I were to die right here, right now, I'd die happy.

"Fuck, so good. So fucking good. So tight, grabbing hold of me." Ashton groaned, remaining completely still as I adjusted to him, his arms at my side holding himself steady over me, and I felt them shaking with the effort. "I'm not going to last."

He thrust into me; deep, powerful strokes that forced me to climb higher and higher, his rhythm becoming wilder, more chaotic, until he screamed out my name, taking me with him.

"Elena!"

His body fell against mine, his skin slick with sweat. Exhausted, I lay in a boneless heap on the bed, my body a tangled mess of sensation, heat, and something else so alien that I couldn't even put a name to it. Never—*never*—had I experienced something like this. His mouth. His tongue. The sharp nips of his teeth against my oversensitive skin. All of it too much, yet not enough.

The sound of ragged pants filled the room. When he finally caught his breath, Ashton reached up and pulled the tie from my wrists, taking each one in his hands, lightly rubbing the chafed skin, bringing circulation back into them.

The feel of his fingers was exquisite. My eyes drifted closed and I allowed myself to revel in his touch. Eventually I felt him leave the bed, only to return moments later. A warm washcloth dipped between my legs, cleaning me up. I smiled, thinking I could get used to someone looking after me, but at the same time hoping that I never did because then the feeling wouldn't be so perfectly . . . right.

The bed sunk under his weight and he pulled me into his chest, settling my face into the crook of his neck. I inhaled, taking in his scent; committing it to memory. I opened my eyes and shifted but he kissed me on the head, his arms clutching me tighter, holding me against him.

"Ashton."

He shushed me. I felt the heat of his breath against my hair.

"It's been a long night for you, Elena. Sleep."

So I did.

CHAPTER 13

Ashton

Elena's body relaxed against me and her breathing evened out. But I was too consumed to sleep, my mind racing with thoughts of the enigma that lay in my arms. She was a paradox. Confident enough to demand my bed, yet submissive enough to relinquish control.

She was perfect.

I hadn't been sure if asking her to submit would be too much. She'd come so far in the last month—asserting herself, making her feelings known. It dawned upon me that I might have set her back. But I wouldn't know for sure until she woke up.

I'd started to lose control the moment she suggested leaving the restaurant. The curve of her hips, the fullness of her breasts . . . they had called to me for weeks. I wanted her more than I could ever remember wanting another woman. Most who claimed they could submit in bed lied.

TRADED

They either tried to dominate both inside and outside the bedroom, or they were submissive all the time. Elena was turning out to be the perfect mix.

Too bad she's married.

Things were changing for Elena, but making the decision to end her marriage had to be her choice. There was always the chance that this was a fluke. That would be disappointing. She could be magnificent.

But would she be?

The buzz coming from the floor pulled me from my thoughts. I knew it wasn't Elena's phone. That was still in her purse, and none of the people who had that number would be calling her now.

Gently moving my arm from underneath her, I climbed out of bed and waited a moment, conscious that she needed her rest. When I was satisfied she wouldn't wake, I searched the floor for my pants, the buzzing continuing somewhere left of the bed. I found them and pulled my phone from the front pocket. It was a text message. Seeing the name on the screen, I groaned.

Elena grunted and turned over in her sleep. Moving quickly, I tugged on my boxers, stepping out the door and quietly shutting it behind me to head downstairs to my office. Before I opened the message I poured myself a drink, taking a large swig that burned going down, bringing a sense of calm with it.

My back hit the couch and I pulled up the text. The quicker I answered, the sooner I could be back in bed.

Dominic: I have tickets for the game tomorrow night. Wanna go?

Of course the bastard would have some kind of super power; some radar that told him I'd slept with his wife. Remembering the way he'd told her to let me practically rape her anytime I wanted made my blood rush in my ears. My jaw worked itself back and forth as I answered his text with the standard response.

Me: I have the club box that night if you want to give away your tickets and meet me there.

Obviously the fucker had money, but there was no way in hell he was getting anywhere near Elena until my three months were up. She at least deserved that much time. I was tempted to ask how much he had, but I'd find out soon enough. His reply came almost instantly.

Dominic: Perfect. I'll meet you there.

Whatever he wanted could wait until the meeting. I sent a text to Brock letting him know he'd be working the next night and then my thoughts drifted back to Elena. I had a feeling the woman had never experienced an orgasm in her entire life. The way she lit up for me almost immediately . . .

The thought had my cock twitching. But she hadn't been the only one affected. My name crossing her lips almost made me come before I got inside of her. Whether or not she'd still be the same feisty woman when she woke up in the morning remained to be seen. If so, the question was: how far could I push her? I could show her a whole new world, open her eyes to sensations the likes of which she'd never seen. But I could only show her and wait for her reaction. I wouldn't force her to do anything. How much she wanted to participate, I didn't know.

A million questions swirling through my head, I tossed back the rest of my drink and left the tumbler on the table. I'd get it in the morning if Julia didn't find it first. Climbing the stairs, I found myself becoming drowsy. Sleep didn't come easy to me. Having to juggle so many aspects of business—both legitimate and otherwise—meant that my mind was almost constantly occupied, making it hard to switch off. Most nights, I couldn't wait for the morning.

I opened the door, hoping not to startle her. I could just make out her shape in the darkness. She was curled on her side, her soft brown hair fanning the pillow. Shedding the boxers, I climbed into bed and pulled the covers up over us, excited and nervous about the prospect of spending the entire night with a warm body against me. While not unusual for me to have a woman in my bed, a sleepover was out of the question, the arrangement being purely sexual.

"Ashton."

I froze, worried I'd woken her, but her eyes remained firmly closed, her words nothing but a murmur—the product of a dream-filled slumber. My heart raced, but as alien a feeling as that was, I was too tired to examine what it meant. Unknowingly, she slid closer, wrapping herself around me until she was contained in my arms again, our limbs a tangled mess, her cheek resting against the left side of my chest. Closing my eyes, I hoped Elena played a starring role in my dreams that night. Thoughts of all the things I planned on doing with her over the next few weeks, floated through my mind and I smiled, gradually drifting off into a deep sleep.

CHAPTER 14

Elena

When I woke, something was off. I moved my legs. The sheets weren't the same as those I'd slept on for the last month. The mattress felt different too—softer.

Ashton's room.

Memories of the night before filtered through my head. I'd let Ashton touch me, and I now understood what every other woman in the world talked about in regards to sex.

Stretching, I glanced around from the bed, looking for my clothes from the night before, muscles I didn't know I had were sore, but in the most delicious way. I looked around the room, seeing Ashton's bedroom properly for the first time. In the days since I arrived, I'd been exploring so I'd known where it was, but never ventured in—not even for a peek while he was out. The room was what could only be described as overtly masculine, the dark color of the woods fitting him perfectly. The chair in the corner had a high back and wide arms, which could easily be used to hold clothes but there was no trace of clutter. The room was immaculate. Not a thing was out of place. He had a housekeeper, but neatness and order were part of who Ashton was so I knew this penchant for tidiness was all him.

Try as I might, I couldn't find my dress or underwear. They were gone. Casting another glance around, something on the end of the bed caught my attention: a pair of yoga pants and a T-shirt.

The room was quiet. No body next to mine in the large bed. No running water coming from the bathroom. Ashton must have collected the clothes for me then gone downstairs. The thoughtful nature of his gesture left me with a warm feeling in my stomach; one that I relished.

I leaned back against the intricately carved headboard, pulling the sheets up and over my body, catching sight of the faintly reddened skin at my wrists, the memories of the silk tie sliding up my skin, connecting me to the bars, rushing forward. Clenching my thighs against the onslaught of need, I grabbed my clothes and went into the bathroom to shower. The bathroom was bigger than the one attached to my room—twice the size of a normal bathroom. With a huge tub in the corner and a glass stall shower next to it, I was torn between which to use, knowing the shower would be quicker and easier, but a nice soak would ease the ache in my tired muscles. My thoughts returned to the man downstairs.

Quick and easy it is.

TRADED

I turned on the water, setting my clothes on the counter. There, next to the sink, was a toothbrush. At first I thought it might be Ashton's, but realized that his was in the holder next to the other sink.

He put that there for me.

Grabbing the toothpaste, I brushed my teeth and hopped into the shower, the warm water running down my body, loosening my muscles. All of the ways Ashton had touched me last night were better than any sex I could remember. The second I gave control over to him, we both assumed our roles; slipping into character, our bodies synchronized as we played our parts to perfection.

I'd been told what to do by a man for most of my adult life and I'd hated it. But last night was different. Every command, every direction, ramped up my desire. His commands were short, direct, but there was no edge of malice, no ulterior motive. And in the end, it hadn't just been about him. Ashton had given.

And given.

And given.

Despite the heat of the water, goose bumps peppered my skin at the memory.

Wondering where he might be, I finished my shower and dressed quickly, checking myself over in the mirror before I went in search of him. Reaching the landing, I smelled breakfast and my stomach growled its appreciation. Following my nose, I found him at the stove, flipping bacon and stirring eggs, his pants hanging low on his hips but he wore no T-shirt, the muscles of his broad shoulders on view.

"Good morning."

His head snapped around and in the blink of an eye, the utensils were placed on the counter and Ashton was standing in front of me.

"Good morning," he whispered, tipping my chin up for a kiss.

The second his lips grazed mine my body pressed against him, loving the feeling of the bare skin of his chest against my hands. His tongue plunged into my mouth and I could taste the coffee that lingered on his lips. The kiss was fleeting and he pulled back, breathless.

"It's an even better morning than I thought." He smirked, taking my hand in his and leading me to the table.

"I think I have to agree." I sucked my bottom lip between my teeth, not sure what else to say.

He groaned and used his thumb to pull my lip free. "If anyone gets to bite that lip, it's me."

My blood heated and I tried to get control of my thoughts. "Ashton," I whispered.

"My name on your lips is one of my favorite sounds. Now sit while I get breakfast, then we can talk."

Ashton wants to talk about last night.

To keep my hands from shaking, I moved them under my thighs until a cup of coffee appeared before me, providing the perfect distraction. I picked up the cup and let the strong brew take away my fears—for a moment anyway.

Ashton placed plates with eggs, bacon, and toast in front of us, taking the seat next to me. Avoiding eye contact, I added pepper to my eggs and concentrated heavily on picking my fork up off of the table.

"Elena, you're nervous. Tell me what's wrong."

Taking a deep breath in and letting it out in a long puff, I glanced up at him. "You said you wanted to talk and I'm nervous about why."

He shook his head. "You don't ever need to be nervous with me. I do want to talk about a few things, *including* last night."

"Okay." My eyes darted back to my food, stabbing a piece of egg to start eating.

"Last night was . . ." I waited to hear how he would describe it.

Mistake.

Okay.

I've had better.

They all popped into my head.

"Incredible."

My gaze snapped to his, my eyes wide and my jaw hanging low.

He covered my thigh with his hand, massaging gently. "You need to move your stuff into my room."

"I *what?*"

With his index finger he pushed my chin up to close my mouth. "I want you to stay in my room while your here."

"Umm . . . I don't think that's a good idea."

"Why not?" he asked, watching me with shrewd eyes.

"Because one night of great sex doesn't mean I'm moving into your room. I may like to be told what to do in your bed, but out here I've learned that I can decide for myself and I won't repeat past mistakes."

Ashton smiled. "Most people wouldn't think to question me. While I want you to stay in my room, I'm thrilled you're willing to stand up to me."

"Of course I am. We're you afraid I'd keep submitting to you?"

"To be honest I was worried, but I hoped I was wrong."

I sat back in my chair and crossed my arms over my chest. "Well you were."

He leaned forward and stole a quick kiss. "I'm glad. Now eat. You need your energy."

I rolled my eyes. "You're lucky I'm hungry."

He chuckled and began eating. Halfway through breakfast, he set his fork down and looked up at me. "I'm meeting Dominic tonight for a payment."

My fork almost to my mouth, my hand froze. "What?" I choked out.

"Dominic text me last night about a payment."

I knew what Ashton did for his father—he'd gone to deal with payments while I'd been living here—but this was different. He was meeting a man I never wanted to see again, if I could avoid it. I knew that wasn't realistic; we were married, after all. If only I could snap my fingers and fix everything.

"He's not going to want me back early, is he?"

"That's not his choice," Ashton growled. "He didn't have the money in time and I

TRADED

refrained from beating him to a bloody pulp because of the deal for you. If he makes that mistake, I'll kick the shit out of him."

I nodded, unable to speak my throat was so dry.

Ashton brushed his thumb across my cheek. "Elena, you do realize you'll have to face him eventually?"

"No. I could just send him the divorce papers in the mail and never see him again."

The corners of his mouth turned down. "I wish it were that simple. If you do it that way you'll always be looking over your shoulder. And you need to show him you're strong. You have to tell him face to face."

I cringed. "I guess I do."

Part of me wanted to disappear into the night, never to face Dominic and all of his bullshit ever again, because the thought of having to go back to him already made my heart ready to pound out of my chest. I feared his words would pull me back into a place I was working my way out of.

"I want to take you to a game one of these days. Just us, no business."

One night a week or so ago, I'd told Ashton about what happened the night of the trade, remembering how excited I'd been to finally see a game. Telling Ashton was so embarrassing, but he hadn't made it awkward. I shivered at the thought of seeing Dominic at the game. He went frequently. How could I be sure he wouldn't be there when I was?

"Don't worry, I don't want you anywhere near that asshole. You stay here for the game tonight, we can deal with him when the time comes."

I nodded and continued with my breakfast, my stomach better. Ashton finished eating long before me and sat sipping another cup of coffee. Picking up our dishes, I walked them to the sink and as I came back to my seat, Ashton's hand grabbed mine, stopping me in my tracks. His glasses were conveniently gone, the green in his eyes even brighter.

He growled and tugged me to him, his mouth devouring mine. Electricity zipped along my nerves when his tongue plunged into my mouth. Demanding. Possessive. Sexy. Braver than I thought I could be, I let my hands slid up his chest, tracing each ridge of his muscled abdomen, the skin silky beneath my fingertips. He pulled away suddenly, and I thought for a minute I'd done something wrong.

Taking hold of my shoulders, he spun me around and my hands fell forward, my palms flat against the table. A primitive desire took hold, my core throbbing with need.

"Ashton."

Fingertips wrapped around the waistband of my pants and they, along with my panties, were yanked down around my thighs. Sensation spread through me. One of Ashton's fingers slipped through my core to circle my clit, the warm heat of his body covering my back as he pressed himself against me.

"You have a sexy ass," he said, taking little nibbles of my shoulder between his words. "And one of these days I'm going to fuck you right *here*." His finger traced around the edge of the

TRADED

one place I'd never considered letting a man go and I gasped, my hips bucking forward. It was scary, yet exciting at the same time. His finger moved away, then there was a slight sting when his hand smacked my ass cheek, the feeling so delicious that my thighs quivered.

"But right now I want hard and fast." The commanding timbre of his voice was almost my undoing.

"Please," I begged, sliding my ass back, searching for him.

Smack!

"Oh no, no, my sweet." His hand gripped my hip, holding me in place, while the thumb of his other hand pressed into my core, the spicy musk that was uniquely Ashton surrounding me. "So fucking ready. You like being told what to do."

"Yes." I whimpered. "Please."

There was a tear of foil; a sound so delicious I clenched in anticipation. Ashton pushed into me in one long thrust, filling me completely.

"Oh God."

"Never get tired of the feel of you around my cock," he grunted.

Each time he sank into me my body tensed, looking for the sweeping pleasure of the previous night.

"I'm so close."

His hand reached around to pinch my clit and sparks shot off through my body, clenching tight, pulling him into me as he continued to thrust. It wasn't long before he his thrusts lost their rhythm and came in short hard bursts, his fingers biting into my skin until, finally, he grunted, pressing himself against me, holding himself there.

For a few minutes, we were both unable to speak. Eventually, he stood, pulling me up with him. "You, my dear, are absolutely amazing," he said against my ear. When I turned my head, his lips once again took possession of mine. The kiss wasn't animalistic in its passion, but it burned me to my toes anyway. He pulled away, breathless, staring at me for a beat before helping me to right my clothes.

"I've got to get ready to leave. I want you to enjoy your day. Don't worry about anything."

"I'll try."

"Do you have to rehearse today?"

"No. They still need one more cast member and the auditions are today."

I was extremely glad I didn't have to go anywhere because the excitement of waking up in Ashton's bed had worn off and I was exhausted. The question of whether or not to move into his room began to swirl through my head. I couldn't make my decision based upon sex. I needed to be smarter than that. And to be smart, I needed headspace.

"Okay. I'm going to head over to the stadium straight from the restaurant so I'll be late. Text me if you need anything." He pressed a brief kiss to my lips and left me alone in the kitchen with nothing but my thoughts.

Deciding to blow off some steam, I went down to the basement and hit the treadmill. With each mile, I wondered if I should feel guilty for sleeping with another man. A little voice in the back of my head said yes, while the rest chanted a resounding *hell no*. Dominic had given me permission to have sex with Ashton. Technically, I was doing as I'd been told.

From the moment I met him, Ashton had encouraged me to stand up for myself, to see myself as worthy. There was no need to feel guilty about a man who treated me the way I deserved to be treated. Not to mention his dominant ways were more of a turn on than I'd ever expected.

Is it too soon to move into his bedroom?

For hours I pondered the answer, but even if I had a hundred valid reasons not to do it, I knew that I wanted to wake up in Ashton's bed every morning. If he planned night after night of delicious torment for me, I was jumping into the deep end with no lifejacket on.

I was done making everyone else happy.

It was time to be a big girl and make decisions for *me*.

CHAPTER 15

Ashton

Walking toward the doors of the restaurant, my mind was completely focused on Elena. Mentioning Dominic to her only hours after she'd spent the night in my bed hadn't been the best move. It was obvious the idea of facing him still made her nervous; something I hoped to help her with before she saw him again.

Even though she shot me down, I had a feeling she was considering my offer to sleep in my room every night. I was thrilled she hadn't caved immediately. It proved she was becoming stronger—standing up for herself. I wasn't kidding when I told her she'd need to face him eventually, and if she had a chance of getting away from him once and for all, she'd need to be able to hold her own.

I really wished I hadn't chosen to conduct these meetings at the games. I used to love to go there and relax, have a few drinks and unwind, but now I'd begun to dread being there. Having to deal with Tolley just made it that much worse. The more time I spent with Elena, the more I realized just how much damage he'd done, and that made it harder to curb the desire to knock his head off.

"Morning, Mr. Hawes."

I rolled my eyes at Dustin, the bartender. No matter how many times I told him to call me Ashton, he never listened. For some reason, he thought it was funny. I failed to see the joke.

I stopped briefly to discuss the liquor order, then headed to my office.

My desk was full of paperwork, which was my own fault. For the past few weeks I'd been leaving early to get home to Elena. It felt weird to hurry home to someone, but so right at the same time. Except there was a shit-ton of guilt attached to it. Never once had I slept with a married woman. I may have a skewed moral compass, but I still had one. And one of the things my father had drilled into us over the years was that you don't cheat on your spouse, or sleep with someone else's. Although Dad didn't seem to have an issue with the current situation.

Pushing the guilt to the back corner of my mind, I began tackling the orders for the next week. It took me longer than normal; thoughts of Elena in my bed every night more than a little distracting.

Maybe Dad was right when he said I felt more for Elena than lust.

I had feelings for Elena that went a whole lot deeper than saving her from a bad situation. Figured that, for the first time in my life, I wanted a woman for more than a few weeks, a woman who happened to be the perfect match for me in every way imaginable, and she was married to a man that gave a new definition to the word asshole.

Everything in my life had been that way. I had the education and experience to become a chef in a high profile restaurant, except that the *business* didn't give me the time to work in a restaurant. My way of overcoming that was to buy my own and make them more successful than anything else in the area.

If there was anyone that could overcome the obstacles that stood in the way of Elena and I making a go of this thing, it was me.

♋︎

The game was in the third inning and still no sign of the rat bastard, though saying that, I'd still have to stay the whole game, even if he'd showed up during the first inning. Leaving right after him would be too suspicious. Dad was adamant we remain cautious if we were to avoid being caught. If the home team was losing, I could sneak out early since half of the stadium would be leaving with me.

Brock called for dinner earlier in the evening and the only thing I could think about were the meals I'd shared with Elena over the last few weeks. There had only been three times, including tonight, where she'd been left to eat alone. I knew she didn't have any friends, except the one from the diner. Dominic had done one hell of a job isolating her from everyone in her life.

"Ashton, what the hell is up with you?"

I peered over my shoulder at Brock to find him staring at me, brows drawn down.

"What do you mean?"

He pointed at my plate with his own fork. "Let's start with the fact that you haven't touched your steak, one of your favorites. Not to mention you haven't paid one bit of attention to the game. You always said the best part of dealing with all of this shit was watching the game in privacy." He moved his fork toward the glass in front of me. "You haven't even noticed that your team is up by four runs."

Glancing toward the scoreboard, I notice the score one to five. How did I miss that? The only number I'd been paying attention to was the inning, wanting the game to be over sooner rather than later. I pulled off my glasses and rubbed my eyes before putting them back in place. "I guess I'm distracted."

"It's the girl, isn't it? I saw the way you looked at her that first night."

I couldn't lie to Brock. He'd been through enough shit with me. He deserved the truth. "Yeah, it's her."

"You know you're walking into a huge pile of shit by getting involved with her, right?"

"Why do you say that?" I growled, feeling my blood pressure rise. Friend or not, he was not going to sit there and bash Elena. She'd been through enough.

"Look at yourself, ready to fight me over another man's wife. Does that even make sense?

And if you're not careful you're going to end up getting sloppy, which you can't afford."

I looked down and saw my hands, clenched into a fist. With an effort, I forced them to relax. "I'm just fucking her—not asking her to marry me."

"Could have fooled me."

"What do you know?" I snapped.

"Look, I've known you for years and I've never seen you this fucked up over a woman. You rarely ever pay them any attention, unless you want to sleep with them, and this time it's all about a *married* woman. What happens when it's time for her to go back to her piece of shit husband?"

I groaned and my head fell against the back of the chair. "I'm still hoping she'll choose not to."

"Can't guarantee that. And do you really want to take on a crazy fucker like Tolley? Any bastard willing to trade his wife to save his own ass must have a few screws loose."

My head snapped up. "I'll bury the son of a bitch if I have to."

"I doubt your father would be real thrilled with that."

I laughed humorlessly. "I wouldn't bet on that. Dad met her last week. Trust me, after hearing what she's been through, I wouldn't be surprised if he did it himself."

"Another David?"

What my father had done to David was worse than death. Even Brock couldn't stomach the stories we'd all heard, and seeing the man first hand made it very clear that most of the rumors were true.

David never walked again after my dad "visited" him. He was missing his left eye and right ear, and one leg had been shattered so badly they'd had to amputate it to save his life. He had third degree burns on his head, neck, chest, and back, but the torture hadn't stopped there. Half of his fingers were broken, the other half cut off, and his tongue was missing. I didn't want to think about what happened to his junk. A shiver ran down my spine thinking about it. How the hell my father had managed to get away with it was beyond me.

"Possibly."

There was a knock on the door.

"Speaking of Tolley," Brock said, getting up to let him in.

The slimy bastard sauntered into the room like he owned the place. He stepped in front of me, holding out a small envelope in his left hand. It was nowhere near big enough to hold the amount of money he owed me. All of my debtors knew they weren't allowed to pay me with anything higher than a fifty.

Why do I get the feeling that the man thinks he has one over on me?

"I'm guessing by the size of this envelope that this isn't even an eighth of what you owe me." I handed the envelope over to Brock to start counting.

"It's ten grand. I'll have the rest by the end of our agreement. I should have thought to trade her sooner. I don't have to use hotels anymore, but I do hate having to clean the apartment." His eyes darted around the room. "Where is the lazy bitch, anyway? She better be doing what I told her to, even though she's a lousy lay."

I leapt from the chair and without a thought let my fist fly. It connected with his face and he stumbled back, bumping into one of the tables. With another punch, I knocked him to the floor, leaping onto his chest. My glasses flew off my face and slid across the room.

"Don't you ever . . . talk about her . . . like that . . . again!"

This wasn't the first time I'd had to make my point with my fist. Hell, it wasn't even the tenth. This piece of shit was lucky it was only my fist I was using. I felt the cold steel of my glock shifting against my hip as I swung back again and again.

I didn't hide behind my muscle. I might have used Brock from time to time, but that was when I had more pressing business, or when the person involved wasn't worthy of me getting my hands dirty. I had a reputation—one I'd earned. You did *not* fuck with me, and Elena was mine, at least for the moment, and therefore this guy did not fuck with her either.

Blood splattered across my hands and arms, my shoulders ached and my knuckles were raw. I reached back to take another swing, not giving two shits about the damage I was doing to him, when strong arms wrapped around my chest, pulling me away.

"He's out cold."

My breaths came in pants. I looked down. One eye was already swollen shut, his hair, stained red, clung to his head, blood dripped from his nose, which now bent at an awkward angle.

"Get him out of here," I snarled. "Call someone to stay with the fucker until he wakes up and make it very clear that if ever talks about Elena that way again, he'll be praying for me to only knock him out."

"Ashton—" Brock started.

"I don't want to fucking hear it," I yelled. "Get that motherfucker out of my sight."

Brock didn't argue further. He quietly scooped up Dominic and pulled him into one of the bathrooms at the back of the clubhouse. There were too many people milling around to get him out of the stadium, but I was too pissed to think rationally. I didn't want to think about the why on that one.

"God-fucking-damn it." I pulled out my other phone, the one that couldn't be traced, knowing the only way to fix the situation was a call to Dad. He was either going to be pissed as hell or agree whole-heartedly.

The phone rang a few times before he finally picked up.

"Hello?"

"Dad, we've got a problem."

"Don't tell me you got arrested." His voice got louder with each word. I heard Mom yelling in the background.

"I didn't get arrested, at least not yet." I searched the room for my missing glasses.

"What do you mean, *not yet*?"

I found them on the other side of the room and placed them on one of the tables to make sure they weren't bent. "Yeah, if you don't get someone over here to help me clean up the mess."

"Well, if you stop with fucking vague-ass bullshit and give me an idea of what we're dealing with, I'll send people over."

I groaned and flopped back into the seat. Now that the adrenaline was wearing off I was exhausted and wanted to get the hell out of there. "Elena's piece of shit husband wanted to make a payment tonight. I met him at the stadium and right off the bat he starting spouting off all kinds of bullshit about her. I lost it."

"Did you kill him?" Dad asked, no emotion in his voice.

"No, but he's out cold. Eye swollen shut, broken nose."

"Sounds like the fucker deserved it." There was some shuffling on the other end of the line. "What inning is it?"

I looked at the scoreboard again.

"Bottom of the fourth."

"Okay, give me about half an hour. I'll have someone over there to deal with it. Is Brock with you?"

"Yeah," I said, just as Brock returned to the seat next to me and stared at the blood on the floor, shaking his head.

"I want you to leave at the top of the ninth. Tell Brock to stay until the end of the game. I'll have a car pick him up."

"All right, I will."

"Stop by tomorrow on your way to the restaurant."

"Okay."

TRADED

We hung up and I stared at the floor. All of the reasons why I wasn't thrilled with being part of my father's business were sitting in front of me. Getting into fights wasn't something I did—at least, not since elementary school. There was a difference between a non-payment and flying off the handle.

A bag of ice appeared in front of me.

"Otherwise you're knuckles will swell and it'll be obvious you were in a fight tonight," Brock explained, his shirt covered in blood. He needed to change too.

Taking the ice from him, I placed it over the bleeding splits. It burned the second the cold touched my skin and I had to hold back the wince. How the hell was I supposed to explain to Elena what happened tonight?

"Thanks."

"Fucker deserved that. Had you not beat his ass, I would have."

"Yeah, except now I have to go home and explain it to Elena."

"If she hasn't learned what a cocksucker her husband is already, this ought to do it."

I sat forward, my arms on my thighs, keeping the ice on my hand. "Oh she knows. I'm more worried about her reaction to me knocking him senseless."

Brock held up his hands. "Look it may not be my place, but I'm going to give you a bit of advice. I may be wrong, but it seems like you're not ready to give this chick up. Maybe it's time to introduce her to what you do—like your dad did. This way she won't be shocked when shit like this happens."

"You do know that if I didn't consider you a friend, you'd be next with comments like that."

Brock smirked. "You wouldn't lay a hand on me."

I rubbed the back of my neck trying to release the tension. "You're probably right though. I was supposed to bring her the other night and decided not to."

"Don't chicken out. Just do it."

I watched the scoreboard count the innings until I could leave. During the seventh inning stretch there was another knock at the door. Dominic hadn't made a sound until the sixth inning and that was just grunts and groans.

Brock got up to answer the door.

"Good evening, Mr. Hawes. I'm Victor, you're father sent me to take care of a mess for you."

"Yes. I guess my father called ahead to the will call booth."

He nodded. "He did. It's almost the top of the eighth. During the change in innings, you should leave while the crowds are out of their seats. I'll send Brock on his way between the eighth and ninth. By then, I'll have everything ready to go."

Whoever this man was, my father obviously trusted him and by the looks of it, dealing with a simple fistfight was probably an easy night.

"Dad said wait until the ninth."

He nodded. "I know. We talked. This would be less obvious."

"Thank you, Victor." I looked around the box.

TRADED

"Go, I got this," Brock offered, holding out my jacket. I shrugged it on, fastening it at the front to cover the bloodstains. "You need to get yourself together before you draw attention to yourself out there." He pointed at my hand. "Make sure you leave that in your pocket until you're in the car.

I nodded curtly. "Good-night."

Without another word, I left the club and stadium behind.

CHAPTER 16

Ashton

Despite the number of people at the game, the parking lot was desolate as I walked to my car, the disarming of my alarm the only sound. I climbed in and started the ignition. My knuckles were still bloody and raw.

"Fuck," I yelled, slamming the palm of my hand into the steering wheel.

Never once had there been an issue with a collection. Obviously there had been incidents like the one with Reynolds, but nothing this bad. They always left on their own two feet, with the understanding that they were to not call attention to themselves. They knew the consequences of not being able to pay back the money. This was the first time I'd had to call for a cleanup.

My hands tightened around the steering wheel until pain flowed up my arm, forcing me to loosen my grip. Backing out of the space, I peeled out of the parking lot; probably not the best way to stay under the radar, but my temper was such that I didn't really give a shit. Thoughts of Elena and the whole fucked up situation paraded through my head. I must have been on autopilot because I was surprised when the turn off for my street came into view.

Pulling up the driveway toward the garage, I noticed the lights at the front of the house were off. Elena must have gone to bed early. The conversation about what happened tonight would have to wait until morning. There was no way I'd wake her up just to upset her.

Quietly, I walked through the door of the garage into the kitchen. I moved through the house cautiously so I didn't run into anything. Light shone from the upstairs, brightening the stairwell enough for me to climb without a problem.

I reached the landing and realized the light was coming from my room. Julia must have left it on for me, knowing I'd be home late. Too bad Elena had told me no when I asked her to stay in my room. My dick grew hard just thinking about her in my bed.

Stepping through the door, I froze in my tracks.

Elena lay asleep in my bed.

"Holy fuck," I whispered. Excitement poured through me.

The sound woke her, her long lashes fluttering open to reveal her warm brown eyes.

"Ashton?" she called, her voice still thick with sleep.

I sat down next to her on the bed and brushed a few wayward strands out of her face. "You said no"

She shook her head. "No, I said I wanted to do it because it was something that I wanted, not to please you. I actually started out in my room tonight and realized that I missed your warmth, the smell of you on the sheets."

My mouth swooped down, taking possession of hers. When her luscious lips parted, I wasted no time slipping my tongue inside for a taste of heaven—exactly what I needed after the night I'd had. Forgetting all about my knuckles, I slid my hand under the little pink nightie she wore to bed and winced when the fabric caught on the raw skin of my knuckles.

I'd hoped she wouldn't notice, but Elena was too smart for that. She pulled back and watched me. "What's wrong?"

"Nothing." I moved my hand out of sight.

"Don't you dare lie to me, Ashton," she warned, sitting up and crossing her arms over her chest. I reached my good hand up toward her face but she smacked it away. "I don't think so. Not until you tell me what's wrong."

Sighing, I pulled my hand out and showed her. The bruising had started to come out and dried blood caked around the cracks.

"What the hell happened?" Without waiting for an answer, she climbed from the bed and went into the bathroom. A few seconds later she brought back a damp washcloth and placed it over my hand.

"Did you just curse at me?" I laughed.

TRADED

"Don't start. What's wrong with your hand?"

"Boy, did you get bossy."

She narrowed her eyes at me and my cock jumped in my pants. Not once in my entire life had a demanding woman ever turned me on. Something about Elena made everything sexy—even angry. Everything was different with her.

"Your asshole husband showed up tonight and couldn't keep his mouth shut."

She flinched at the mention of Dominic. "What did he say?"

I shook my head, really not wanting to tell her, but I knew she'd push after the way she'd acted so far. "A bunch of shit about you that no husband should ever say about his wife. I lost it."

"You defended me?"

"Of course I did. What would you expect?"

"I'm just not used to it." Her eyes sparkled. "I have to say I like it. You're not going to get in trouble are you?"

"No. My dad sent someone down to the stadium to take care of it."

Gently peeling away the washcloth, she examined the cuts, the heat from her hands warming the cold skin, and all I could think about was those delicate fingers wrapped around my cock.

"Elena."

Her eyes darkened but she made no move to touch me. Not once since the first time I tasted her lips had she taken the lead. Probably another fucked up thing her *husband* taught her.

I plunged my hands into her hair, ignoring the pain, and captured her lips with mine. The taste of strawberry mingled with the flavor of whiskey on my tongue and her hands slipped up my chest, stopping there.

Nipping at her bottom lip, I sat back on my heels and began unbuttoning my dress shirt. Her breath hitched when I popped the last one and pulled the shirt off, dropping it to the floor. Elena's hand came forward, abruptly stopping and dropping to the bed. I caught the longing in her gaze before her eyes shifted away from me.

"Put your hands on me, Elena."

Her head jerked up. Questioning eyes caught mine. Taking her hand from the bed, I placed it on my chest. Her eyes rounded and I needed to know how deep it went. "You've never touched a man?"

Her head shook, eyes filling with moisture. "Not like this. I wasn't . . . wasn't allowed. Dominic told me where to touch."

Fuck.

Her hand trembled under mine as I held it against my body. Without breaking eye contact, I told her, "That man doesn't deserve anything other than someone's fist or a fucking branding iron. I want your hands on me anytime you want to put them on me. Unless I have you tied up." I leaned forward and licked her quivering bottom lip. "And then, that's only because I want to bring you to heights of unmatched pleasure."

She moaned at my words, the sound going straight to my cock. Her body responded to me but I had a feeling if I let go she'd take her hands back, and that wasn't happening. Using my own to guide her, we traced over the skin of my chest. I let her explore without fear. My muscles jumped when her hands grazed over my nipples. It took all of my self-restraint to keep from bucking my hips, afraid of destroying the progress we were making. Not to mention the fact I found the whole situation erotic.

When her hands continued to explore on their own, I moved mine to remove my belt and open the button on my pants. Freeing my dick, I breathed a sigh of relief. Pulling a few fast strokes, I noticed Elena's hands had once again frozen, her eyes wide but she didn't look shocked.

She looked aroused.

I took hold of her hand again, guiding it down my body. Our hands reached my cock and I bent forward, close to her ear.

"Touch me."

If felt weird to have those words roll of my tongue, yet for some reason they felt right.

Her delicate fingers wrapped around my shaft and stroked lightly. Everything about it was tentative, but that just made it so—much—better. Sensation traveled everywhere, igniting a firestorm in my body and the desire to flip her to her back and plunge into her over and over again surged through me. Gritting my teeth, I kept my ass rooted to the bed.

Tonight was about Elena.

Tonight, *she* was in control.

Hooded, molten brown eyes watched me, her chest rose and fell with shallow breaths, her breathing keeping time with each stroke. Our bodies were in sync. The atmosphere in the room turned electric, and something flipped in her gaze, and when she leaned forward and for the first time kissed me there was no way I could keep my hands completely to myself. Cupping her face, I tilted her head to gain better access to her mouth.

Passion ignited and she pushed me back onto the bed, and a low growl rumbled up my throat. She pulled back from the kiss and I opened my eyes to find hers wide, her fingers pressed to her lips.

"I—"

"Don't stop now."

I guided her back down. Our lips connected and the heat returned.

Suddenly she sat up again but when I opened my mouth to protest she covered my mouth with her finger. I stilled and waited for her to make her next move. Her hands went to the hem of her nightie, pulling the skimpy material over her head and letting it drop to the floor. Her panties quickly followed.

I lunged off the bed, removing the rest of my clothing and grabbing a condom from the drawer. Taking her hand, I placed the foil in her open palm and closed her fingers over it. Her nose scrunched.

"Tonight is about what you want. I want you to take control." To show her I was serious I lay back on the bed, hands behind my head.

Her eyes searched mine. "And if I don't want you to keep your hands to yourself?"

I laughed, my dick bobbing against my stomach with the movement. "Oh sweetheart, I have no intention of keeping my hands or any other part of my body to myself. I simply want you to take you lead. If you haven't noticed," her eyes followed mine as they ran down my body towards my cock, "everything you've done up to this point has me harder than nails."

"Then touch me, please."

Reaching up I cupped her breast, rubbing the pad of my thumb over her already hard nipple. A soft whimper passed her lips. Her hands landed on my chest and her leg slipped over my stomach to straddle me, the weight of her body pressing down on me only heightening the pleasure. Her wet core slid over my shaft and I had to grip the sheets to keep from thrusting up and finding my way inside her delectable body.

I noticed the glint in her eyes and knew I was in serious shit. Whatever had been holding her back before, she'd obviously pushed it to the back of her mind. Bending down she ran her tongue over my nipple.

"Oh fuck, Elena."

Her tongue traced a path down my chest and back up, laving the other nipple with the same attention and the shocks that raced through my body had me wondering if I was going to die before the night ended. She licked back up my chest, her tongue trailing from the hollow of my throat, up my neck, until she captured my mouth. Letting my eyes slide closed, she devoured my lips, hunger and passion leading the way. Some small functioning part of my brain recognized that this is what women felt when I had their gorgeous bodies below me. Fuck, it was amazing.

"Do you like that?" she whispered against my lips.

"Feel for yourself."

As she pushed my desire higher, my cock grew harder, and my body began to tremble. "Oh

God, Elena, if I don't get inside you soon, I'm going to come all over my stomach."

She nipped at my ear. "We wouldn't want that, would we?"

Leaning back, she ripped open the foil pack and her hands shook as she attempted to roll the condom down over my shaft.

"Relax, you're doing just fine."

She watched me for a moment then nodded. She took a deep breath and her eyes focused on my cock, seamlessly gliding the rubber along my length, the gentle squeeze of her fingers making my stomach ache. Clenching my eyes shut, I held the orgasm back before it exploded with the soft touch of her fingers. Lifting up, she held herself over me, pausing for a moment before she slammed her body down on mine.

"Holy hell."

"Shit, that feels good." My eyes popped open and I watched in wonder as her face flooded with something indescribable and her eyes hooded with lust.

"Cursing twice in one night." I chuckled, unable to hold it back.

She cocked a brow. "You feel like laughing?"

Oh shit.

She lifted up like she might get off, but the breath punched out of my lungs as Elena began to ride me. I held my hands up for her to grip. Her pace picked up and I felt my body building faster than ever in my life.

TRADED

"Please tell me you're close," I begged, my words hissing out from between my clenched teeth.

"So close," she panted.

I reached down to thumb her clit and her back arched, her pussy gripping my cock as she exploded around me. It was all I needed to follow her. Finally, her body settled and she collapsed on top of me. I brushed the hair from her face and placed a kiss to her upturned lips.

"I knew you had it in you."

She shook her head, her eyes drifting closed. "I didn't."

Her breathing evened out. After one, truly fantastic round of sex, sleep sounded perfect. I slipped from beneath Elena to clean up and ditch the condom. I needed to talk to her about getting tested. Elena I trusted; the fuckwad she was married to, not so much. Tolley probably couldn't keep it in his pants, but hopefully he'd worn a condom with his other women.

She was still in the same spot when I crawled back into bed. Not a sound traveled through the house. Gathering her in my arms, she cuddled against my chest and the moment was so perfect that it was hard to consider that any of this might temporary. But the decision was Elena's. Whatever she decided, I'd just have to wait and see.

CHAPTER 17

Elena

My body felt lighter than it had in a long time. The bed felt different: bigger, softer, warmer. I kept my eyes shut, letting myself enjoy everything about the moment. For the first time in as long as I could remember, I didn't have the overwhelming dread that came each time I opened my eyes—or the exhaustion. Every morning since I arrived, the weight seemed to get a bit lighter.

This morning it was completely gone.

I felt a featherlight touch across my back and my eyes fluttered open; the desire to see Ashton flowing through me so strong it was almost too much to handle. Deep, mesmerizing green eyes connected with mine.

"Good morning." His voice was a sultry whisper and it sent chills up my spine. Good chills though; the kind that made my heart swell.

"Morning."

TRADED

Now fully awake, my nerves kicked in. I was safe with Ashton, but with everything that had happened the night before, instinct took over and I braced myself for the reaction I knew in my heart wasn't coming.

He held me captive with a glance and lifted his hand to caress my face. "I like waking up next to you."

The second the words passed his lips, I melted into his touch. "Me too."

Thoughts of more mornings like this paraded through my head. If only the situation wasn't temporary. Ashton called to me on a level no man ever had. A dream: that's what staying with him was. Then again, I never thought I'd be on stage, singing the way I'd always wanted to. Dreams could come true, when you got yourself out of a bad situation.

His finger caressed my rapidly hardening nipples and despite all that we'd done thus far, here in the bright light of day, I wanted to hide my nakedness from his gaze. His touch was simple, yet exposing. Without the heat of the moment, my confidence deserted me.

"Don't be shy. Not after last night."

I broke the connection of our eyes. "I don't know what I'm doing."

His hand continued its ministrations while the other slipped around my nape. "You do, but there's a million things I want to show you," he said against my lips, before taking possession of them in a heated kiss.

Our tongues danced until we needed to breathe. Ashton lifted his head to watch me. "Your first rehearsal is today, right?"

"Yeah." I peeked over at the clock. "I have about an hour and a half until I have to be there."

"I'd start right now, but I don't want you to be late."

I attempted to sit up and throw my legs over the side of the bed but Ashton pushed me back down.

"Stay here," he demanded, standing and pulling on a pair of track pants. "I'm going to bring you breakfast. You're going to relax until you have to get ready."

He didn't give me a chance to argue. Spinning on his heel, he darted out of the room and down the stairs.

The problem with lying alone in the silence was that it gave me too much time to think. My mind wandered back to earlier in the morning.

Am I falling for Ashton?

No. It wasn't possible. My emotions must stem from convenience. He was showing me a better life, filling me with confidence, renewing my dreams. It was normal to feel some gratitude toward him. That was what I was feeling.

Gratitude.

If that were the case, then why did my heart lift when I saw him? In fact, I didn't even have to see him. Just seeing a text from him was enough for that fluttery feeling to take over my stomach. As soon as I knew he was on his way home, I couldn't concentrate on anything else.

I tucked my hand underneath the pillow, pulling the sheets up over my shoulders, but I knew there was no way I'd be able to sleep.

TRADED

Thoughts, feelings, thoughts *about* feelings; they all ran through my head.

Within moments I was kicking off the sheets, my temperature spiking and falling at a rate whereby it was near impossible to get comfortable. I pulled myself up, my back against the headboard, and let out an audible sigh, thankful that Ashton was far enough away for him not to hear because if he did then he would surely question it. There was a word that kept taunting me, teasing me with its significance, dancing around in the back of my mind so that I was unable to ignore it, yet unable to justify its use given the newness of whatever Ashton and I had.

It was an unusual situation; one I hadn't even considered. And that was scary. There had to be another word for this.

There had to.

I needed to find a way to deal with Ashton without giving my thoughts away. He couldn't know that I'd even considered the possibility. I didn't need pity. Since leaving Dominic I'd worked really hard to push and become someone stronger.

I heard Ashton coming down the hall and did my best to school my features, sitting up in the bed, pulling the sheet tighter around my chest.

"Tsk, tsk. I'd love to watch those breasts as you eat."

He set the tray in front of me and dipped his finger into the hollow between my breasts, slowing pulling the sheet away. I felt exposed and sexy all at the same time—something only Ashton had ever made me feel.

Needing to focus on something other than his hands, I looked at the tray, noticing that he'd made me his special omelet. Ashton picked up the fork and slid it into my fingers, which was strangely erotic. Picking up a piece of the omelet, his eyes followed the path the fork took all the way to my mouth. A groan escaped him as the fork left my lips.

"Shit, watching you eat like that is incredibly fucking sexy." He reached down to adjust himself. "I'm going to do my best to keep my hands to myself and let you eat, but I make no guarantees because right now I want to flip you over and fuck you until neither of us can move."

The moan slipped out before I could pull it back. Images of all the things I'd like Ashton to do to me but was too shy to ask for ran through my head.

"Elena," he said, his voice throaty. "I don't want you to be late and I see the look in your eyes. I'm going to go take a really fucking cold shower, but tonight you're mine." He captured my lips, stealing my breath, and left through the door to the bathroom.

My eyes darted back and forth between the food in front of me and the door, where I could hear the shower running.

Squirming in the bed, I shoveled down the omelet and got up to make my way into the bathroom.

The outline of his body was visible through the frosted glass and my nipples hardened into tight little buds. With one arm up on the wall in front of him, he was the picture of raw sensuality. And I wanted to have a taste.

Stepping into the shower behind him I wrapped my arms around his waist. Taking him into one of my hands, I gave his hard length a few slow strokes. His head dropped forward for a second before he turned around. I didn't want to give him a chance to stop me so, stealing myself, I dropped to my knees, taking him into my mouth.

"Elena," he hissed. "You don't—"

I sucked him deeper, effectively cutting off any argument he planned to make. It was my first time giving a blowjob where each stroke didn't come with an insult. Dominic would tell me what a bad job I was doing. Strange that, considering he always managed to get off. The sounds of Ashton's satisfied grunts and groans led me to believe I was doing something right.

When my tongue drew small circles around the tip, Ashton slid his hands into my hair, his fingers clenching, tugging. It stung, but not in a bad way. His skin was silky against my tongue as I sucked him deeper. His hips pistoned forward and he stopped suddenly.

"Elena, I'm sorry—"

Not wanting to let go, I grabbed his ass cheeks, pulling him to me. He took the hint and began to slide in out of my mouth. All the while, I cupped his balls, rolling them around in my hands. His movements sped up, becoming stuttered and without rhythm.

"I'm gonna come, Elena," he panted.

I knew why he was warning me, but I wanted it. I drew him into the back of my throat, gripping his ass, making sure he couldn't pull out as I brought him over, his essence spilling into my mouth and down my throat. The second he finished I was yanked up and his mouth was on mine, my lips covered and possessed by his.

Lips parted.

Tongues dueled.

It was sensational.

He broke the kiss and pressed his forehead to mine. "You didn't have to do that," he whispered, his breathing still labored.

"I wanted to."

"Mmm . . . feel free to do that anytime you want."

Those simple words banished more of the fear and insecurity.

"I will."

He caressed down my stomach. I knew what he had in mind. Taking hold of his hand, I brought his palm to my lips. "You can have me tonight. Otherwise we'll both be late."

He kissed me quickly. "I hate it when you're right."

We finished our shower and got ready to face the day. Ashton's would be much longer than mine, but there was something I needed to take care of when I got home from rehearsal.

~~~~~

Rehearsal went better than I expected; the only problem being how quickly it flew by. Nerves hit me. Although probably the easiest of all my problems to deal with, I wasn't sure if I was quite ready to face more demons.

TRADED

After Lewis dropped me off at the house, I sat in the living room staring at the phone. Not dialing, or talking on. Simply staring at the phone in my hand. My fingers trembled as I pressed each button and my stomach churned up the contents of my lunch.

What would they say? I hadn't talked to them in five years. Had they given up and disowned me? Would they even still have the same number? The call connected and I almost puked. A soft, female voice answered.

"Hello?"

I took a deep breath and spoke. "Mom?"

"Laney?"

Hearing her use the name I'd grown up with made my throat close and I couldn't breathe.

"Laney, is that you?"

"It's me," I croaked.

"Oh my God." This was a muffled scraping and then Mom was yelling. "Lance. Lance. Our Laney is on the phone."

There was more shouting.

"Put her on speaker," my dad said.

"Laney, are you still there?"

I had to laugh at their antics. In five years, nothing about them had changed. "Yeah, I'm still here."

"Where are you?" Mom asked the same time Dad said, "Are you still with that asshole?"

I sighed. "I'm still in Colorado and *technically* yes, but I'm going to start divorce proceedings."

"Oh thank God," my mother chanted. "What changed?"

I fiddled with the edge of the pillow. "I met a man—"

"You met someone?" Her voice was a little giddy. "Are you and Dominic separated?"

She had never been a fan of Dominic. When I'd called to tell her we'd eloped, she cried, but they hadn't been tears of joy. That was when Dominic began whispering in my ear, telling me my mother didn't want me to be happy; saying that if she did, she would have been as excited as I was. It was the first step down a very treacherous path that left me alone in the world, except for Dominic.

If I'd only known.

"Yes, we've been living apart for the last month or so." My parents didn't need any more information than that. "And I did. He's charming and handsome."

"Oh, honey," her voice held a hint of sadness. "You thought Dominic was all of those things too."

"Yes, but . . . " Just the thought of Ashton brightened my day. "He's so different. He cares about what *I* want, and what *I* need. He listens when I talk and refuses to let me help with dishes when we have dinner together. And you'll never guess what else he did?"

She sniffed down the line.

"He helped me get an audition for an off Broadway show and I got one of the lead roles."

My mother didn't answer, but I could hear her sobbing when my father did. "Oh, Laney, that's wonderful."

TRADED

"Mom, are you okay?" Why was she crying? She knew when I went to college this was what I wanted to do.

"I—" She drew in a sharp breath. "I . . . just never th-thought we'd hear from . . . you again," she sobbed.

Tears sprang to my eyes faster than I could stop them and I let them run, unchecked, down my face. "Oh, Mom, I'm so sorry."

"Baby girl, you have nothing to be sorry for," Mom argued. "He warped all of your views."

"That's one thing I'm learning. Ashton is a good teacher."

"When do we get to meet this mysterious man?" Mom asked, and I could almost hear her smile.

Shit.

That was something I hadn't thought about. Obviously, I could explain to my parents that the situation was temporary—how I ended up here in the first place—but that was something I'd rather they not know. But Ashton had already done so much for me. Could I really ask more and ask him to meet them?

"I don't know. But I'll work on finding time to come and see you both. I miss you so much," I cried.

"We miss you too, sweetheart."

The conversation continued. My parents asked questions about what I'd been doing but, afraid of their reaction to just how bad my life had been, I left out many of the details. They, in turn, filled me in on what was going on with my family back East. Eventually, I noticed the time and knew Ashton would be home from work soon. As a surprise I wanted to have dinner ready when he got here. He might be annoyed that I was cooking but tough, it was my choice. Something I *wanted* to do.

"Okay, Mom. I promise I'll try and call at least once a week."

"You better, otherwise your mother will drive me nuts," Dad said with a laugh.

"Okay, okay."

"Laney?" Mom piped up.

"Yeah?"

"I'm so happy you called."

"Me too, Mom. Me too."

We said our good-byes and I was just hurrying into the kitchen when Ashton walked through the door from the garage.

"Damn," I cursed.

"Language," he mock reprimanded me. Reaching up, he gently took my bottom lip between his thumb and forefinger. "Want to tell me what this pout is for?"

"I was going to make you dinner, but I ran late."

I barely had time to finish my sentence before I found myself in his embrace, the taste of his lips on mine. We were breathless when the kiss ended.

"Now that's better," he said.

"What is?"

He ran his thumb along my lip again. "No more pouts. Now go upstairs and change. We're going out tonight. You can cook tomorrow." He winked.

And that was what I loved about Ashton. *Loved?*

Shit
shit
shit.

How could I be letting myself fall again? I couldn't do it. No way. Whatever I was feeling would need to be pushed way down deep. My life had finally become something to enjoy.

I wouldn't let anything ruin that.

CHAPTER 18

Ashton

Something flashed through Elena's eyes, but just as quickly, it was gone. She pasted a smile on her face and asked, "What should I wear?"

"Semi-casual."

I'd made reservations at my favorite steakhouse earlier in the day. I planned on taking her to see a movie afterwards. Elena hadn't been to the movies in God knew how long and I wanted to take her. So many times we'd watched something that I'd seen a million times but she hadn't even heard of it. And they weren't smaller indie films but huge box office, blockbusters.

"Okay, give me about fifteen minutes," she smiled.

"Take your time. I want to get changed too."

Nodding, she started up the stairs and I followed a little slower behind. Watching her ass sway as she walked made me hard. Memories of the shower that morning took over all of my thoughts. Never in a million years had I expected her to do that, but damn did the woman know how to use her mouth.

Stopping about halfway up, I watched her disappear into the room and I took the time to adjust myself. Only a few more hours then I could have her. She deserved to not be treated as a sex slave, but I had every intention of showing her a world of pleasure, and that would require lengthy lessons.

By the time I made it through the doorway Elena had finished changing and was in the bathroom fixing her hair. Probably a good thing—if I saw her naked we'd never leave the house.

My tie was the first thing to go. While it might make good bondage later, I had other plans for that in one of my dresser drawers. Stripping down to my boxers, I dug out a pair of jeans and a gray button down. I changed quickly and went downstairs to remove myself from temptation. About another ten minutes passed before Elena joined me. I held my breath when I saw her. The way they accentuated her curves, the jeans looked custom made.

We needed to get out of the house before I ruined all my plans for the night and ravaged her right there on the living room floor. Around her, all of the self-control I prided myself on went flying out the window. With Elena it was never enough. No matter how many times I had her, I still wanted more.

In every position.
In every room.

Over and over.

Normally I could wait; anticipate, pour my attention into one session, taking hours bringing a woman to unparalleled heights of passion. Not with her. With Elena, I found myself lucky if I didn't come in my pants. Watching her crash over the edge was just . . .

My dick twitched uncomfortably.

Tonight, that would change. I didn't care how hard it was, I would hold out and show her it all.

Holding out my hand to her, I said, "Let's go."

"Where are we heading?"

Once she was seated in the car, I went around to my side to climb in and answer her question. "I have reservations at my favorite steakhouse, then I'm taking you to a movie."

Her eyes lit up. It still amazed me how the simple things in life brought her a world of joy. "What movie are we seeing?"

I pulled out onto the street. "I figured I'd let you decide when we get there."

She settled back into her seat. "I think that sounds like the perfect night out."

We pulled into the parking lot and I made sure to beat her around the front. I always enjoyed the way her eyes lit up when I opened a door for her, or did something any gentleman should be doing. Not that I was always a gentleman, but Elena was different. The minute we walked into the door we were shown to our seats. Ever the gentleman around her, I pulled Elena's chair out.

"Thank you."

TRADED

By the time I took my seat the waiter had appeared. Knowing Elena hated to order wine, I browsed the selections.

"We'll have a bottle of the Chateau Montelena Cabernet 2010."

"Excellent choice. I'll be back to take your orders."

I nodded to the waiter and he left. I and turned my attention back to Elena, who was studying the menu. "I have no idea what to choose," she laughed.

"Not a surprise." I chuckled. "Is there a type of steak you like?"

She shrugged and her eyes shadowed. "I haven't really had much steak."

The statement, simple and honest, reminded me why I did things like this for her. She'd missed out on so much in life. It made me want to grind my teeth, but I held myself in check to avoid upsetting her.

"Want me to pick for you?"

The smile returned to her face. "I would. You always have better taste anyway."

"Not always. Look at the swordfish?"

She giggled. "That's true."

"All right," I said, opening the menu. "Let's see what you'll like."

"Okay."

Guys like you don't deserve girls like her.

The thought burned in my brain. It was true. The kind of guy I wanted to be deserved this woman. Elena deserved someone who could give her good, clean, and stable—everything I was not. But the kind of guy I was wouldn't give her back. That kind of guy didn't extend his chivalry that far. I was going to take her, even if she deserved more.

I closed the menu. "Pick out what sides you want and I'll order the steaks."

She pinned me with her gaze, waiting for more. When I didn't answer and continued to stare, she rolled her eyes and looked down at the menu. The waiter brought back the wine. I took the glass he offered me, taking a sip and giving the waiter a curt nod. He poured us both a glass.

The waiter took our orders left the table. Before I could ask Elena about her day, my phone vibrated. I held it up and jerked my head away from the table.

"Go ahead." She nodded at the phone. "It could be someone from one of the restaurants."

Unlikely.

I flicked the screen on as I walked away from our table and there was a text from my dad. What a way to ruin a good day.

Dad: Did you want to use the box tomorrow?"

"Shit," I muttered under my breath.

Me: Sure. Thanks.

I hit the phone to silent like I should have done before we left the house.

"Is everything okay?" Elena asked when I returned. Concern creased her brow.

"Dad needs me to meet with a client tomorrow night."

"Okay, don't you do that all the time?"

TRADED

The time had come to lay my cards on the table and see her reaction. "Not by choice."

She gasped. "You mean your father *makes* you do it?"

"No." I rubbed the back of my neck, massaging the muscles there. "Not exactly, anyway. After Dad finished paying for me to go to culinary school, he asked me to take over this part of the business. He'd given me so much, I felt like I couldn't tell him no."

Lifting her glass, she took a sip and set it back down. "I'll be honest, I don't understand that. Every day you push me to make my own choices—to do what makes me happy. Yet you don't do the same."

"It's not the same. I do it because I love my dad, and he loves me."

Her head twisted to the side as she slid back in her chair. "That was low."

"Shit." I reached out toward her. "That's not what I meant."

She pulled away and her eyes focused on something to the side of the room. "Then explain, because it really sounded like you were reminding me how stupid I was to do all of those things for Dominic when he treated me like crap."

"Elena, look at me."

She glanced over at me. "Don't you dare think that's going to work on me here. You can talk to me like that in the bedroom, not in the middle of an argument."

I'd been reaching for my glass, when her words froze my hand. No one, man or woman, had ever spoken to me that way, and while it shouldn't have it made me rock hard it did. "Excuse me?"

Crossing her arms over her chest, she snapped, "What, didn't think I had it in me?"

"I'm wondering why you're speaking to me that way," I countered, mimicking her pose.

Her shoulders remained tense, like she was preparing for battle. "Your point?"

Fuck, she isn't going to give me an inch.

"I was trying to tell you before you bit my head off, that wasn't the way I meant it."

"Then how did you mean it?"

I ground my teeth together, trying to keep some semblance of control. The rational part of my brain knew that she needed to stand up for herself. That didn't matter when my temper was in play. It had been set loose and it was looking for blood. With all of my effort to rein it in.

"My dad gave Miller and I everything, so when he asked us to take over parts of his business, we may not have liked it, but we couldn't say no. His family has been doing it for decades. Right or wrong, it's all I know."

"You know how to cook. Very well, I might add."

"Yes, but he's my dad."

Silence stretched between us. I swilled my wine around in my glass, taking a sip then looking for the waiter to refill it. The tension slowly leaked from her body.

"I called my parents today."

Holy shit. I didn't see that one coming. "What did they say?"

TRADED

Her eyes filled with tears. "That they missed me, and were so happy to hear that I wasn't living with Dominic right now."

Thoughts of her living with me assaulted my brain. "Did you tell them about the show?"

Her smile broke through the tears. "I did. They're really proud of me. Said they wish they could see it."

"Why can't they? Where do they live?"

"Delaware. It's an expensive plane ride for just one show."

"But they're your parents?'

"Yeah. You have to remember my parents don't have the kind of money yours do. A ticket like that would cost over six hundred—*each*. And that's not including hotel."

An idea formed. I just needed to see if I could pull it off. "I didn't realize the flights were that expensive," I said lamely, hoping she wouldn't catch on to what I was thinking.

The waiter returned, bringing her salad. He noticed my glass and by the time I looked back at it again, it was full.

The rest of our meal arrived, and we began to eat in silence. Halfway through, Elena set her fork down and watched me. "I think if you talked to your dad and told him how you felt, he wouldn't be mad that you wanted to stop. All you need is the courage to talk to him. And if I can talk to my dad, you can talk to yours."

"Drop it, Elena." It was impossible to keep the annoyance out of my voice.

Her jaw dropped, likely at my tone, but she replied, "Fine. It's your life," and went straight back to eating.

Great. Now she was pissed at me.

As dinner progressed, Elena and I made small talk, which eventually helped us both settle somewhat. When the plates were cleared and coffee brought to the table, I finally began to relax for the first time since the text from my dad.

I checked my watch. "Should we go? We can do dessert on the way home from the movies?"

"That sounds perfect," she said. "I don't think I could eat another bite right now. The steak you chose was perfect."

After paying the bill, I stood and walked around to pull out her chair. "I'm glad you enjoyed dinner," I whispered in her ear, feeling her shiver.

We drove over to the theater and stood in front of the marquee while Elena chose a movie. There was only one romantic comedy listed. I didn't expect her to pick it, but there was a first time for everything.

Thankfully, she didn't.

I stepped up to the counter and ordered the tickets. Even though Elena swore she was full at the restaurant, she still wanted chocolate covered raisins. Who was I to tell her no?

She would be my dessert later.

* * *

"That was better than I expected it to be."

She looped her arm through mine and smiled up at me. "Really? I loved it."

TRADED

"When there's that much hype surrounding a movie, you never know whether the trailer had all the best parts."

"Oh, don't be a downer," she said, and her laughter was such a beautiful sound. I wondered if I'd ever get used to hearing it.

"A downer?" I turned to face her, the car at her back. Using my body, I pushed her up against the door. "Aren't you full of spunk tonight."

"Can you blame me? Any movie with Matt Damon is a winner in my book."

"Matt Damon? Is that what has your attention," I asked, crowding her body with my own.

"No," she rasped. "I definitely have other things on my mind."

Her hand gripped me through the fabric of my jeans. Such bold behavior had my hips jutting forward to get closer to her as my mouth came down on hers, possessive and needy. The second her lips parted, my tongue dipped inside needing to taste her.

Oh, how much more I'd taste later.

"Mr. Hawes?"

The unfamiliar voice pulled me out of the lust-induced haze Elena had a way of creating. Adjusting the obvious hard on, I spun around to face whoever had interrupted my night and froze. My shoulders tightened.

Schooling my features, I replied, "I'm sorry, I'm not sure we've been introduced."

"Ashton?" Elena stood right behind me.

The voice took two steps forward, letting the lights from the parking lot cast down on his face. "Mr. Hawes, it's me, Drake Palmer. I owe you money, sir."

Motherfucker.

No matter what, I couldn't react and beat the ever-loving piss out of the moron. Fists clenched at my side, I faced off with the idiot. "You have the wrong guy." Reaching back, I took hold of Elena's trembling fingers.

He took another step forward, his hands shaking visibly under the yellowing light. "I'm sorry to interrupt your night out, but I'm having trouble making my payment." His voice was low, nervous. And he had every reason to be.

"Not me," I growled, but he kept talking.

"I heard you might be willing to trade." He nodded toward where Elena stood.

No. I wasn't doing this here. Sure, Elena knew what I did, but this was *my* time. We were on a date, for fuck's sake. I worked hard to keep that side of my life contained. There was no way I was letting it spill over.

Not now.

Not ever.

Letting go of her hand I took two steps forward, putting myself directly in front of him. I had at least a few inches on him and by the looks of his scrawny figure, there would be no contest. He was the kind of guy I usually punted to Brock.

"Listen here you motherfucker, I have no idea who you're talking about but if you don't get out of here in the next five seconds, I'm going to consider it a threat. And trust me when I say you do *not* want to threaten a guy like me."

His eyes went wide and his body jerked. I went to open my mouth but he'd vanished, racing off into the night. My body still on alert, I looked around but there was no one else there.

With an effort, I unclenched my fists. I needed to see if Elena was okay.

She was white as a sheet, trembling from head to toe. I reached out my hand but she recoiled, which hurt worse then I'd imagined it would.

"Elena, look at me."

Her eyes panned up to mine, unfocused, and I knew nothing would get through to her. I had to get her home, away from the bullshit.

I placed my hands on her shoulders and gently maneuvered her into the car. She didn't speak a word as she mindlessly buckled her seatbelt and waited. I stood at the back of the car, whipping out my cell and shooting a text to Brock.

Me: I need a favor. Meet me at mine in 20?
Brock: I'll be there

His reply didn't surprise me. I paid him and paid him well to be available wherever, whenever. Palmer would understand how to contact me correctly by the time Brock finished with him. Under normal circumstances, I'd do it myself. If he'd stopped when I'd asked him to I would have let it go, but he pushed it. There was nothing I'd enjoy more than seeing to it that the guy never upset another woman as much as he'd upset Elena, but my attention needed to be with her, so Brock would have to relay the message on my behalf.

Hurrying around the front of the car, I peeled out of the parking lot. Concern pulled my attention to her. She sat facing forward, her hands clutched in her lap. Taking her hand, I moved it to my lips, placing a soft kiss on it.

"Elena, talk to me.

"No."

"What can I do?"

She swallowed hard. "Does stuff like that always happen?"

Everything in me said I wanted Elena to stay after the three months was up. To do that, I not only needed her to leave her husband, but to feel comfortable with me. I couldn't lie to her. "It's happened once or twice before. Most of the clients know and understand the rules before they borrow the money. And if they don't, we remind them."

She shivered and I squeezed her hand tighter.

"I don't hurt them—not right away at least. So far most have obeyed the rules after the first conversation. Those that don't are no longer an issue."

She didn't reply, but I could see her lower lip trembling.

"I'd never hurt you, Elena. You have to know that. It's just business."

"Is it? You told me earlier in the night, you only work for your dad because you feel like you have too."

I groaned. It was supposed to be the perfect date, not an analysis on wants and desires. "And I do. Me enforcing the rules doesn't change anything."

TRADED

"Maybe for me it does."

I slammed my fist into the wheel. "You knew what I did when you first climbed into my bed."

That snapped whatever had been keeping her temper in check. "So that makes it okay for me to have it thrown in my face that I'm your latest fucktoy?"

And there it was—the comparison to Tolley. Because he treated her as nothing but a slave, that's what I was going to do, no matter what I did to prove I wasn't the same man.

What was the point? I'd worked my ass off to show her that I wasn't him; that I could offer her more. I hadn't been that guy ever. Hell, I was a better guy for her than I'd been to any woman. She saw Ashton Hawes 2.0—the nice guy. So why, after everything, would she think me a liar?

I didn't know why she thought that way, but I'd be damned if I would let it continue.

CHAPTER 19

Ashton

"Goddamn it, Elena. Why would you say that?"

I pulled into the drive and slammed on the brakes, sending us both flying forward.

"Ashton," she screamed, grabbing the belt.

I turned toward her, grasping her chin to move her head to face me. "Do I have your attention now?" I snarled.

"What?" she snapped.

"I have never, nor will I ever consider you a *fucktoy*. If that were the case, I'd use your body for what I needed like your piece of shit husband suggested instead of having you sleep in my bed because I like you there. I would not set up auditions for you. I would not take you to dinner. And I would *never* sit through a movie with you, no matter how good you were at giving head."

I didn't give her a chance to think, much less to reply. Lowering my head, I took her lips in a brutal kiss. I needed her to believe me. I needed her to know that what we had was no longer a product of circumstance. I put everything into the kiss.

I claimed her.

And with each passing moment she slowly tempered, her lips molding to mine, her body going limp in the seat. I broke away.

"I want you to be so much more than a temporary distraction. It's why I've done everything I can to bring out the real Elena—the one who stands up for herself. I want you to make your own choices. I want you to choose me. I don't care how you came to me, I just want you."

She stared at me for a beat then left the car, walking into the house, leaving the door wide open. I went to follow but was stopped by the purring rumble of Brock's '69 Chevelle SS. I climbed out and leaned against my door, needing the conversation with Brock over and done with.

"Ashton, what's up man? It's not like you to call out of the blue."

"Drake Palmer has become a problem," I growled.

"You had a drop tonight?" His brows dropped down over his, dark, almost black eyes.

"No." I began to pace the driveway. "Fucker approached us outside the movie theater."

"Shit. Wait—us? Elena was with you?"

"Unfortunately, because not only did the asshole bring up business in public, he also made it very clear he knew about my deal with Tolley."

"What the fuck?" Brock's shoulders rolled back like he was bracing for a fight. "You want me to handle this?" The drop in tone of his voice signaled he was done talking unless I reined him in.

"I want you to go have a *chat* with Palmer. Make it clear he's one tiny slip up away from spending months not hours in the hospital, and if that happens, it'll be me who deals with him. While you're there, find out who told him about the deal."

"Who else besides us and Tolley knows?"

"No one. I know it was that prick, but I need to know how far that shit's spread. Elena is pissed and I don't like that. The other thing I don't like is weak little piss-ants like Palmer thinking they can buy time by pimping out their girlfriends. Before you know it, every one of them will have some ridiculous reason why they can't pay and offer something equally as stupid. We can't have that shit."

"I'll take care of it." Brock crossed his arms over his massive chest, a move design to intimidate, but I knew better. "You sure she's strong enough for this? I know I said I thought she was tough, but maybe—"

"Back the fuck off," I warned. "I've had enough shit tonight."

The more I thought about that fucker running around claiming he pulled one over on me, the more I wanted to hunt his ass down. But I had bigger things to deal with.

"I'll deal with this asshole," Brock said, backing up toward his car. "You should go deal with Elena."

TRADED

"Fuck!" I took a few deep breaths trying to calm down. "Stop by tomorrow with an update."

"Will do," he walked back to his car.

I watched Brock pull out of the drive. He'd get the results I needed. Drake Palmer would soon learn what happened to people who didn't pay their debts and ran their mouths off.

Throwing the door open, I sent it crashing into the frame. Angry didn't describe how I felt about the night being ruined by that little prick. None of it was Elena's fault, yet she was the one upset. I needed to talk to her; needed to explain. Before I climbed those stairs I needed to calm the fuck down.

* * *

A couple of shots of whiskey later, I climbed the stairs. Even though I knew we'd have to have it out eventually, my time downstairs had given me an idea. When I reached the top of the landing, I heard the shower in my room running.

At least she hadn't gone back to the guest room.

Hoping to catch her when she got out, I peeled off my clothes and went to the table next to the bed. My goal was to make her forget for a little while. To soften her up so we could talk this shit out.

It was time to introduce Elena to some of my more exotic tastes in the bedroom.

Grabbing the items I wanted, I lay them on the table and covered them with a small towel. The second the water turned off, I went to the door of the bathroom and threw it open.

"Ashton," she screamed, pulling the towel tighter to her body.

Before she could say another word, I backed her against the vanity. Sinking my hands into her hair, I let the taste of her lips wash over me, the kiss igniting a burning heat throughout my body, the simple act of my tongue gliding into her mouth only a small representation of what I planned on doing to her later.

Needing air, I broke the kiss and leaned back to take in the flush that had worked its way up her body and onto her cheeks. The towel lay on the floor, forgotten. In one swift motion, I scooped her into my arms.

"Put me down," she squealed, her words sharp.

"Not until I erase the shit from earlier."

The way her body molded to mine the moment I let her legs slide to the floor made my dick jerk. If he were the brains I'd already be buried balls deep.

"Ashton," she attempted come off stern. "We need to talk."

"Later."

I needed more.

Bending down, I kissed the skin right behind her ear, then sucked a path down her neck, down her chest, until my tongue slid over the hardened peak of her nipple.

"Oh," she moaned, her body vibrating with the sound.

As I grazed my teeth across the tip, her hand slipped around my neck, holding my head there. I gave her what she wanted, alternately nipping and licking. Her sharp moans filled the air. Slowly, I stood and looked her dead in the eye.

"I want to play with you tonight. Once we start I'm in charge. If something is too much, say so. Can you agree to that?"

Her chest rose and fell with her heavy breaths. She searched my face, settling on my lips for a moment before bringing her gaze back up to mine.

"Yes."

It was the only word I wanted to hear out of her mouth. In a heartbeat, I twisted her to face away from me and guided her down onto the mattress. Raking my fingers down her back, she shivered beneath my touch and I took a moment to watch her, not quite believing that all of her soft smooth skin was mine to touch and caress.

My hands gripped her hips, grinding my hard length against her ass, showing her what she did to me every—damn—time. Taking a firm hold of her ass, spreading the cheeks to see the virgin entrance, my breath caught in my throat. One day I'd be the first man to take her there.

But not tonight.

"So fucking sexy. Every time I see you in my bed, I want you more and more."

I let my thumb graze over her forbidden entrance. She had no idea how much pleasure I could wring from her. She gasped at my touch.

"I think we'll play here a bit tonight."

Her head lifted from the bed and she glanced over her shoulder, uncertainty clear in her eyes. "I've never—"

"I know." I bent down to whisper in her ear, sliding my thumb over the tiny hole. "We won't get there tonight, but I want to try something new. Something you've never done. Trust me."

"I do."

She lowered her head back to the mattress. Tension still tightened her muscles, but she relaxed imperceptibly with my reminder.

Reaching over, I moved the towel to the side and took the three things I thought she'd enjoy the most. My cock pulsed at the images they stirred in my head. With a soft groan, I flipped the top on the bottle and poured the cool liquid on my fingertips before sliding them down her crease, letting my thumb slip inside.

She clenched, holding me tightly. Starting at the base of her spine, I tasted her skin, licking a path up her back. "You taste as sweet as you look."

"Oh God." Her soft moan was muffled by the sheets.

When I felt her relax I moved my thumb, in a bit and back out again, letting her grow accustom to the sensation. She writhed on the bed when I stretched my index finger forward to brush over her clit. The moment her body pushed back trying to pull in more, I knew she was ready.

Letting my finger slip from her body, I picked up the brand new plug and coated it to make entry easier on her. I placed the small sliver plug at her entrance, all the while using my fingers to tease her center. Fire raced through me watching the plug slip inside.

"Oh, that's—oh!" Her words became incoherent babble when I circled the little nub.

"Sweetheart, that's nothing."

TRADED

Gripping her hips, I rolled her head to face me. I raised an eyebrow, letting the question hang in the air.

Her eyes burned with lust. "Feels full."

"It's about to get better."

I flipped her to her back, bending my head and sucking her nipple into my mouth, bringing it to a stiff peak. While I paid the same attention to her other tight bud, I connected the clamp.

"Ashton," she whimpered, her back arching off the bed.

"You like that."

"Yes. Yes. Yes."

I connected the other clamp, the thin silver chain a delicate contrast to ivory skin and gave it a quick tug, my dick surging at the sight of her. She was so responsive. I tried to be patient, but I'd hit my limit. All I wanted was to slide into the warm heat of her pussy and feel the delicious friction of the plug, stretching her for me.

I entered her in one smooth thrust.

"Holy shit," she cried out. "Oh my God, I—"

A quick thrust in and out and all conversation was forgotten. I captured her lips, sliding my tongue inside. My body moved in the same rhythm: taking and giving. Each groan and cry from her lips pushed me further, the tugs on the chain making her clamp down on me harder. The tight heat was almost too much to bear.

I wouldn't make it much longer, and by the way her body undulated against mine I knew she was close too. Gliding my hand down her ribs, I slipped it between our bodies, thumbing her clit until she went off like an explosion. Her pussy rippled around me, combined with the pressure from the plug and I couldn't hold back. Two more sharp thrusts and I emptied myself inside her body.

She lay there, panting, a dazed look in her eyes. I pulled the plug from her, eliciting a groan, and carefully removed the clamps. There wasn't a part of her that wouldn't be sensitive tonight. Taking the toys to the bathroom, I grabbed a washcloth to clean her up. I ran the warm cloth over her body while she lay there, unmoving, completely sated.

I knew you were perfect.

By the time I climbed into bed next to her, she was sound asleep. I coaxed her over into my arms and, just like always, the minute her body touched mine, she curled up against me.

There was something in that gesture, and I knew things had gotten further than I'd ever expected them to. Elena meant more and more to me each day.

Was it love? I didn't know.

But I was willing to find out.

♋♋♋

The mountain of paperwork never seemed to end. The reality was I needed to spend more time at my other two establishments. Lately, I spent most of my time in La Tratoria, neglecting The Bluewater Grill and Indigo. It was the first restaurant I opened and would always be the most special. However, the other two also earned me money; something they wouldn't continue to do if I neglected them.

TRADED

Leaning my head against the back of the chair, I remembered the way Elena looked wrapped around me this morning as she slept, all of her delicious curves on display. She'd fallen asleep, so we hadn't talked. I'd have to try after work.

The knock on my door pulled me from my fantasies.

"Come in," I called out, sitting up and leaning forward on the desk.

Miller's head popped around the door. "Hey, man. Thought I'd stop by and see how Elena's doing." He waggled his brows up and down.

I pointed to the door. "Back the fuck off or shut the fuck up."

He laughed. "You slept with her, didn't you?"

"And what makes you think I'm telling you anything?"

"You tell me about every chick you fuck," he said sitting down on the sofa in the corner of my office. "What makes her different?"

I turned back to the computer screen.

Great guffaws of laughter burst from Miller as he slumped down on the couch clutching his stomach. "You . . . you . . ." He couldn't speak.

"What the hell are you laughing at?" The sound didn't stop which annoyed me. "You know what? I don't want to know. Just get out so I can get some work done."

When he got himself under a bit of control, he spoke. "I was right about you that night at Dad's."

"Right about what?"

"You want her, and not for a quick screw. You want that woman long-term."

"Says who?"

He smirked. "It's written all over you."

I no longer held the relaxed position of someone who didn't care. My hand was clenched around my bicep, my fingers tapping against my arm.

"Fine. I want her. Happy?"

"Not really. It's the first time you've wanted someone longer than the time it takes to play and get yourselves off. What gives? What makes Elena different?"

A good question. What made me want to give her the world on a silver platter when the most I cared for a woman before was whether or not she was interested in what I liked. "She's different."

I was saved by another knock on the door. "What?" I snapped, irritated with all of the interruptions.

Brock stepped into the room, his jaw clenched so tight I thought it might break under the strain. He acknowledged us as he stepped into the room.

"Who pissed in your cheerios?" Miller was still having trouble keeping himself from laughing.

Brock growled at Miller. Before he had a chance to strangle him, I redirected Brock's attention to me. "What do you have for me?"

No small talk, no preamble.

TRADED

"Palmer is completely aware of how he should and shouldn't behave in the future, if he wants that future to be a bright and happy one."

"I had a feeling he'd understand once you'd had a nice discussion with him." As much as I hated doing any of the business at the restaurant, the whole situation needed to be handled immediately.

"We had a nice long *chat* about how he remembers hearing certain things about Elena."

That sobered Miller up. "What happened with Elena?"

I sighed, not wanting to explain it but knowing Miller wouldn't let it lie if I tried to push him off. "Some dipshit client approached us outside the movies last night, wanting to talk about the money he owes."

"Jesus Christ. I hope you told him to fuck off."

He was now sitting up straight, his eyes bouncing back and forth between Brock and myself. Miller was almost always a hothead. He probably would have done a lot more to Palmer.

Brock took the seat next to Miller. "Palmer and Tolley bet at the same place downtown. Sports. Not your place. Miller," he added. "Way Palmer told it, Tolley was in there boasting about how he pulled one over on you. That no one in their right mind would want his dumbass wife."

I slammed my fist down onto the desk. "You've got to be fucking kidding me? How has someone not seen to this asshole before? He must have enemies."

Brock shook his head and I knew he was as puzzled as I was as to why Dominic Tolley was still walking, let alone breathing. In our business, guys with big mouths didn't last long. It only took one piece of information to fall into the wrong hands, and the whole house of cards could come crashing down.

And trust me—no one wanted to be *that* guy.

"How did Elena take that?" Miller asked.

I scoffed. "Not well. Claimed I was using her as a fucktoy and didn't really want her."

"Jesus. That some fucked up shit. What the hell are you going to do about it?"

I moved to face Brock. "I want you to pay that bastard a visit *today*. Make it very clear that he'll owe me every goddamn dollar if he doesn't stop sharing our deal with the fucking world. If I didn't think I'd take it too far I'd visit myself. But we need this guy breathing."

Brock stood. "Will do. I'll make sure he understands." There was no mistaking the menace in his tone.

Once Brock closed the door behind him, Miller moved to the chair in front of my desk. "What are you going to do to fix shit with Elena?"

"I fixed it last night."

"No, brother, you put a Band-Aid on it. Something that big doesn't get sorted overnight. If she means as much to you as I think she does you need to make it very clear that she's your priority. That you want her above anything else."

"And how do I do that?"

He shrugged. "I don't know. Take her somewhere she's never been. Do something that shows her you pay attention. That she's on your mind."

Maybe Miller had a point. "When did you get so soft?"

"Fuck you. I paid a lot of attention to Mom and Dad. We work in a business that would scare the shit out of most women. You find a good one, you'll want to keep her. If you want to keep her, you need to show her that you won't let the business interfere with your life with her. That you can separate the two. Keep her safe."

A plan began to form in my mind. Something she'd never done and probably wouldn't get the chance to do again, unless she stayed with me. The question was whether I could pull it off or not.

CHAPTER 20

Elena

"Wake up, sleepyhead."

My eyes opened slowly to find Ashton sitting on the side of the bed. In a suit he was sexy; in a pair of jeans and a tight T-shirt, he was what dreams were made of.

"Morning." A quick glimpse at the window and I got confused. "Umm . . . or night? What time is it?"

"It's almost three in the morning."

He pulled back the covers and I did my best not to swallow my tongue at the way his jeans stretched across the curve of his ass. I sat up and attempted to straighten the rumpled mess that was my hair, making myself somewhat more presentable. In comparison to him, I'd never come close. He gripped my fingers and pulled them up to his lips.

"Don't. You're always beautiful."

TRADED

He left no room for argument, although it didn't stop the blush from staining my cheeks.

"Thank you." Still not great at accepting compliments, I attempted to change the subject. "Why are you up and dressed?"

Picking up the bag at the end of the bed. "I have a surprise. I need you to get up and get dressed."

"But—"

"No buts. Get your sexy ass out of that bed and get dressed. I'll wait for you downstairs, otherwise we'll never get out of the house." His heated gaze traveled down my body. Reaching down he adjusted himself, staring at me longingly as he sucked in a deep breath, before walking out the door.

I sat for a moment, feeling my heart dance in my chest as I wondered what on earth he could have planned. There had been so many surprises—each one more wonderful than the last. I pulled the sheets up to my face and grinned.

"Hurry up!" he called from the stairwell.

Jumping from the bed, I washed up quickly and threw on the jeans and T-shirt Ashton had left on the bed. I'd been too busy staring to notice the outfit earlier. Pushing my phone into the back pocket of my jeans, I took the stairs two at a time. It might be the crack of dawn, but it had been a long time since anyone surprised me. And with Ashton, each surprise was better than the last.

"Ready?" he asked, shaking the car keys.

"Yeah."

I reached for the bag at his feet, but he pushed my hand away and picked it up himself. "Are you going to tell me where we're going?" I asked as we walked down the steps to the Bentley already waiting in front.

"Nope."

I stuck my bottom lip out, hoping it would get me more information, but after he'd loaded the bag into the trunk and rounded the car to open my door, his thumb swiped over my bottom lip.

"It won't work, Elena." He opened the passenger door and gestured inside the car.

"Fine." I slipped into the seat, listening to his belly laugh all the way around the front and into his own seat. It was hard to keep up the pretense and not laugh with him. By the time we pulled out of the drive, I'd given up and giggled right along.

I had a hard time sitting still during the whole drive. Theories about where we might be heading flipped through my head at such speed, I could barely keep up with them. Ashton turned the car into a small airport, pulling up and parking behind one of the hangers.

"Flying?"

"We are, but I'm not telling you any more."

We climbed out of the car at the same time and Ashton grabbed the bag from the back on his way to meet me. Threading his fingers through mine, I gasped at the gesture because the slight pressure on my hand settled my nerves. It was weird how well he knew me.

TRADED

We walked hand in hand to the hanger. The front was open, the plane already out on the tarmac.

"Ashton." A man with cropped red hair came through the door. "You made good time."

"We did," Ashton said, extending his hand. "Once someone got out of bed." He looked over and winked at me.

"It's the middle of the night," I protested.

They both laughed. "John, this is Elena." Ashton brought me forward. "Elena, this is John. Dad keeps him on retainer for special flights."

"It's a pleasure." John kissed the back of my hand. He lingered a little longer than necessary.

"John," Ashton warned.

John raised his hands, his eyes raking down my body. Despite Ashton's warning, his gaze lingered on my breasts. "You can't blame me for getting carried away."

"Then you can't blame me for what'll happen next."

"Fair point." John started to back toward the door. "Plane's fueled. Checks done. Flight's cleared. We can take off whenever you're ready."

Ashton glanced over at me, obviously seeing the pleading in my eyes. "We're ready now."

"Stairs are down. Help yourself. I'll be up in a minute." John took off, jogging out the door.

"It was nice to meet you," I called out into the night. Turning to face Ashton, I added. "You scared the crap out of him."

He scoffed. "I don't give a shit. I pay him to fly a plane, not grope the woman I'm trying to impress."

I rolled my eyes and let Ashton lead me to the steps, which were already extended. "A private plane?"

"The only way to get where we're going. The airport is small and the next largest one is three hours away."

Geography was never my best subject. I racked my brain for where he might be talking about.

"Stop trying to figure it out," he said softly next to my ear. "You'll spoil the surprise."

He placed the bag in one of the compartments near the front, then showed me to one of the seats, each a large leather recliner. This plane looked nothing like the jets where they shove three people in a section that is really only big enough for two. Taking a seat, I was surprised at how comfortable the seats were.

"I've only ever flown coach."

"How many times have you flown?"

I glanced down to the floor. "Once, when we left for Vegas."

Ashton's head snapped in my direction. "Are you telling me you've only flown once in your entire life?"

I nodded, unsure how to respond. Humiliation swept through me. "Yeah, we drove from there to Colorado. Dominic wanted to start afresh somewhere new."

"I thought your parents lived on the East coast. You didn't visit them?" His tone was harsh.

TRADED

"Dominic always said we didn't have the money to make the long flight." I looked at the carpet for so long I began to memorize the pattern. "Besides, we lost contact, remember?"

He caught my chin between his thumb and forefinger, bringing my face up to his. "Elena, you're not to blame. It's just that every time you let me in, I'm disgusted with how callous and selfish that man is."

So many thoughts ran through my head. Whether it was right or wrong, I decided to tell Ashton about my plans.

"I've decided to file for divorce. I just need to find a good lawyer."

A wicked grin crossed his lips and he swooped, taking my lips in a demanding kiss. Swirling tongues fought burning fires and I momentarily forgot where we were until he sat back, panting, "I want you. Can't. Not yet, at least."

My chest heaved. It still amazed me how quickly Ashton could reduce me to a mass of nerves and no brainpower. All it took was a simple kiss. The man had a very talented tongue. Wherever he used it.

John stepped into the plane at that moment, averting his gaze. "Buckle up, we're cleared to take off."

My face flushed with the idea of being caught.

"He didn't see anything," Ashton whispered. "And he'll miss the rest of the show when he's stuck behind that door, flying the plane." He gave me a salacious grin.

Every nerve ending tingled with his carnal promise. "We can't do *that* on the plane."

His hand slipped underneath my shirt. "Oh we can. And we will. You've done nothing but tease me since I woke you up. I'm done waiting."

"Oh God."

"That's right. You'll be screaming that a lot in a bit. But, my name will do just fine for now."

"Wait . . . did you say that *I've* been teasing *you?*" All of the comments, looks, not to mention the kiss flashed before me. "You've—" He covered my lips with his fingers.

"Don't deny it. I saw you staring at my ass earlier. What's a man supposed to do?" I wanted to protest that he happened to be the one who took my clothes off last night, but his fingers never moved. "Since we can't do what I want to do yet, let's talk more about your divorce."

His fingers moved away from my lips but I only managed to get out, "Last night," before he covered them again.

"Uh-uh. We're talking divorce, not your teasing ways."

I rolled my eyes and nodded. Once again, his fingers fell away. "I want to start divorce proceedings. I don't want to wait another minute to be free of him. I should have left before, but I didn't know any better. I'm glad that now I do. I just need to find a lawyer."

"I have a law firm on retainer. We can go see them this week."

"You don't have to do that."

TRADED

The plane started taxiing toward the runway. "I want to. The idea of you completely free of that asshole makes me hard as a rock. Plus, they're on a retainer. They may as well do something for their money."

The plane picked up speed and we rocketed down the runway. At the same time, Ashton took my hand, placing it over the bulge in his pants.

"Ashton," I whispered.

He captured my mouth as the plane began its ascent, and the floating sensation filling my body had nothing to do with takeoff. Ashton and his talented tongue sent me soaring to new heights. All thoughts of protesting flew right out the window. His mouth trailed down my cheek to my neck, lightly sucking on the pulse point.

My body was already alight with sensation when Ashton's fingers stroked across my stomach, snaking up and under my shirt to cover my breast. His thumb teased me above the fabric.

"More," I begged.

"More?" His fingers teased my nipples. "You weren't sure you wanted to do this."

Needing less talking and more touching, I threaded my fingers into the hair at his nape and pulled his mouth to mine.

He didn't disappoint.

When his tongue slid back into my mouth and his fingers dipped below the fabric of my bra, a small voice in the back of my head tried to scream that I must be crazy to go along with this. Except the voice was so small it could be a whisper.

The throbbing, my core begging for more. Suddenly, my seatbelt unfastened and I was hauled over into Ashton's lap, nothing breaking the connection of our lips. The hard length of his erection pushed into me, creating a delicious friction. Desire, hot and heavy, filled me. Using my free hand, I reached down to unfasten the button and zipper of his jeans. He taught me that: that I could touch him and enjoy it.

That's exactly what I wanted—to touch and enjoy. A groan left his lips, the moment my hand slipped inside and wrapped around him.

"Oh fuck, Elena."

My hand moved up and down for a few strokes before Ashton grabbed my shoulders and flipped me around on his lap. One hand went up my shirt and back to my nipples, while the other snaked down my front to open my jeans and slip inside. Ashton slid his fingers down through my slick wet heat. My hips bucked up, trying to get his fingers where I needed them. His teeth scraped across the back of my neck.

"Ashton."

"That's exactly what I wanted to hear. So responsive." His finger caressed my clit and the muscles in my body tightened in anticipation, all the while his tongue traced patterns across my nape. The combination became too much and fireworks exploded behind my eyes as I gave in to the urge and let go, screaming out Ashton's name.

Aftershocks flashed through my body so strongly, I barely noticed him push my pants down my thighs. He lifted me a bit higher and slid home. Both of our tests had come back negative and I was on the pill, so there was no need for a condom.

"You're so fucking wet. It makes me want to come, knowing how badly you want me. I want to fuck you hard and fast right now."

"Do it," I moaned.

Ashton didn't need to be told twice. He gripped my hips, thrusting rapidly. My body moved in sync with his.

"Damn, damn, damn," I cried, my body pushing itself toward another orgasm quicker than I could have imagined.

Ashton lost his rhythm right before slamming into me one last time. Sensations were the only thing I paid attention to as my orgasm ripped through me.

As our bodies cooled, Ashton placed sweet soft kisses to the back of my neck. Glancing down, I noticed our partial state of undress. Drained, I leaned back against Ashton, enjoying the soft movements around my stomach.

"You are so passionate and responsive. Everything I need," he whispered in my ear.

"Mmm."

"Did I steal your strength?" he chuckled.

I nodded, too tired to speak.

"Let's get you dressed, then you can sleep the rest of the flight. I'll wake you when we get there."

"Where is there?"

"Oh no, you're still not getting it out of me with your sleepy ramblings."

"I tried," I mumbled.

He laughed and stood, his arms wound around my middle. He helped me adjust my clothes and then tucked himself back into his jeans. I sat back down in my seat, wondering how I'd be comfortable enough to sleep sitting up. Ashton was digging through a cabinet in the back and came back with a pillow and a blanket.

"Thank you," I said, taking the pillow from his hands and placing it behind my head.

He laughed and shook his head at me. "Let me help." He reached down on the side of the seat. Slowly, the seat began to recline. When it finally stopped moving, I was lying down and knew I'd be asleep in no time. Ashton covered me with the blanket, then placed a soft kiss on my head.

"Sleep."

Too tired to argue or attempt to get answers from him, I let my eyes drift closed.

༺༻

The jerk of the wheels hitting the ground woke me. Like a kid on Christmas morning, I was instantly alert. Sitting up, I found Ashton lounging in the seat next to me. His glasses were on the top of his head, a book in his hand.

"Are we nearly there?"

He lowered the book to his lap and pulled his glasses back down over his eyes. "We should be at the hanger soon, then we just need to wait for permission to disembark."

He stood, stretching, all of his lean muscles on display underneath his T-shirt. "You can stop staring now. If you want to touch . . ."

He glanced at me out of the corner of his eyes, a smirk crossing his lips.

TRADED

I glanced away but then looked back. Why shouldn't I touch him? After all, we'd done much worse on this flight. Soon we'd been wherever it was he'd taken me—who knew when I'd next get a chance like this.

Standing, I stepped up and placed my hands on his abs and his eyes darkened instantly. His reaction had me feeling brave and I didn't give him a chance to do anything before I leaned up on my toes and pressed my lips to his. His hand on my lower back pressed me closer to him. When he leaned back, he watched me for a minute then admitted, "You make me feel things I never thought I would."

Unsure how to respond I opened and closed my mouth a few times, willing the words to come. But I was interrupted when the door to the front compartment swung open.

"You guys can exit the plane whenever you're ready. The car . . ." John seemed to notice something going on between us and trailed off.

"Thanks, John. I'll text you when we're ready to head back," Ashton answered over his shoulder. Letting out a breath, I thanked my lucky stars. Saved by the bell.

"Ashton."

He stepped toward the front, where he'd stored the bag earlier. Oh man, had I messed this up? My stomach began to churn. He'd taken the time to plan this and there I was, sticking my foot in my mouth.

I followed him, hesitantly. These sorts of situations always made me nervous, and with Ashton I didn't know where I stood. Dominic would have just flown into a rage, and rage I could cope with. I wasn't used to brooding.

Ashton was standing at the door, just looking at the stairs. For a moment, I thought he might change his mind and call John to take us back. Then he turned and held out a hand to me, the mysterious bag in the other. I felt the tension leave my body, all of my insecurities of a moment ago faded away.

My hand slipped into his, weaving our fingers together. The warmth infused my skin, chasing away the cold. We walked the steps hand in hand, toward the jeep that sat on the tarmac in front of us.

"Here, you might need this." He reached into the bag and pulled out a hooded sweatshirt.

"Thank you." I put the sweatshirt on and climbed into the jeep.

Once he was settled in the driver's seat, I looked over at him. He was such a handsome man. I had to force myself to believe I wasn't dreaming. "Still not going to tell me where we are."

"You'll see in a minute." He started the car and took off toward the front gate.

When we passed through, I thought my eyes might fall out of my head. I couldn't have seen the sign correctly. Reaching over, he placed a finger under my chin and closed my mouth.

"Close your mouth, before the bugs fly in."

"The Grand Canyon? You brought me to the Grand Canyon?"

It was a place I'd always wanted to go, but never in a million years thought I'd find myself.

TRADED

"I had a feeling you'd never been here, and I thought sunrise would a spectacular way for you to see it the first time."

The tears came on so fast I had no chance of stopping them and they leaked down my cheeks, blurring my vision and making it hard for me to draw a full breath. Ashton glanced over at me. "Don't cry, Elena."

"I can't help it. I've never been so happy."

The sky was still dark and it was hard to see. My heart pounding in my chest the longer we drove. I knew we were getting closer.

Ashton pulled the jeep to a stop and jumped out to grab the bag. Stepping out of the car, I was surprised by the drop in temperature.

"Wow, it's cold."

"Until the sun comes up." He lifted the bag in his hand. "I brought things to keep us warm. Come on, I don't want you to miss any of it."

He flicked on a flashlight and led the way, the light seeming extraordinarily bright in the darkness. I was used to nighttime, obviously, but I didn't know if it was the change in location or something else, but everything seemed . . . *more*. The air was colder, the night darker. I caught up to Ashton, looping my arm through his as we followed the trail and the feel of him against me was just the same.

More.

We weren't the only ones there. Voices could be heard all around us. When we finally stopped walking, I was glad Ashton had me put sneakers on. He lay out a blanket and pulled another from his bag. Taking a seat in the center, he gestured in front of himself.

"Sit with me. This is the best place to see the sunrise this time of year."

Shivering at the cold I sat between his legs, leaning against his chest and he wrapped the other blanket around the two of us, holding me tight to him. It felt so right, sitting here with him like this. But it was hard to concentrate on anything but the beauty surrounding me. As we sat watching, the sky changed from a light blue to orange and eventually a pink.

Then, in the most unforgettable moment of my life, wrapped in the arms of the man who saved me from the hell I'd been living in, I watched the sun peak over the horizon.

"It's beautiful."

I didn't dare move my eyes from the sky, knowing this was a once in a lifetime moment. I didn't want to miss a single second. Nothing could make the moment any better.

"Yes," Ashton said, resting his chin on my shoulder, his mouth right by my ear. "You are."

CHAPTER 21

Ashton

The awe in Elena's voice made everything worth it. No one had ever bothered to treat her like a princess. My dad read me like a book the first night I brought Elena to his house for dinner—something about her called to me. I didn't know what, I didn't know why. I just knew. At first I told myself that it was all about saving her, but the reality was she'd found a way past the barriers I put up.

I watched her as we sat there waiting for the sun to come up, studying the curve of her jaw, the way her hair flowed around her, thinking Elena was beauty and elegance wrapped into one package but she didn't realize it. It baffled me.

The sun continued its ascent and Elena sat watching, completely enthralled. All I wanted was my hands somewhere on her body; it didn't matter where, as long as I was touching. I could have tried to tell myself it was about the feel of her body, the sex, but I knew it wasn't. Every moment I spent with Elena, I found myself changing, becoming a man worthy of being with her.

I had so much more planned for the day: hiking, lunch in a fabulous restaurant not far from the park, then a quick plane ride back for the baseball game. I decided against taking her to the box; too many bad memories. They were things she might have to face eventually, but she didn't have to deal with it yet. Not on our date, anyway. To avoid this, I'd bought seats behind the dugout, on the first base line. If she really wanted to watch the game, there were no better seats.

Thinking about the box, and everything it signified, brought my mood low. At some point I needed to decide if this was something I could keep doing for my dad. Did I want to continue to be the loan shark, or simply be the restaurateur and chef? Was it possible to do both?

The sun had fully risen in the sky. Elena turned her head to face me. "Thank you," she said softly, placing a brief kiss on my lips.

"You're so very welcome."

She turned to gaze back over the summit. "Do we have to leave yet?"

"Nope." I stood and reached my hand down to her and helped her to her feet. "I thought we might do a little hiking first."

I produced a water bottle each and the smile on her lips was brighter than the newly emerged sun.

"Are you ready?" I asked, watching her take in her surroundings.

TRADED

"I've never been more ready for anything in my life."

For the next few hours we hiked different trails, sticking to the easier ones. Elena hadn't hiked before and I was afraid one of the harder trails might be too much. About an hour in, we stopped for a drink of water and to rest our legs for a moment.

Seated on the rock below mine, she looked up at me. "Can I ask you a question?"

"Of course."

She gestured to my face with the water bottle. "The glasses."

"What about them?"

"Well, I noticed on the plane you weren't wearing them while you were reading. You had them on top of your head."

"Oh." I chuckled. "I don't need them for seeing things up close, only things in the distance. It's just easier to wear them all of the time than only when I need to see far away."

"Well, that makes sense." She lifted her bottle to her lips again, taking a sip of the water and I was glad that she was no longer speaking because all I could think about was how much I wanted those lips wrapped around my dick.

Later, Ashton. Be patient.

"What about contacts?"

I snapped myself out of my fantasies. "Never had much luck with them. I own a set, but after a few hours they're not very comfortable." I wouldn't mention my slightly narcissistic side. I knew many women had a thing for men with glasses—stylish glasses at least.

"Shall we finish up and head back to the car? I have more surprises planned."

Her gaze snapped to mine. "More?"

"Yep. The first is a special place for lunch but you'll see when we get there."

"Okay." Her smile was infectious and I found myself grinning inanely, something I didn't do a lot.

It took us about a half an hour to reach the car. I loaded the bag into the back seat and climbed in the driver side. Elena had already climbed in the car before I had the chance to open her door.

"What did you think?" I asked as I drove down to the restaurant.

"It was perfect. I can't think of a better reason to get up at three in the morning." She paused and smirked. "Well, maybe one other reason..."

"Elena," I groaned. "If you keep up with those comments, I'm going to pull the car over."

When her hand landed on my thigh, I stopped the car on the side of the road, looking over at her and trying to remember all the reasons I shouldn't push her.

But goddamn...

She'd removed the sweatshirt during the hike. The T-shirt she wore only defined her breasts even more, right down to the hard nipples, visible through the thin fabric.

The blood raced to my cock and reason flew out the window. Putting the car in drive I turned down a deserted side street and pulled over as far into the trees as possible. Without a word, I got out of the car and jogged around to her side, yanking open the door and popping her belt, hauling her out of the car. Her eyes flashed as I spun her around and pushed her torso down on the seat.

"I warned you," I whispered, my hand snaking between us to unbutton and unzip her jeans.

"Please," she begged.

Dipping my hand past the waistband of her panties, I sunk my fingers into her. I nipped her earlobe. "You're already dripping wet for me."

My fingers continued to slip through her body's juices. I locked her wrists in one of my hands, thoughts of dropping her pants right then and fucking her senseless crossing my mind. Instead, I plunged two fingers inside, rocking them in and out of her body, creating a delicious friction that I wished was on my dick and not my fingers.

She moaned from the back of her throat, pushing back against my fingers.

"Harder?"

"Oh God, please."

"Only 'cause you said please."

Done with the foreplay, both of our bodies screaming to connect, I pushed her pants down to her knees. Lowering my own zipper, I freed my cock and pulled a couple strokes off before I thrust forward. Her body clenched around mine, pulling me in deep, creating a sensation that made me half demented with need.

"That's it," she groaned.

My body slammed into hers hard and fast, each thrust making my cock leak and beg for relief as I brought her up and over the edge with me, coming hard, over and over again into her body.

"Ashton," she said, her body collapsing on the seat.

A quick hard fuck: exactly what I needed before I brought her home tonight and introduced her to more of the fun things I kept in my bedroom.

Our bodies still connected, I slowly pulled out and tucked myself back into my jeans. Elena stood, her eyes widening as she took in our surroundings.

"Oh my God, I can't believe we just did that on the side of the road—in broad daylight!" she said, quickly righting her clothes.

I wound my arm around her, drawing her up against my body. "Oh, sweetheart, there are so many ways I want to and will take you. This is just the start."

"I've never done anything like this." She blushed furiously.

"I know. And I'm so happy that you're doing it all with me."

"Ashton, I—" I covered her lips with my own.

"Don't say anything. Just enjoy the moment." I gave her ass a quick slap. "Now get in the car and stop distracting me."

Elena raised her brows, but climbed into the car without another word. We both buckled up and I made a quick U-turn and put us back on the road to the restaurant. A soft, rumbling sound came from the passenger side of the car.

"Hungry?" I asked, glancing at her out of the corner of my eye.

TRADED

"Starved." She rubbed her hand over her stomach. "The protein bar wore off. I need real food."

"Good thing we're on our way to eat."

"Definitely."

Elena had completely overcome her need to eat salads and small portions. Gone were the days when she had to worry about the overweight prick convincing her she weighed too much. She had a wide-ranging palate and was always willing to try something new, even if she thought it didn't sound appetizing. I'd decided against taking her away from the Grand Canyon. For Elena, it wasn't about the number of stars the restaurant had; she was more concerned with the atmosphere. Not to say she didn't enjoy fine dining, but a fancy restaurant didn't fit the day's plans.

Driving into the lot, I found a parking space and Elena stared at the building before us. Designed like a hunting lodge, the restaurant was rustic and had a log cabin type of feel. The place was rumored to have the most spectacular view of the Grand Canyon, besides being on one of the trails.

She looked over at me. "This doesn't seem like your normal choice of restaurant."

"It's not, *if* I were in the city but we, my dear, are in the middle of the desert. It seemed like the perfect place for lunch."

"I couldn't agree more."

"Well then, let's go inside and see if it's as perfect as you think."

Her eyes lit up. "Let's go."

I led her inside. We were quickly seated. The place had the same decor inside as it did out. Rustic hunting lodge meets sit down dining. Elena gushed over everything she saw, even the animal heads mounted high on the walls.

The waitress was prompt in taking our order, something I appreciated, and quickly brought us our drinks. Elena picked up the bottle of beer, turning it around in her hand.

"I thought you preferred dark beers?"

Taking a sip, I savored the taste of the local brewery. "I do, but sometimes local brewed beers taste even better. Try it." I nodded toward the bottle.

She lifted it to her lips, drinking down the liquid. "Oh, that's really good."

"I told you."

Elena peeked up at me through her lashes. "Is it going to be bad, you missing so many days of work to spend time with me?"

I shook my head. "Not at all. Remember I own the restaurants; I can be out a few days. Besides, everyday you've been at rehearsals, I've been working. These are your last few days off before the show begins. I want you to enjoy yourself."

"Thank you," she said simply.

"Are you excited about the start of the show?"

She beamed. "I am. I never thought I'd be up there under the lights. After Dominic and I got married it didn't seem possible. Now here I am, a few days from taking the stage."

Her excitement was contagious. I already had plans for that night, but was keeping it all a secret. "Yeah, Alan still curses me out every time I see him for not bringing you to him sooner. I'm excited to see your first performance."

"You're coming?"

"I have front row seats."

"But . . . I'm really excited . . . but I don't want you to feel like you *have* to go."

"Elena, have you ever known me to do something I didn't want to do?"

I thought she might say something about the conversation we had the other night about our parents, but she left it alone. "No. Unless you count getting stuck with me."

Covering her hand with mine, I got lost in her eyes for a moment. "I didn't get *stuck* with you. If I hadn't wanted to help you, I wouldn't have taken Dominic's offer. I would have dealt with him the way I normally handle that situation. And, I want to see you up there. Trust me when I tell you that."

"I do trust you," she said, solemnly.

Our food arrived not long after and we slipped into easy conversation. I still didn't understand the connection with Elena. She'd been so shy in the beginning, now there she sat, offering me her trust. It was perfectly obvious at that point—I wanted Elena even after the three months were up. I had to come clean, but how?

Was it about getting her away from Tolley? Hell fucking yes. But more than that, I wanted her for myself, even if I couldn't define it, or knew what that meant.

"I want to go and see Gretchen sometime next week."

The only thing I knew about Gretchen was that she worked with Elena at the diner. They'd been friends since Elena started there three years ago, and the smart woman continually pushed for her to leave Tolley.

"Okay. I'm guessing she'll be glad to know I'm not keeping you locked up somewhere."

She giggled, the sound rushing over me. "I told her you weren't some crazy creep when I called to tell her I was taking some time off." She gave me a pointed look.

She'd been upset the night I told her I'd talked to her boss at the diner and told him she was resigning, although, she'd tried to hide it. I explained that I wanted to help her find something better. At the time, I hadn't known how good she was at acting. I never imagined she'd be working downtown in one of the theaters.

"That sounds like a good idea. You can tell her all about your new job. When are you going to meet her?"

"I was thinking that I'd meet her at the diner in a day or two."

That caught my attention. "Do you think that's a good idea?" I knew Tolley lived only a few blocks from the diner, and if he knew she was there he might visit, starting shit when I wouldn't be there to protect her.

"Why wouldn't it be? I worked there for years."

"Yes, but at that time you weren't considering getting a divorce."

She shrugged. "I'm stronger than I was."

That certainly was the truth, but . . .

TRADED

"Elena, please don't take this the wrong way, because you are a hell of a lot stronger than you were, but you haven't seen him since the night he left you with me. I have, and trust me when I say there's nothing you need to hear from his mouth."

Her eyes flashed. "You don't think I can stand up to him?"

There was a small piece of me that worried she might cave if he pulled the same bullshit as the other night. Then again, I knew she needed to do it for her to ever be completely free of him. "No, it's not that. He's a complete asshole and I don't want you to have to deal with him. If it were up to me, I'd keep you as far away from the fucker as possible."

The tension left her shoulders. "Yeah, I'd like to never see him again, but that's not realistic. We live in the same city—I could see him anywhere. And like you said, I'll probably have to see him for the divorce proceedings."

The thought of it made me want to punch something. Not that I had any idea how any of that shit worked, but I'd be doing my research. "Doesn't mean I have to like it. How about you invite Gretchen to La Tratoria for lunch? Then she can meet me—see for herself that I'm not some pervert, holding you hostage for sexual favors."

She laughed and I knew we were in the clear again. I hadn't meant to get her all pissed off on a day where my goal was to impress her.

"How about Thursday?"

"I can do that. I'll set up the table myself." I lifted her hand from the table to my lips.

"That was delicious," she said, setting her napkin down on her now empty plate.

"Well, we did work up an appetite."

"That we did."

As far as she'd come, I still enjoyed the slightly shy woman who appeared every so often. It was both adorable and sexy—a very interesting combination. When the waitress brought the check, I pulled out my phone and sent a quick text to John to have the plane ready to head back home. There was still more to come, but I wanted to get Elena home to rest for a bit first.

I paid the bill and stood with my hand out. "Ready?"

CHAPTER 22

Elena

"Where to now?"

"Back to the airport."

I didn't want to admit it, but I was slightly disappointed that the day was over. Ashton probably needed to be at one of the restaurants that night. "Okay."

He laughed. "You can get that look off your face. I have other stuff planned for tonight, but first I want to take you home. You need a nap. I did get you up at the crack of dawn."

"You can say that again."

He led me out to the jeep and we took off for the airport. John was waiting for us when we pulled up to the hanger. He didn't spend more than a few minutes talking to Ashton. The flight back seemed longer, maybe because I spent it curled up against Ashton instead of sleeping, but it was a much more enjoyable way to spend the flight.

Well, second to sex in the air.

When we arrived back at the house, I followed after Ashton, who was entirely too energetic given the amount of sleep he'd had, dragging my heels. A yawn escaped my lips.

"I have a few phone calls to make. Why don't you go and rest? I'll be up in a few minutes."

"Sounds perfect."

Ashton followed me up the stairs. For a moment I thought he was going to try something, but then he pulled back the sheets and helped me in, pulling them up and over my shoulders, tucking me in. It was a sweet gesture.

"How long before I have to get ready," I asked sleepily.

"A few hours. I'll be up to join you as soon as I make sure everything is ready for tonight."

And as exhausted as I was, I barely saw Ashton leave the room before my lids grew heavy and I drifted off to sleep.

⚋⚋⚋

A buzzing noise came from the dresser. It took me a minute to realize it was Ashton's phone. I opened my eyes and saw him reach out and shut off the sound. The sky was still light, but nowhere near as bright as it had been earlier.

"What time is it?"

I heard the familiar sound of his hand tapping around on top of the table, looking for his glasses. His hand finally smacked them and the bed moved as he rolled to his side. "Five."

"I guess we need to get up."

TRADED

Reaching out, he curled his body around mine. "As much as I want to strip you naked, there'll be time for that later. You can get in the shower first."

"Okay." I sat up and looked at him. "Any clues as to what I should put on?"

"Something casual. I'm wearing a pair of cargo shorts. Not sure if you'll be cold later on tonight."

What does he have up his sleeve this time?

"I'm guessing we'll be outside again?"

"You guessed right. Just throw on a tank top for now. I have something for you to wear."

"Another surprise? You're spoiling me."

His hand came up to caress my face. "You deserve to be spoiled, and I like doing it."

"I like that it's you spoiling me," I said, not looking at him. Truth was, I was a little embarrassed about just how much he was doing. I didn't lie—I loved that he wanted to spoil me. I just didn't quite understand why.

I wondered how it was going to feel when I left. Ashton hadn't mentioned me staying and no matter how connected I thought we were, I'd never assume that he'd want me there. It would be very easy to get used to all the trappings of this lifestyle.

I grabbed a white tank and a pair of jean shorts and closed myself in the bathroom, the whole time feeling Ashton's gaze on my body. Whatever he had planned, I was sure it included naked time together.

After my shower, I dressed quickly and finished drying my hair before stepping out of the bathroom. In the first week or so after leaving Dominic, it felt weird to care about my appearance. Even taking more than ten minutes to get dressed caught me off guard. I'd learned that I enjoyed taking the time to look nice, not for anyone else, but for myself. It made me feel more confident.

Ashton sat on the edge of the bed, a box in his hands. He wore a pair of khaki cargo shorts and a simple white T-shirt. Not what I expected. He lifted the box up.

"I want you to wear this tonight."

Curious, I took the box from him and removed the bow holding it closed. Inside the box sat a purple Rockies T-shirt. Taking the shirt from the box, thoughts of the last time I stepped foot into the stadium flashed before me. Without a word, I pulled the tank top over my head and switched it for the T-shirt. It fit perfectly. I noticed Ashton had also pulled on a jersey.

"Ready?" he asked, watching me.

"I guess."

Did I want to go back to place where everything I knew got turned on its head? It might have been for the better, but that didn't mean I wanted to remember the things that were said in that room. Things I'd worked really hard in the last two months to overcome.

"You're nervous," he muttered.

"Kind of." I stared off into the corner of the room.

"Would it make you feel better if I told you we're not going to the box tonight?"

My eyes snapped to his.

"Because we're not."

TRADED

My stomach settled and filled with excitement; the same excitement I'd felt the first night I thought I'd get to see a game. I pushed those thoughts aside. Had it not been for that night I wouldn't be with Ashton now.

"Then, I'm very ready."

He held his hand out for me. "Let's go."

The entire ride to the stadium, my knee bounced up and down, only stopping when Ashton lay his hand on my thigh, sliding it up to the hem of my shorts. The air was still hot, and my body grew even hotter with each one of Ashton's caresses.

Walking into the stadium was even more nerve-racking than I'd expected. Even knowing we were heading to different seats, I couldn't stop the slight tremble of my hand. Ashton gave my hand a reassuring squeeze as he led us down the stairs.

He led me passed rows and rows of seats until I finally realized where he was taking me.

"We're sitting behind the dugout?"

The corners of his mouth curved up. "I figured if you've never been to a game then you needed to have the perfect view."

We took our seats directly behind the dugout on the first base line, or at least that was how Ashton described it to me. For me, someone who didn't really understand baseball, they were just seats but Ashton went out of his way to explain things.

As great a view as we had, I was having more fun watching the Jumbotron; at least, until the kiss cam started. Not in a million years did I expect the camera to end up on us, but with the way Ashton made sure to lean toward me the entire night, I should have.

The second our faces appeared on the big screen, Ashton ran his hand up around my nape, bringing my lips to his. The moment his tongue slipped into my mouth the stadium around us fell away. His thumb lightly tickled my neck, sending sparks everywhere. It wasn't until the catcalls started around us that we finally broke the kiss.

Ashton's face didn't move far from mine. "Now the whole world knows how badly I want you."

Emotions I didn't want to acknowledge filled me. How I wished that Ashton felt more than a desire to have me in his bed. In reality, it was a pipe dream. I wouldn't let it ruin what happened to be the best day of my life. Ashton had planned the perfect date. Smiling, I stole a brief kiss and cuddled into the crook of his arm to watch the game.

After the seventh inning stretch, I excused myself to head to the ladies room. The Rockies were only ahead by one run and I didn't want to miss too much of the game. Dodging the people heading for beer and food, I was a few steps away from the restroom when someone grabbed my arm, jerking me to a stop.

"When I said you should spread your legs for Ashton, I didn't mean you should practically fuck him in public," a familiar voice snarled in my ear.

My head snapped around.

"Dominic?" I squeaked. It pissed me off that I let him affect me like this, but the shock of seeing him sent my mind into a frenzy. He yanked my arm and I was trapped, caught in his gaze. His eyes were cold. "Maybe I need to remind you who you belong to."

Before I had a chance to respond, his mouth came down on mine in a bruising kiss. It might have been the first time Dominic had kissed me in at least five years, but it wasn't done out of love. That kiss was meant to punish and degrade me. Shock held me immobile, until he tried to stick his tongue in my mouth. Shoving at him with all my strength, I managed to push him off of me.

"What are you doing?" I wiped my hand across my lips, trying to get rid of his touch.

He sneered. "Reminding you who you'll be coming home to in two weeks."

I shook my head, taking a step back. "No."

"No, what?" he snapped.

Wrapping my arms around myself, I took another step back. "I'm filing for divorce."

"What?" he shouted, a vein pulsing at his temple.

The sight of his hands clenched into fists kicked in my fight or flight response, but when I tried to move I couldn't because I was backed into the wall; the sound of cheers erupting in the stadium drowned out by the sound of the pounding of my heart.

Dominic grabbed my arms, pulling me toward the exit.

"You're mine. There will be no divorce." His voice sent chills down my spine and everything instinct I'd fought so hard to quash during the two months I'd been away returned in full force.

"What are you doing?" someone yelled from behind me.

"We're not done," he snarled, giving me a shove and I fell backward, hitting the ground awkwardly. I wrapped my arms around myself, watching him take off as two guys ran over.

"Are you okay," the taller one asked.

"I am," I answered, carefully hiding my trembling hands. "Just an ex who doesn't understand he's an ex."

"Do you need us to walk you back to your seat?" the other chimed in.

I shook my head. All I wanted was to get back to Ashton as quick as possible. "No. I'm pretty sure you guys scared him away. Thank you." I forced a smile, hoping to make it more convincing.

The tall one looked around, scanning the crowd. "If you're sure. Can I at least walk you to your section?"

"I'm right across the concourse."

Forgetting about the ladies room, I let them lead me across the way to my section, my eyes darting everywhere, wondering if Dominic had really left, or if he was somewhere nearby, watching me.

"Be careful," they said and I nodded before walking through the entry and down the stairs toward my seat.

"You missed—" Ashton looked over at me and froze. "What happened?" His eyes searched mine.

"Nothing." I linked my fingers through his. "Let's watch the game."

TRADED

"Don't pull that shit, Elena. Look at you—you're shaking. Something happened and I want to know what it is." His tone left no room for argument.

I swallowed and my voice shook as I said, "I ran into Dominic."

"Jesus Christ."

He lifted his hands to touch me and I couldn't help it; I flinched.

"Fuck."

His hands dropped to his sides but I could see the tension in his body. He took a deep breath then asked, "Are you okay?"

I shook my head.

"Okay," he said, but his voice was so low I knew he wasn't talking to me. "I've dealt with him enough to know that you don't just run into Dominic without him saying something stupid. Want to tell me what he said?"

"He . . . umm . . ."

Ashton reached up and pushed the stray hair out of my face and behind my ear. I wasn't entirely comfortable but I allowed it, knowing that he wouldn't hurt me.

"Elena, it's okay. I'm right here. I won't let him get to you again."

Needing the comfort, I leaned into his side. "At first he yelled at me for kissing you on screen, then he kissed me."

Ashton was out of his seat and halfway up the stairs before I could stop him. Leaving our things by our seats, I raced after him. He beat me to the concourse.

"Ashton!"

He stood about ten feet in front of me. The reflection on his glasses from the lights above was not enough to mask the cold determination in his eyes. Needing to be close to him, I ran over and slipped my hand in his.

"Don't leave me," I begged. I didn't care how desperate I sounded. I didn't want to be alone. And I definitely didn't want him doing anything stupid.

When he turned to me his features softened. "I won't leave you, but I also won't stand by and let that prick put his lips on you."

"I told him I was filing for divorce."

"You did?" Ashton's face was a mixture of confusion and wonder. He paused for a second, thinking something over before he asked, "How did he take it?"

"He said he wouldn't allow that and pushed me up against the wall near the ladies' room."

He ground his teeth together. "I'm going to kill that bastard when I get my hands on him."

I was still freaked out and just wanted to push it out of my mind. Focusing on the fun we'd had would help. "It's been a perfect day. Can we just watch the game and worry about Dominic later?"

Ashton took my face in his hands, placing the sweetest, softest kiss ever on my lips. "Okay. Let's go." He took my hand and walked me back to our seats. I could see the tension in his shoulders, but knew he was trying to hide it—for me.

The second we sat down, Ashton pulled out his phone. His fingers flew across the keys as he sent text after text. A few minutes later, he put it away and sighed.

"We're getting you self-defense lessons."

I thought about arguing, but it couldn't hurt. Even if I never had to use the skills I'd learn, knowing that I'd be able to overpower Dominic if he ever came at me again would give me some comfort. Ashton wouldn't be around forever. It was the smart thing to do.

I nodded and Ashton turned his head back to the game.

There was only one inning left so it ended pretty quickly. Since it had been such a close game, people stayed all the way through, it took longer to get out of there. Once we reached the exit gate, I noticed Brock standing there waiting for us.

"Ashton. Elena. I hear you had some trouble tonight."

"A bit," I answered.

"Brock will drive us home. In case we have to deal with Dominic again, I don't want you left alone."

All of it sounded so possessive and protective. Ashton and I climbed into the backseat of the car and waited for Brock to pull out of the lot. Ashton sat so rigidly that it made me want to scream in frustration. I couldn't let my problems ruin an absolutely wonderful day. I knew talking wouldn't solve anything, but there was one thing that would help ease the tension.

I ran my hand up his leg, knee to thigh, my palm coming to rest over his zipper. His sharp intake of breath told me I was doing something right and I let my fingers slide down his other leg, then retraced my path. His hand covered mine.

"If you keep that up, we'll give Brock a show," he whispered in my ear.

The heat rose to my cheeks but was quickly forgotten as Ashton cupped my jaw and took possession of my lips. Opening my mouth, he slid his tongue inside, tasting every square inch. Absorbed in the kiss, I didn't notice when we pulled up in front of the house until Ashton released my seatbelt and lifted me out of the car.

We made our way into the house and up the stairs. Heat blazed in his eyes when he finally set me down and I knew I'd succeeded in making him forget about Dominic, if only for the moment. Ashton's mouth returned to mine as he lowered me to the bed.

The perfect end to the perfect day.

CHAPTER 23

Elena

Ashton made sure to come out and show me to the table himself, and it was obvious it was the best table in the house. Secluded for private conversation, but still in the midst of everything. I looked down at my watch.

Fifteen minutes.

Fifteen minutes until Gretchen arrived.

I was excited to finally see her again. We'd exchanged text messages after Ashton got me the phone, but neither replaced the face-to-face conversations we used to have. So many things had changed since I last saw her; some good, while others . . . well, let's just say the jury was still out on those.

"Elena." Her voice was so loud, almost every head in the restaurant turned to stare. Thank God it was only the lunch crowd.

"Gretchen." I waved, hoping to calm her until she got to the table.

But that was Gretchen. She didn't apologize for who she was. It was often said that opposites attract, and this was true in the sense the Gretchen was everything I wished I could be. She was strong to my weak, confident to my cowardice. In the past, when she'd spoken about me leaving Dominic, she'd made it sound so easy, and every time I left after one of those conversations, I'd be full of good intentions; wanting to head home and let him know how unhappy I was, and ask him to change. Then I see him and all my fire would die. Yet, even though this to and fro happened often, she never despaired of me. She was always there in the background helping me, keeping me sane. And for that I'd be forever grateful.

Ashton was nowhere in sight, then again, I had a feeling he wasn't faraway because he'd promised to come over and meet Gretchen at some point during lunch, and help set her mind at ease.

"Oh my God."

Suddenly I was yanked from my seat into a crushing embrace, squeezed to the point where I couldn't draw breath. "I missed you so much, you had me so worried."

"I text you all the time," I forced out.

She let go. "Sorry, I didn't mean to squish you."

"It's okay," I laughed. My stomach settled and I felt myself relax.

"I was just so worried," she rambled, taking her seat. "You sent me texts but anyone could have the phone, claiming they're you. And you could have been tied up in some creepy basement dungeon with whips and canes and God only knows what else."

A throat cleared behind me. Gretchen's eyes snapped up and her mouth dropped open. Then a warm hand curled over my shoulder and blood rushed to my face.

"Elena." There was a hint of amusement in his voice. Oh God, how much of that had he heard?

"Ashton."

He squeezed my shoulder then stepped into view. Reaching out, he offered his hand.

"And you must be Gretchen." Slowly, she lifted her hand and took his. "It's a pleasure to meet you."

"It's a . . . a . . . a—" Gretchen swallowed hard. "Nice to meet you too."

He brought her hand to his lips and her cheeks went pink.

"Excuse me, ladies, I need to take care of something, but I'll be back. I just wanted to introduce myself."

He placed a soft kiss to my lips and stepped away. Gretchen sat there, nodding dumbly. I snapped my fingers in her face, trying to get her attention. When her eyes returned to mine, I couldn't stop the laugh that escaped my lips.

Her expression. Not often was Gretchen speechless. Her eyes were practically popping out of her head when she looked back at me.

"That's him?"

"Yeah, that's Ashton."

She gave her head a quick shake. "Holy shit. It's about time you found someone like him."

I rolled my eyes. "I'm glad you approve, but he's not exactly mine."

"I wouldn't be so sure about that." She watched me for a moment. "Although, I'm kinda liking this new snarky attitude you've got going on."

Watching my finger trace patterns on the tablecloth, I said, "I've learned a lot in the last two months."

"Hey." I looked up into soft, understanding eyes. "It's never easy to see what's wrong when we want it to be right."

Tears blurred my vision. "I'm so sorry I didn't listen to you."

She shook her head. "It's not your fault. That jerk had your mind so warped and twisted with his bullshit and lies that you couldn't see what I was saying. What matters now is that you finally see the truth."

"I do. Ashton helped."

Gretchen peeked over at him and smiled. "Now I've seen for myself that he's not abusing you in some underground room of pain, I want to know what you've been up to. You have so much time now that you don't have to take shifts at the diner—what do you do all day?"

I hadn't thought about those early mornings in a long while. For the longest time, the only thing that kept me going was my routine. Not that I didn't still have a routine; this one was just markedly different. The corners of my mouth lifted.

"Actually, Ashton got me an audition for the new musical opening up in the theater district in a few weeks."

Her head tilted to the side. "An audition?"

"I guess I never told you what I went to college for."

"I didn't even know you'd been to college."

"Dominic and I got married right after graduation. Up until then, I wanted to sing on Broadway."

"Really?"

"From the time I was a little girl."

"Okay," she said nodding. "When is this audition?"

The waiter came over, interrupting the conversation. In his hand he held a bottle of wine, resting in an ice bucket. He set it up on a stand next to the table before presenting me with the bottle and popping the cork.

"Compliments of Mr. Hawes."

I glanced over my shoulder; Ashton's eyes were on me. He lifted his chin slightly, gave me a wink, and turned back to what he was doing. When I turned back to the table, the waiter had poured a glass. He held it out to me. Swirling the liquid like Ashton taught me, I took a sip, savoring the flavor.

"Perfect. Tell Mr. Hawes he has good taste."

The waiter took our lunch order and after handing over the menu, I looked at Gretchen, who was gaping at me. "Look at you being a flirt."

"I wasn't."

"Oh yes you were."

Maybe I was, but I wouldn't admit that to her. "What were we talking about before?"

She laughed. "That quickly that man fried your brain cells."

I ignored her comments. "Auditions, wasn't it? Well, I already auditioned and got the part."

"You did?" she squealed, my reaction to Ashton completely forgotten.

"Yes. It opens in two weeks. Will you come?" I asked, shyly.

"You bet your ass I'll be there."

"Thank you. I could use some familiar faces in the audience. It's been a long time since I've been under those lights."

The waiter brought over our salads and Gretchen picked up her fork to eat. Pointing it at me, she said, "I'm sure Ashton will be there."

"He will, but the more the merrier."

She studied me for a moment. "What aren't you telling me?"

I shook my head, hoping she would see how it was so much more than flirting with Ashton for me. "Nothing."

She gave me a dubious look. "Okay, fine. Since you won't 'fess up, tell me more about Ashton and what you do outside your time between the sheets."

My face flamed. "I never said we'd slept together," I whispered harshly.

The corner of her eyes crinkled and she laughed. "You don't have to. I can see the sparks from here." She grabbed her napkin and started fanning herself.

TRADED

"Oh my God. Stop that." I grabbed the napkin from her hand. "We don't have that kind of chemistry. He's just really sweet."

She scoffed and lowered her voice. "You just called a loan shark sweet."

"How else should I describe him? Ruthless, conniving, maybe selfish? Because he's been none of those to me."

Gretchen covered my clenched fist on the table. "Calm down, Elena. That's not what I meant. It only seems like an oxymoron. 'Loan shark' and 'sweet' definitely don't go together—unless you happen to be Ashton Hawes, who is obviously different."

"He is."

We finished our salads just in time for lunch to be delivered to the table. The waiter placed Gretchen's in front of her and when I looked up, Ashton set my lunch in front of me with a flourish. "Enjoy, sweetheart," he whispered, before disappearing again.

"Hello sexual tension," Gretchen whispered at me.

Ignoring her, I cut one of the large raviolis into smaller bite size pieces, thoughts of his endearment tickling all of my nerve endings. It gave me chills every time he spoke to me like that. After a bite or two, Gretchen started again.

"You never answered my question about what you and Ashton do together."

I sighed thinking about the trip a few days ago.

"Did you just sigh?"

I giggled. "I guess I did. Well, he took me to see the sunrise at the Grand Canyon."

Gretchen's fork slid from her fingers. "He did *what?*"

"He took me to see the sunrise at the Grand Canyon. We had lunch there before coming back for the baseball game." Gretchen winced and I quickly added, "He got seats right behind the dugout. It was perfect."

"Oh shit," she whispered.

My gaze snapped back to hers. "What? What is it? Are you okay?"

"You're already in love with him, aren't you?"

I froze. Why would she think that? "I'm not. It's just an infatuation. He's helped me so much. Guys like him don't fall in love."

"Oh, sweetie, even I can see it's more than an infatuation. Why are you so afraid to admit it?"

Tears welled in my eyes and I hoped to God Ashton wasn't anywhere near to see it. "The last time I thought I was in love, look where I ended up."

"Yes, but the man over there," she nodded to her left, "is nothing like the dickhead you married. For crying out loud, he flew you to Arizona for sunrise. Dominic wouldn't even take you out to dinner."

I sniffled. "I don't want to get hurt again."

"Elena?" Ashton's worried tone came from right beside me. He took one look at my face and pulled me from the chair and into his arms, sending a glare Gretchen's way.

"What's wrong?"

TRADED

I tried to collect myself. "We were talking about what a fool I was when it came to Dominic." At least it was a half-truth.

He brushed the tears from my eyes with his thumbs. "You're not a fool. That fucker has no idea what he had. He will never get his hands on you again. You're mine."

Time froze. The restaurant could have burned down around me as I glanced up into Ashton's eyes. Even through his glasses, I could see something there. Something more than sex, or helping out a poor abused woman. He opened his mouth to say more when suddenly our bubble was burst.

"Mr. Hawes," the maître d' said, now standing next to us.

"Yes, Pierre?"

"Sir, I'm sorry to interrupt, but we have a problem."

Ashton glanced back and forth between the two of us. He sighed. "I'll be right there, Pierre." He waited for Pierre to walk away before saying, "Elena, I'm sorry I have to take care of this."

"I understand." While that was true, it didn't mean I liked it. But he had a restaurant to run. I took my seat and reached for my drink, needing to do something with my shaking hands.

"We need to talk when I get home tonight."

It wasn't a request. "Okay."

"I shouldn't be too late. Wait up for me, please?"

"All right," I squeaked out. An empty feeling settled at the pit of my stomach.

What could he want to talk to me about?

Gretchen smirked at me over the rim of her glass. "You're an idiot."

"Thanks a lot. Ashton just caught me crying in his restaurant and now he wants to *talk*." I said using air quotes. "On top of all that, you're calling me an idiot. This day just keeps getting better and better."

"Well, you *are* an idiot if you can't see what's right in front of your face. That man is so into you it's unreal. I'm pretty sure he was just about to tell you so when you were interrupted."

My mouth popped open. "No he wasn't."

"Oh, babe, he was. At some point you're going to have to realize you can be loved without being hurt, otherwise you're going to push everyone away and end up alone."

Alone.

I'd been alone for a long time. Living with someone who didn't spend time with me, only talking to me when they had to was possibly *more* lonely than actually being on my own. My nerves were shot and if we continued the conversation, I was likely to puke all over the table.

"Can we just drop it for now?" I pleaded.

She nodded and set her glass down. The meal continued with us both avoiding anything to do with Ashton, although, I did find my gaze straying as we talked, trying to get a glimpse of the man who occupied my thoughts.

The waiter brought our dessert over without us ordering: chocolate mousse cake. Ashton knew it was my weakness and the fact that he'd known to send it over made more questions swirl through my head.

Sooner than I liked, lunch was over.

"I miss spending time with you," Gretchen said as we walked out of the restaurant. "We need to do this again."

"We do." I tried to smile, but it felt forced. "And you'll come for opening night?"

"I will definitely be there."

"Great. I'll leave your ticket at will call."

She wrapped me in an embrace. "Give him a chance. And tell him thank you for lunch."

"I will, and I'll try."

We said our good-byes and Gretchen headed to the parking lot, while I turned to the front. Lewis was waiting with the car, ready to take me to rehearsal.

"Elena," he greeted as he opened the door. It had taken me a while but I'd finally managed to convince Lewis to stop using my last name. I hated the reminder of Dominic.

Lewis pulled out into traffic and in no time at all, he was dropping me off at the stage entrance.

Rehearsals went smoothly; all thoughts of Ashton pushed to the back of my mind. But that only lasted as long as my attention was elsewhere. As soon as rehearsal was over, I began worrying about what Ashton might have to say to me.

By the time I got back to the house I was so jittery that I decided that a long hot bath was in order. The warm water soothed my aching muscles, the steam clearing my head. I lay back and closed my eyes.

As the temperature cooled, I knew it was time to leave my little cocoon and face whatever Ashton had to tell me.

Dressing, I went downstairs. The house was still quiet and none of the lights were on. Wanting the conversation over with sooner rather than later, I walked down the hall to Ashton's office. Still nothing. He'd said he wouldn't be late. Something must have kept him at the restaurant.

The sound of the garage door opening made the desire to sprint down the hall overwhelming. With a deep calming breath, I forced myself to walk slowly into the kitchen, but when the door opened, it wasn't Ashton who greeted me.

"Miller. What are you doing here?"

"Ashton got stuck at one of the restaurants so I thought I'd keep you company." He produced two takeout bags from The Bluewater Grill.

I laughed. "Let me guess, Ashton sent you over here with dinner so you could watch over me until he gets home."

"Busted." He set the bags on the counter and began pulling out plates and forks from the cabinets. "But can you blame him after what happened the other night?"

I cringed at how much he knew about my screwed up situation and went to the wine cooler to cover my reaction. I pulled out a Chardonnay that Ashton liked with seafood, along with two glasses. "Dominic has no idea where Ashton lives . . . but, no, I can't really blame him."

Miller opened the takeout boxes and placed each meal on a plate, throwing the containers into the trash. "Hungry?" He gestured to the food.

"Yes," I said, taking a seat at the kitchen table. Ashton had sent my favorite dish: crab sautéed in a white wine sauce. "Delicious. He always knows what to pick for me."

Miller smirked, which I decided to ignore. "Yes, he does."

Miller dived right into his food. I might have been hungry, but it was hard to think about food when all I wanted to know was what Ashton needed to tell me. Pushing my food around on my plate, I didn't notice Miller trying to get my attention until he tapped me on the arm.

"What's wrong?" he asked. "You haven't touched your food. Ashton swore this was your favorite."

"He's right, it is my favorite. I'm just having a hard time pushing something else out of my mind and it's stealing my appetite." I wasn't sure sitting there having a conversation about his brother was a great idea. How much would he tell Ashton?

"Come on, you can tell me. You won't be able to stop thinking about it until you do."

For a few minutes I sat there in silence, battling with my conscience while Miller looked on. What would be the harm in talking to him? On the one hand, he might tell Ashton everything I said. On the other, he'd known Ashton since the day he was born.

Deciding I needed to get it off my chest, I put it out there.

"Today at lunch, Ashton asked me to wait up for him because there was something he wanted to talk to me about and I'm afraid he wants to make sure I'll be out of his life in two weeks, when the three months is up. I'm just not sure if I'm ready for that."

Miller's glass was halfway to his lips but he quickly set it down as he burst into laughter, the sound making the hairs on the back of my neck stand on end.

I knew talking to him was a mistake.

Gathering up my plate and glass, I pushed away from the table to move to the dining room where I could sit and eat in peace, when Miller reached out a hand to stop me.

"Please don't leave. I'm sorry for laughing." He wiped at his eyes. "It's just the idea of Ashton wanting you to leave is absolutely ridiculous."

I placed my stuff back down on the table, but stayed on my feet. "Why would you say that?"

He shrugged. "I've never seen Ashton react to a woman the way he does to you. Take the night we all had dinner at my parents' house. He threatened me more than once for looking at you the wrong way. He even punched me."

"He *punched* you?" I asked, my eyes wide. "Why would he do that?"

"He thought I was going to make a play for you after you talked to Aunt Veronica. Which was just stupid. He was already falling for you then."

My mouth dropped open. "What are you talking about? I've only known Ashton for a little over two months. And only because my *husband* can't stop gambling."

Miller smirked. "A husband who I hear will be out of the picture very soon."

TRADED

"How do you know that? I only told Ashton the other day. I haven't even met with the lawyer yet."

"Ashton told me the morning after you told him. He's normally so calm and collected. He doesn't let his emotions rule him . . . except with you."

"But . . . but he . . . he doesn't—"

His hand came up to cover mine. "Don't stress. My brother cares more about you than he's admitted so far. I'm sure he won't be able to keep it in much longer."

Miller's words had me breathing a little easier. Could Ashton really care as much about me as I did about him? Only time would tell.

Lost in my thoughts I began to eat my dinner. Miller did the same.

"How's the show coming along?" he asked between bites.

"Good. I really like working with Alan."

He rolled his eyes. "The two of them have been friends for forever. Dumbasses got themselves into a lot of trouble growing up."

I couldn't help my curiosity. "Oh *really?*"

"Mmm hmm. The stories I could tell you."

"Please do."

Miller and I finished dinner. It took longer than normal since I had to stop multiple times to laugh at Miller's stories of Ashton as a child. It was easy, yet hard to hear about him being so carefree. I'd seen glimpses of both parts of his personality, but I was starting to think I was one of only a few who did.

"Since you're stuck here until Ashton gets home, should we watch a movie?" I asked, loading the remaining dishes into the dishwasher. Yes, Ashton had a housekeeper, but some habits just wouldn't die.

"Sounds good to me." Miller winked.

I followed him down the hall and watched as he selected a movie, moving around the room with an ease that suggested he had been here many a time and was more than comfortable in his surroundings. I tried to focus on the screen, but my eyes strayed to the doorway every so often.

By the time the movie finished, Ashton still wasn't home. Miller put another one on and I curled up under a blanket on the couch, all the anxiety of the last few hours catching up with me. My lids got heavy but I fought to keep them open. I had to know what Ashton wanted.

At the moment, nothing seemed more important.

Not even sleep.

CHAPTER 24

Ashton

Frustrated.

No other word could accurately describe how I felt on the drive home. There were so many things I had to tell Elena. The three months were almost up and I'd yet to ask her to stay. My plan had been to beat her home, make dinner, then tell her how I felt.

Then shit went downhill.

It started when the alcohol order for The Bluewater Grill didn't come in and I spent the whole damn night trying to balance two bars of liquor between three restaurants. Then it only got worse when Pierre called me away. I had no idea that it was to deal with a debtor.

* * *

"Mr. Hawes, there is a gentleman asking for you? Says he owes you money."

"What the fuck?" slipped from my lips before I had a chance to rein it in.

Pierre raised his hands, helpless. "I don't know, sir. I'm sorry, I tried to dissuade him from staying. He wasn't listening. Refused to stop making a scene at his table until I got you."

"Thank you, Pierre," I said, my hands shoved in my pockets to hide that they were balled into fists. "Point me to him and I'll take care of it."

Take care of it was right. I could pretty much guarantee that he would be leaving in worse shape than he arrived.

Pierre pointed to the table in the corner, where the man sat, arms crossed over his chest, a smirk playing about his lips.

Fuck.

I was going to kill someone. Using all my self-control, I walked over to him. Bastard was sitting alone. When I was sure I was close enough to be out of earshot. I bent down and said softly, "You will follow me to my office right now." His eyes widened at my tone. "And if you even attempt to do anything but that, I will find you later and I guarantee I will be even less pleasant than I am right now.

He swallowed hard and nodded.

Spinning on my heel, I walked toward the kitchen door and down the back hallway to my office.

Stepping through the door, I turned and waited for him to follow me. The minute he was over the threshold, I shut the door and turned on him.

TRADED

Grabbing his wrist, I wrenched it behind his back and stepped up into his body. If he moved, he would shatter his own wrist. A cry of pain slipped past his lips.

"You motherfucker. You crossed a line coming here today. I'm not sure what makes you think it's okay for you to come here to handle our business, but I can guarantee you were fucking wrong." I kept my voice low and controlled so as not to alert my staff.

"But, I—"

"I don't want to hear another goddamn word from your mouth. You went too fucking far." With an extra push down, I heard the bones of his wrist crack at the same time his knees buckled.

Blood seeped from between his lips, from biting either the inside of his cheek or his tongue. Either way, at that moment, I didn't give a shit.

"I see you're wise enough not to call any more attention to yourself. Let's see if you can continue to use your brain."

He nodded once, sharply.

"You're going to walk out of here like nothing is wrong. Later you're going to get your wrist checked out, and tell them you caught yourself with it when you tripped. Finally you're going to meet me at the designated meeting place the next home game. That's where we'll discuss your loan and the increased interest rate. Do I make myself clear?

"Yes," he choked out.

"Good, now get the fuck out of my sight before you leave with more than a broken wrist."

He walked out and I flopped down into the couch in my office. I'd let anger control me again. I didn't like the man I was without Elena and that bullshit kept me from seeing her before she left, pushing me over the edge.

***

At the stoplight, I glanced down at the clock. It was long after midnight. When I realized there was no way I'd be getting home at a reasonable hour, I'd called Miller and asked him to go over to my house and keep her company. After the bullshit with Palmer a few nights ago and now people coming to the restaurant to discuss business, I didn't feel comfortable leaving her alone—even with all the security I had on the house. I'm sure she'd already noticed the fact that Brock or Lewis went with her everywhere she went. Unless I was there, obviously.

Hitting the button to connect the phone to the car, I called Miller.

"Yo, bro, you on your way finally?"

"No *hello?*"

"Hey, I spent the night hanging out with your woman, and since you won't let me have a go at her I kind of want to go out and find one of my own."

My fingers clenched around the wheel. "You son of a bitch, you better keep your hands to yourself. I hope she kicks you in the balls for saying that."

He burst into laughter. "Do you think I'm stupid? I like her. I don't want her to hate me. She fell asleep on the couch about an hour ago."

TRADED

I sighed. I'd missed my chance . . . again. The words had almost slipped out in the restaurant, until Pierre interrupted.

Fucking hell.

"All right. I'll be home in ten."

I hit the *end* button before he said anything else to piss me off. Elena had been through so much. I just wanted everything to be perfect. She deserved it. The sight of the garage door was like a weight off my shoulders.

I quickly found Miller and Elena in the great room; Elena curled up at one end of the couch, Miller reclining in one of the chairs. Even asleep she was the sexiest woman I'd ever had.

With a nod to Miller, I walked over and scooped Elena up into my arms. For a moment I thought she'd wake up, but she only cuddled closer to my chest. Warmth spread through me at the trust she showed me every day when, given her history, she'd be within her right to be afraid to trust anyone.

"I'll be right back," I whispered.

Elena was light as a feather and I had no trouble carrying her up the stairs. I quietly tucked her into our bed.

Our bed.

I fucking loved the way that sounded.

I went back downstairs to talk to Miller. The second I stepped into the room, he put a glass of scotch in my hand.

I dropped down into one of the recliners, too exhausted to bother taking off my jacket or tie, and sank the entire glass in one.

"That bad?" he asked, lifting his own glass to his lips.

"You could say that." The liquor burned my throat and I felt its warmth spread through my body. Setting the tumbler on the side table, I took my glasses off to rub at my eyes. "Adam Thompson showed up during the lunch rush to talk about the money he owes me that he doesn't have."

Miller's jaw clenched. "What is with these fuckers?" he said through gritted teeth.

"I have no idea, but I sent a very clear message. I still have to deal with the rest of the inventory mess in the morning."

"Good. Hopefully after word gets out about Palmer and Thompson that will be the end of it.

"I hope so." I put my glasses back on and looked at Miller. "Was she upset I got stuck at work?"

Miller sighed. "Yes and no. She would have been fine had you not got her all worked up about needing to talk to her."

I sat up so fast, I thought I'd fall out of the chair. "Goddamn it."

"What were you going to tell her anyway?"

"I'm going to ask her to stay. I know she plans on leaving that piece of shit and I want her to stay her with me."

He chuckled. "I figured that was it. She's afraid, you know?"

I ran a hand through my hair and got to my feet, pacing the floor. "How could she not be? Look at what she's dealt with up until now. Anyone would have reservations jumping into something else so quickly, not to mention trusting someone."

TRADED

"I knew you were falling for her." He smirked.

I stopped in my tracks. "Can you be serious for a moment?"

"Yes, and my serious answer is you need to tell her how you feel. She's not going to trust it until she hears it from your lips."

"I'll tell her tomorrow."

Miller rolled his eyes. "Good, because the both of you are driving me crazy with your lovesick ways."

I glared at him. "Didn't you say you had plans?"

"Yes, yes I did." He drained his glass and turned toward the hall, looking back to say, "Seriously, big brother, tell her. She's the first woman to make you smile in a long time."

I felt that in my chest, because he was right. It was true that I'd had more than a few bed-partners, but none could compare to Elena. None had staying power. Until she'd come into my life I'd wondered if I would ever settle down; I'm sure my family had questioned the same. But being with her made me want different things. I wanted to give her the life she deserved.

"Thanks for staying with her tonight."

"Anytime." He nodded and left.

I sat back down, alone with my thoughts for the first time all day. No matter how crazy life got, I knew I needed to tell her what I wanted.

The sooner the better.

♋♋♋

But the time was never right.

The next day came and went with no chance to speak. Then rehearsals got longer. Things at the restaurants just got busier and busier, requiring more and more of my time. Add in self-defense classes and there was no time for anything. We'd barely spent any time together; much less had a chance to talk.

Before I knew it, two weeks had passed. Time was almost up. And Elena still didn't know I wanted her to stay; and not just until she got her feet on the ground.

Forever.

Miller gave me shit every time I saw him, but he conveniently forgot that not once in my whole life had I wanted a woman to move into my place and become a part of my life. It wouldn't be something I jumped into lightly. There had to be a right time to tell her, and I was determined to find it.

"Ashton," her soft voice called from down the hall.

"In here."

A few seconds later, her head popped around the corner, her glossy dark hair falling to the side. "I'm getting ready to head over to the theater. Are you sure you want to come?"

Elena might want to play it off like she wasn't nervous as hell about her opening night, but after so many weeks together, I could see it. The small fidgety things she did: wringing her hands, trying to make it look like she was cracking her knuckles, or continually tucking the same strand of hair behind her ear. They were like a bright flashing neon sign to me, even as she did everything in her power to hide them.

TRADED

I moved from my desk and took her hand, pulling her into the room with me and cupping her face in my hands, I traced my thumb across her cheek. The words *I love you* almost slipped from my lips but I realized that if on the small chance she didn't want to hear them, I'd ruin whatever calm she'd built up for the performance. Whatever my feelings, they could wait until afterward.

"I told you, I can't wait to see you perform. Are you sure you want me there?"

"Yes," she breathed. "It'll be nice to have support in the audience, besides Gretchen."

What she didn't know was that I'd arranged for her parents to fly out and see the show, as well as my own. Mr. and Mrs. Brighton had been staying in a hotel for the last two days, doing everything they could to hide their presence from their daughter until later tonight at the party I'd arranged at La Tratoria.

"Then I'll be there."

Bending down, I brushed my lips over hers. If I couldn't tell her that I loved her, I'd at least show her before she left. A shudder ran through my body at the touch of her fingers as they brushed over my abs and up my chest, eventually finding their way into my hair. The moment her tongue slipped into my mouth to tangle with mine, I lost all control of what had started out as a gentle kiss. Breathless and disappointed it had to end, I broke the kiss. She narrowed her eyes at me.

"If we keep going we'll end up in the bedroom, and then you'll never make it to the theater."

I reached down and adjusted myself, making it clear just how serious I was. She blushed and started to back out of the room. "I'll see you at the theater, then I'm all yours." With a wink, she turned and walked back down the hall.

I heard the front door open and close. Lewis should be waiting for her out front. Not once had she questioned why whenever she went somewhere she was always accompanied by someone, but I was just grateful that she was. I needed her to be safe, and if that meant being a tad on the cautious side, then that's what I'd do.

Moving back to my desk, I dropped down into the chair. The whole situation was frustrating the hell out of me. Used to being in control, I found it hard to have so little control when it came to Elena.

My phone vibrated on my desk. Swiping my finger across the screen I answered. "Why hello, my dear, I haven't seen you in so long."

Her laugh was melodic. "I figured this was the safer way to talk since you can't keep your hands to yourself."

"I can't keep my hands to myself," I scoffed. "I seem to remember *you* being the one to push things further that time."

"What can I say? You're irresistible." I heard a smack. "Oh God, did I just say that out loud?"

I pictured Elena, smacking herself in the head, her face the color of a stoplight. "That's okay. I find you pretty irresistible myself."

She sighed but the sound was joyful instead of annoyed. I did everything in my power to focus on what she was saying instead of the image of her naked beneath me, screaming my name as orgasm overtook her.

"I . . ." her voice sounded husky. After clearing her throat she continued. "I wanted to tell you that I heard from one of the lawyers. They attempted to deliver the papers yesterday, but Dominic didn't answer the door. They'll try again on Monday, starting with his work."

Those were words I wanted to hear. "Good. The sooner the better."

"I couldn't agree more. I figured you could use another positive thought while you work your way through that mountain of paperwork on your desk."

The mountain was higher than it needed to be, mostly contracts for a new liquor distributor. "You can say that again. Why didn't you tell me before you left?"

She laughed. "Umm . . . did you forget your threat to take me upstairs and make me late?"

"Good point. But just think of the fun we'd have had."

"We will later."

"I'll keep that in mind to help me through the boring paperwork."

"You do that."

"I'll see you tonight. Break a leg." I'd gotten an hour-long lecture from Alan as to why I had to say break a leg instead of good luck. It happened to be a history lesson I could have done without, but if it helped Elena then so be it.

"Thank you. I'll see you after the show. 'Bye."

"'Bye."

I disconnected the call and dialed the number of the hotel where Elena's parents were staying.

"Hello," a soft voice answered.

"Mrs. Brighton?"

"Yes. Is that you Ashton?"

"It is. I wanted to let you know the car will be there around six to pick you and Mr. Brighton up."

"Thank you and, please, call me Elizabeth. I can't wait to see her."

I smiled, thinking back to one of our conversations about her parents. "I know she'll be thrilled to see you."

"I hope so," she said wistfully. "It's been more than five years since we've had even a glimpse of our daughter."

"Then I'm glad I could make that happen."

"Thank you, Ashton. I look forward to meeting you tonight."

When the call ended I tried to focus on the paperwork. After the debacle a few weeks ago, I didn't want a repeat. Taking a sip of the coffee I'd brought with me, I began sifting through contract after contract.

* * *

It took me most of the day, but I eventually found someone to use. Setting aside his application for Monday, I looked over at the clock. It was time to get ready to leave. Halfway through buttoning my shirt, a soft vibration came from my dresser. I picked up the phone to see a new text message.

TRADED

A. Newell: Hey just got tickets for the game on Tuesday. Wanna go?

Damn it.
Sooner or later I'd need to introduce Elena to all of this world, although, I had a pretty good idea she knew what she would be getting herself into if she stayed with me. It was, after all, how she came to me.

Me: I think I have box seats that night if you want to join me.
A. Newell: That sounds even better. I'll see if anyone at work wants these.

With the meeting set, I pulled on my jacket and walked out the door. I made sure Elena had taken a dress with her; telling her we'd celebrate after the show. What she didn't know was who would be joining us.
I arrived at the theater, hoping that everyone else was already there. I had Alan set the tickets aside at will call so they could pick them up as they arrived and didn't have to wait for me.
"Ashton," my mother's voice called from somewhere in the crowd.
Scanning the lobby I finally saw Dad, a head above most people in the room. I made my way to them, bending down and placing a kiss on Mom's cheek.
"Thanks for coming, I know she's really nervous."

"Of course we'd be here. You haven't told her yet, have you?"

I groaned. "Why is everyone on my case about this?"

"Don't talk to your mother like that," Dad snapped.

"Sorry," I said, feeling like a five year old being reprimanded in school. "I didn't mean it to sound like that. It's just Miller's bugged me every day for the last two weeks. I was going to tell her today before she left, but she was already so nervous I decided to wait until after."

Mom cupped my face in her hands. "My baby's fallen in love."

"Never expected it in a million years."

"Never expected what?" Miller walked up to us.

"That your brother would find the right woman." Mom beamed. She turned back to me. "I'm so happy for you."

"Did you finally grow a set and tell her?"

"Miller!" Mom scolded.

"I'm telling her after the show."

Miller rolled his eyes at me and, thankfully, just the thought of punching him satisfied my desire to actually do it. I wouldn't cause a scene. I couldn't do it to Elena. Not to mention knowing what my mother would do if I did hit Miller. He looked over at Mom and Dad.

"Mom, this is Katelyn. Katelyn, this is my Mom and Dad."

"It's a pleasure to meet you," the voluptuous blonde at his side said, reaching out her hand.

TRADED

Miller finished the introductions but I wasn't entirely sure why he bothered—she'd be old news by next week.

I glanced at my watch. "I think we should go in."

I'd bought center stage orchestra seats, a few rows back, on Alan's advice. After climbing down to the orchestra level, we found Aunt Veronica and Samuel along with another couple, who could only be the Brightons. Elena was the perfect mix of her parents, getting her dark hair from her father and chocolate eyes from her mother.

"Mr. and Mrs. Brighton?"

The man stood, his hand extended. "Yes, and you must be Ashton."

I returned his handshake. "I am. It's a pleasure to meet both of you."

Mrs. Brighton stood when her husband let go of my hands, wrapping her arms around my waist, practically squeezing the air from my lungs. "Thank you so much for helping us to share this with our daughter. We couldn't be happier she found a wonderful man like you. I'm sure things will be easier, now that the papers have been filed."

I had to remind myself they knew nothing of the circumstances surrounding Elena coming to live me, including what I did for the family business—and it would stay that way. Her parents didn't need to know how bad it had become with Tolley, or that I was involved in illegal activities. I wanted them to like me. They'd worried about their daughter for long enough. I wouldn't give them any further reason."

The lights flashed above us. "You're welcome. We'll get more time to talk at dinner."

She nodded and we took our seats. It might not have been me up on that stage, but my heart started to race nonetheless. Elena still hadn't let me hear her sing, telling me I had to wait for opening night.

The curtain opened on the stage and the music began. I was captivated by the whole experience. Then a woman broke out in song. I didn't need to see the singer to know that the unbelievably gorgeous voice belonged to Elena. She stepped onto the stage and I wanted to jump to my feet and applaud.

I glanced around at the awed expressions on the faces of my family. They were just as surprised as I was at how beautifully she sang. It took a moment to reconcile this Elena with the pathologically shy woman who first came to stay with me.

The only two people not in a state of shock were her parents. Tears streamed down her mother's cheeks, her face filled with pride. Her father's look was almost identical. They were proud, and not afraid to show it.

And I was too. I was simply awestruck at the amount of raw talent Elena possessed. No wonder Alan had yelled at me.

"Ashton!"

I spun around, looking for the source of the voice to see Alan coming toward me. We were standing in the lobby waiting for the second act to begin. "Alan. Great show." I reached out to clasp his hand in mine.

"Thank you. She's amazing isn't she?"

TRADED

My eyes were still wide with surprise. "I had no idea."

"Please tell me she's going to stick around for a while? I keep thinking of different shows I could do with a voice like hers."

"That's the plan."

He watched me for a moment. "Ashton, we've known each other for a long time, and I can tell when something isn't right with you, so spit it out."

He was right. Alan and I had known each other for forever. We didn't really have secrets between us. "I'm asking Elena to move in with me. I really think she's the one."

"Holy shit. Really?"

"Tell me about it. Never saw it coming until she hit me like a freight train. If she says yes, she'll be around as long as I can keep her here."

"Wow, that's a big step. Elena's good for you, though. In all the years I've known you, I've never seen you so relaxed."

"She is."

The lights inside the theater flashed. "I've got to get back up there. We'll talk more at the party."

I nodded and made my way back to my seat.

The second half of the show was even better than the first; almost like she'd been building her confidence through the first act and found it by the second. When the show ended, everyone quickly left to head over to the restaurant. They didn't want to give away anything by being seen at the theater.

I waited for Elena in the back hall by the dressing room. It was my turn to fidget as I paced back and forth outside her door. After about fifteen minutes, it swung open to reveal Elena in a sapphire blue strapless cocktail dress. The color gave her skin a healthy glow.

"Hi," she said, a bit on the shy side.

Wanting to take away her fear, I quickly wrapped her in my arms. "You were fantastic. I've never seen anything like that."

A blush rose on her cheeks. "I'm so glad you liked it."

"I loved it." Taking her hand, I led her to the front of the theater and down the steps, all the while recounting my favorite parts of the show.

I brought her to the fountain across the street. She looked around, confused.

"There's something I want to talk to you about," I said, and she nodded, taking a seat at the edge of the fountain, staring down at the coins resting on the bottom. Taking the seat next to her, I used my finger to lift her chin to face me, tucking a small strand of hair behind her ear and saying, "Elena, remember how I told you that you could stay with me as long as you needed to get yourself on your feet again.

She swallowed hard. "Yes."

"I don't want that anymore."

Her eyes instantly filled with tears and she tried to stand up and walk away, but I took her hand in mine and stopped her, urging her to sit back down. "That didn't come out right. Please stay and listen." I was annoyed with myself. Not once in my life had I had trouble talking to women, but right now I sounded like a tongue-tied idiot. "What I'm trying to say is that I don't want you to leave. Even when you get back on your feet, I want you to stay and be mine."

Her eyes widened and I watched as her body went tight.

"I love you, Elena."

CHAPTER 25

Elena

"What?"

My voice came out all breathy, so much so that I questioned whether or not it was audible. Did Ashton just say he loved me? Pieces of the conversation I had with Miller a few weeks ago came back to me.

"He was already falling for you."

"I am completely in love with you, Elena," he said, his gaze never leaving mine.

The words both scared and excited me. They were the ones I'd longed to hear from Ashton's lips, but I knew I couldn't return them. Even though he'd never shown me anything but care and compassion, the fear of rejection still festered, buried deep within me. As much as I willed them to come, no words would leave my mouth. I didn't know what to say.

Did I want to stay with Ashton? More than anything. But would he still want me if I couldn't utter those three little words? There was only one way to find out. I was tired of living in fear.

"I want to stay with you, more than you can even imagine . . . but I need more time—"

His fingers covered my lips.

"You don't have to say it back. Take all the time you need."

Cupping my face in his hands, he slanted his lips over mine in a passionate kiss. The soft, slow movements were more about sharing ourselves than lust. When his tongue slid across my lips, tasting every inch, I groaned. There, on the ledge of the fountain, I ignored the world around us. The only thing that mattered was Ashton, and the happiness he'd brought to my life.

Our lips parted, the corners of his mouth pulling up into a smile. He stood and reached a hand out to me. "Come on. I believe I owe you a celebration dinner."

"You do." I winked and placed my hand in his.

On the way back to the car, I noticed Ashton's shoulders had relaxed. Even his breathing seemed lighter.

I glanced over at him as he pulled the car out onto the road. "Ashton?"

He took hold of my hand and linked our fingers together, bringing my hand up to his lips. "Yes?"

"Were you afraid to ask me to stay? I noticed you seem more relaxed now that it's out in the open."

He smirked. "A little. I didn't think you'd tell me no, but with everything you've been through I wasn't sure. Plus, I wanted to find the perfect time to tell you."

"I didn't need the perfect time. I just need you."

"You may not have needed the perfect time, but you deserved it."

"Thank you. And I—"

Once again he cut me off. "Not until you're ready. I can wait."

We pulled up outside La Tratoria. Every time I saw the place, it always amazed me with it elegance. "A special dinner for two?"

"Something like that."

He hopped out of the car and opened my door before I had a chance to unbuckle myself. We walked into the restaurant hand in hand and it felt nice to be on the arm of a man who cherished me—who *loved* me. I felt strange just thinking it. The man holding my hand was in love . . . with *me*. The feeling of pride that swelled in my chest was like nothing I'd ever felt. It was a delicious sensation; one I knew I'd never tire of.

Bypassing the main dining room, I was confused. We'd eaten at the same table each time we'd dined there so, naturally, I assumed we'd be sitting there. I didn't question him, just went where he led. When we came to a door in the back, Ashton opened it with a flourish. We stepped into the room and I froze.

My parents.

My *parents*.

Oh my God.

The air left my lungs in a whoosh, the hand not in Ashton's now clasped over my mouth. My knees began to buckle and I felt him slide closer, knowing that if he hadn't been holding me, there was no way I would still be on my feet. I hadn't seen them in so long, yet it felt like yesterday. Mom's hair was shorter, her eyes more tired, but she was still the same woman who'd blown on my cuts and grazes, talked to me about boys, and helped me curl my hair for prom. Dad was slightly grayer, but it suited him. He'd filled out a bit too. But his smile was exactly the same. I loved that smile nearly as much as I loved my dad.

Mom ran up to me crying, wrapping me in the tightest hug imaginable. The back of my throat burned as I tried to hold onto my emotions, but it was impossible and the tears fell down my cheeks. Ashton quietly stepped away, giving me a few minutes alone with my mother and father.

Mom leaned back to look me in the eye. "You were amazing tonight, Laney. We are so very proud of you."

She pulled me in close again, her face tucked into my neck, and her arms around me were joined by Dad's. "I'm so happy we got to see your first performance."

"How?—when? Oh my God, I can't believe you're here," I squealed when I eventually moved out of their embrace, my head bouncing back and forth between the two of them.

Mom's smile warmed me all the way to my toes. "Ashton called us and asked if we wanted to come."

"But you guys can't afford to come here for just a weekend. I'm thrilled you're here, but you didn't need to do that."

"Don't worry, babydoll, Ashton covered all our expenses."

My hand flew to my chest. "He did?"

I searched the room for Ashton. I didn't know if he'd come back, but I wanted him to know how thankful I was. Before my eyes could find him, Dad took hold of my shoulders and turned me to face him. "You've got yourself a good man there. I'm glad to see you so happy."

"Ashton makes me happier than I've ever been."

"That's all we could ask for."

A tap on my shoulder made me turn. "You were amazing," Mrs. Hawes gushed.

"Thank you so much, Mrs. Hawes." She lifted her brows and waited. "Sorry, Faith."

"That's better." She smiled. "I'm so excited to see it again next week."

"You're coming again?"

"Absolutely!"

Mr. Hawes stepped up behind his wife, resting his hands on her shoulders. "Don't try and deter her. She wouldn't miss it for the world." He wrapped me in a hug of his own. "You were excellent."

"She was, wasn't she?" Ashton slid his arm around my waist, pulling me tight to him. "The kitchen should be ready with dinner, if we want to take our seats."

Everyone moved toward the dining room, but I held back. Not wanting to hold up dinner I didn't speak. I just placed a gentle kiss to the corner of his mouth and said, "Thank you . . . so much."

TRADED

And then I went to eat dinner with my family.

* * *

Dinner passed in a blur of wonderful conversation and celebration. It was more than I could have ever asked for, and I told Ashton as much on the drive home.

"I still can't believe you flew my parents all the way out here."

He lifted our linked hands to his lips. "Haven't you figured out yet that I'll do anything to make you happy."

"It's occurred to me once or twice." I laughed.

"Keep up your cheek and I promise you'll pay for it."

"Oh *really*," I said, trying to egg him on. Like he'd actually have enough self-control to hold back long enough to make me pay."

The second we parked in the garage Ashton was out of the car, ripping open my door, picking me up, and throwing me over his shoulder like a sack of potatoes. I squirmed, but nothing helped.

"Put me down, Ashton." I tried to sound stern but my giggles were a dead giveaway.

Still trying to wriggle my way down, I let out a sharp yelp when his hand connected with my ass. Liquid heat pooled at my core. All I could think about was him, pressed between my thighs. Twice more on our way up the stairs his hand landed on my ass. By the third time, I let the moan escape—one hundred percent positive Ashton knew what he was doing to me.

When we made it to the bedroom. Ashton let me slide down his body, and immediately after my feet touched the floor he gripped the hem of my dress and pulled it up and over my head. My underwear followed right behind. Then Ashton's mouth was on mine, as he lowered me to the bed and all conscious thought left me. His right hand caressed up and down my side, eventually gliding up my arm to my wrist, holding it in place until something cool and leather wrapped around it.

Swiftly, and before I spoke a word, Ashton had my other arm up and closed the leather cuff around my wrist. "I told you teasing me wouldn't be a good thing," he said as his fingers tickled down my side, caressing over my breast until he pinched my nipple between his fingers. Sensation shot through my body, my lower half squirming on the bed.

"Tsk, tsk, tsk. I think you can move too much," he whispered in my ear.

I had no idea what he was talking about. The idea of begging crossed my mind for one brief moment but the reality was, I wanted to see how it would play out. His hands continued their path down my chest and through my core. God, I needed his fingers to stay there longer. But they moved slowly down my thighs, capturing one of my ankles, his thumbs digging into the arch of my foot.

"Ashton," I sighed.

That's when I felt the cool leather again and heard the click as my ankle was attached to the bed and just like with my wrists, Ashton wasted no time cuffing my other ankle. I looked up. His eyes were hooded, his pupils dilated so wide that I could barely see what color his eyes were.

Lust.

"Oh, Elena. How fucking sexy you look spread-eagle on my bed." His hands grazed down my exposed stomach. "Now I want to see how much you can handle."

I trembled at his words and watched to see what he would do. Somehow, without me seeing, Ashton had managed to get a vibrator out onto the bed. The sound alone made the anticipation grow. "Please," I begged.

"Oh don't worry, it's all for you." His voice was husky as he touched the vibrator to my clit.

I'd never felt anything like it. Desire poured through me like wildfire. Within minutes I was crashing over the edge. "Oh God, don't . . . don't stop," I managed to pant out.

"I don't plan on it."

The speed increased, making the vibrations come quicker and long before I expected it, my body built up again to that peak where it's a choice: let the torture continue or fall off the cliff. This time when the explosion came, my vision grayed out and my body tightened almost to the point of pain.

As my body started to come down, I noticed my muscles tightening up again. Ashton had left the vibrator in place, except this time, he plunged two fingers into my wet heat, letting my body ride and clench them.

"Again. I love watching you come. The way your back arches as your mouth drops open . . ." He made a noise and it was quite possibly the most erotic sound I'd ever heard. Unsure how much I could handle before my body became too sensitive, I braced, my core quivering in anticipation.

On and on it went.

I begged Ashton for relief, but I didn't mean it. The combination of pleasure and pain was utterly overwhelming—and I loved every minute.

After my third or fourth orgasm—I'd lost count—my ankles were freed, followed by my wrists. Ashton took the slightly chafed skin in his hands, rubbing some of the feeling back into them.

"You did so well, babe, but now I need you."

Somewhere in the midst of everything, Ashton had removed his clothes and glasses. He placed me over his lap, and I sank down, his swollen shaft sliding into me easily. The tiredness that had begun to claim me left hurriedly the minute he started to move inside me; my body and mind lost to the passion. Soon, I pushed everything aside and took over, riding him like I'd never get enough of being with him that way.

"Fuck, Elena, please tell me you're close," he pleaded, and I could feel his cock hardening, stretching my walls.

I dropped my head to his shoulder. "I can't come again."

"You can and you will." The demand in his tone and his thumb on my clit forced my body into action, my body tightening around his, pulsing over and over again.

"Oh God!"

Ashton grabbed my hips, thrusting himself up into me until he shouted out his release. Exhausted, we both dropped to the bed and curled up in each other's arms.

"I love you, Elena," he whispered softly into my hair. "Welcome home."

The three words were so poignant, they brought tears to my eyes. After many years, I'd finally found my place.

A place I could call home.

CHAPTER 26

Ashton

"I told you she was ready," Miller said laughing, his ass on the couch on the other side of my office. "Did you two even leave the house this weekend?"

It was my turn to smirk at him. "Yes. She had a matinee yesterday. Then we went home and ate in."

"Lucky bastard," he muttered.

I finished scrolling through the email on my computer and leaned back in my chair. "I'm still not sure how she'll deal with everything, after the last time we were there. She was scared. Things got a little violent."

"Have you taken her since then like Dad suggested? She needs to see that's not what happens every time."

Rubbing the muscles in the back of my neck, I took my glasses off and dropped them on the desk. "No, I didn't want to freak her out."

TRADED

"You need to take her."

Everyone had the grand idea that I should take Elena with me to collect another debt. That it would show her what she needed to know and suddenly she'd understand what we did and why, and be able to accept it. Like it was the best thing for her.

But what if it wasn't the best thing—for either of us?

"Ever considered *not* doing it?"

"Not doing what?"

"You know I never wanted this."

Miller leaned forward, resting his forearms on his thighs. "It's part of who we are," he said simply.

Was it though? Maybe Miller and Dad were right. It might be in our blood—without it, I never would have been able to open one restaurant much less three—but there was this small part of me that just wished . . .

"Yeah. Yeah, I guess you're right."

"Of course I am. Embrace it. No one will ever fuck with Elena now. She's yours, which means everyone will leave her alone so they don't have to deal with us."

He had a point. Elena would be safe from all of the bullshit she'd dealt with in the past. "You're right. I have a drop on Tuesday. I'll take her with me."

Miller shrugged. "There's got to be something to the theory. Mom's kept Dad all these years without kicking his ass to the curb."

My phone buzzed on the desk. "Speaking of Dad."

"His ears must be ringing. I've got a meeting with Max Taran. Fucker better have his shit together. I'm not helping his ass this time."

It always amazed me how different Miller became when dealing with clients. He was cold, calculating. There were no second chances with Miller. Either you paid him the money or left with at least one broken bone, if not more. You'd never though that side existed when you spoke with him, but it was there, lingering just under the surface.

"We'll talk later," I said, picking up the phone.

Miller waved and closed the door behind him.

I swiped my finger across the screen. "Hello?"

"Ashton, have you seen your brother. He's not answering his phone."

I chuckled. "Idiot probably has it on silent again. He just left to deal with Max Taran."

"Good. I wasn't sure if he'd remember." I heard yelling in the background. "Your mother wants me to tell you she can't wait to see Elena again."

"I saw the show again on Sunday. I had no idea she was that good."

"You two looked awful cozy together on Saturday night," he accused.

The thought of how she'd stayed by my side brought a smile to my face. "She's moving in with me."

Dad didn't pull any punches. "Have you taken her on a collection or loan yet?"

TRADED

"Dad, she's already seen it. Hell, she's been in the middle of it."

"As a client—not from the other side of the fence."

I sighed. "Miller said the same thing. That she needs to know because it's part of who we are."

"And he's right. You can't expect her to understand your life if you don't show it to her."

The question from earlier came smashing back into me.

Is this really my life?

"Why did you want me to do this?"

Silence.

I could picture him staring at the phone. His brows would be drawn down and a frown on his face. "Because I knew you could. Miller never wanted anything but to be part of the business and, call me selfish, but I wanted you to be there too. I knew you could do both. Now you have the restaurants on top of what you do for the family. Besides, you wouldn't have met Elena if it weren't for all of this."

He had a point. Without any of this, Elena wouldn't be sleeping in my bed every night, so I had something to be thankful for, besides the financial aspect.

Dad and I talked a little longer before he hung up. Our conversation gave me a lot to think about as I sat at my desk, going over the books.

How in the hell had I managed to get this far behind? Oh right—I'd been wining and dining Elena in the hope that if and when she left her husband she might want to stay with me. The books were up to date, and so were the orders.

Mainly, it was a lot of calls to return for catering and the dreaded filling. Not to mention meeting with the new distributor. Damn, Joanne needed to come back from vacation before the paperwork got worse. Then I could go back to what I loved.

The last two nights I'd watched Elena up on that stage, a part of me was a little jealous. She was getting to be everything she always wanted to be. Not that I wasn't successful, but over the years I'd found myself moving further and further from what I loved about running a restaurant. Spending all of my time collecting debts for my dad had got me to where I was, and now so much of the money loaned was my own that I knew I couldn't really step away until I figured out a way to bring my dad back in to take over. Either way, I was going to start making being a chef and the other things I wanted to do in the restaurant a priority.

Picking up the phone, I began to dial the first number when a knock sounded on my door. Pierre opened it, followed by another man.

"Ben is here to meet with you about liquor distribution."

I stood and reached out a hand, which he took in a polite handshake. "Nice to meet you, would you like to take a seat?"

"Thank you. I hope I have a quick solution to your problem."

"I hope so."

We took our seats and began to discuss his facilities and supplies when yelling and banging caught my attention. I dropped the pen in my hand and darted from the office toward the front, hoping no one was hurt. The second I stepped through the doors, a hand landed on my shoulder, twisting me and throwing me up against the wall.

"Ashton Hawes?"

A cop stood next to me, at least a dozen more throughout the restaurant, tearing the place up.

Just fucking great.

What in the hell were they looking for in the restaurant? Nothing here would be worth their time. I would never taint this business.

"That's me." My voice was muffled against the hard surface of the wall.

"Mr. Hawes, we're bringing you in for questioning in the kidnapping of Mrs. Elena Tolley."

I tried to swing around to get a good look at his face, but the officers held tight until the cuffs were snapped into place. It never occurred to me to ask about the cuffs if I was only being questioned.

"What the fuck are you talking about? Elena's down at the theater practicing for the new Sondheim show."

"We'll send a car over."

It took two of them but eventually they had me moving, marching me across the restaurant, toward the door. Most of my staff had looks of disbelief on their faces: mouths open, eyes rounded. Fuck, I'd have to come up with an explanation for them and hoped they didn't run for the hills. And the customers. This shit could ruin my business. I needed to get it cleared up—fast.

"Dustin, call my father and tell him what happened."

"You got it, Ashton," he answered and I was extremely grateful he didn't have some ridiculous remark to go with it.

The cops pushed through the front door and helped me into the backseat; not easy with my hands locked behind my back. One reason I never used metal cuffs in all of my games, they were way too uncomfortable. Although, I tried to get more information out of the officers, none of them were budging. It wasn't until we walked through the front doors of the station that so much became clear.

Tolley.

The lousy piece of shit sat at one of the desks. When he looked up, his eyes still black and blue, he gave me a cold smirk. The bastard had orchestrated all of this. Would Elena take his side? A small part of me worried that might be the case, except the rest of my brain pushed it away. Not the new Elena. That worthless son of a bitch was in for a rude awakening when she got here.

Tolley jumped from his chair, playing the victim so well. "That bastard stole my wife." Two of the cops restrained him, offering him comfort. Thoughts of shaking off the cops' grip and finishing what I'd started a few weeks ago was more than a little appealing but, unfortunately, if I wanted to walk out of there sooner rather than later, I needed to keep my hands to myself and be on my best behavior.

Grinding my teeth, I didn't fight the officers as they led me into an interview room, closing the door behind me, two cops still inside. On the far wall, I could see myself in the two-way mirror. They sat me down in the chair and moved the cuffs from the back to the front. A few minutes later the door opened and in walked another cop, dressed in a suit. He took the seat across from me as the other two left.

"Mr. Hawes," he said opening the folder in front of him. "Where is Mrs. Tolley?"

My natural instinct was to tell this guy to shove it up his ass and get me a phone to call my lawyer. It was what Dad had drilled into our heads from the time we were little.

Not this time.

I hadn't kidnapped anyone, and the sooner they found Elena, the sooner they would let my ass go.

"Like I told the *gentlemen* who brought me in, Elena's at the Canterbury Theater downtown. She's got a part in the one of the new productions."

"Damn, you're making my life easy." He shook his head, a shit-eating grin on his face.

Arrogant bastard thought he had me. I leaned back in the chair and waited for all of it to play out in front of me. As long as the idiot didn't figure out the real reason why Elena was currently in my care, I would be walking out of there in no time.

"Want to tell me why you kidnapped Mrs. Tolley in the first place?" he asked, not looking up from his paper, waiting to write down whatever I said for later.

"I didn't." It happened to be the only answer he would get out of me, until either Elena or my lawyer showed up.

"You told us exactly where to find her, and yet you say you didn't kidnap her."

"Exactly."

The door swung opened and Arthur, my father's lawyer, stepped through. "That's enough of the questions. I'm Mr. Colburn, Mr. Hawes's attorney. From what I understand, he's given you the information to prove he is innocent. At this time, he will not answer any more questions until you stop treating him like the accused and instead realize that he's actually the victim."

The detective clenched his jaw, but made no attempt to correct Arthur, instead, leaving the room, the door crashing into its frame as he slammed it behind him.

Arthur took the chair next to me. "What the fuck happened, Ashton? Your father is ready to storm the place."

"I take it Dad's here?"

"You could say that. I'm not the only lawyer he brought. Now do you want to tell me what the fuck happened so I can go out there and calm him down, *before* he makes any of this worse on either of you?"

"The soon-to-be ex-husband of the woman I'm seeing claims I kidnapped her."

"Elena?"

I nodded, curious as to how Arthur knew that.

"Don't look surprised. Your father told me all about her. Now let me go out there and calm him down."

TRADED

Before he had a chance to stand, screaming could be heard from the main lobby and it happened to be the only voice I wanted to hear.

CHAPTER 27

Elena

"From the top," Alan called from somewhere near the back. "Vince, remember where we made the changes to the blocking."

We'd been rehearsing the same number for the last three days when Alan decided that the scene didn't work and we needed to start from scratch. My feet were sore from all the dancing, not to mention my throat was scratchy. At some point Alan would need to give up and give us a break.

The intro to the music started and I counted the beats. I was the first to come in. I heard my cue and started to sing. Suddenly, the door was flung open, the heavy metal handle crashing against the wall and startling everyone in the room. Six police officers ran through the door, guns drawn.

TRADED

Alan jumped from his seat and into the aisle, his hands raised. "I'm not sure what's happened, but I think you have the wrong place."

The one in the front took a step forward, calling out, "Elena Tolley?" and all heads, excluding those of the police officers, snapped in my direction.

"I'm Elena Tolley," my voice squeaked out.

He holstered his gun and came toward me. "You'll have to come with us, ma'am."

I crossed my arms over my chest and stood stock-still. "I'm not going anywhere with anyone until someone explains what is going on."

"Ma'am, we have Ashton Hawes in custody. He is being questioned regarding your disappearance. Kidnapping," he clarified.

My eyes practically popped out of my head. "You what?" I yelled.

Alan ran up onto the stage. "You arrested Ashton?" he asked, a bit more calmly than me.

Why in the hell would they think that Ashton kidnapped me? I was only clueless for a fleeting moment because the answer slapped me in the face.

Dominic.

Asshole was still finding ways to ruin my life.

"Officer, I can assure you Ashton did not kidnap me. I'm with him of my own free will."

The officers looked at me like I was crazy, probably thinking I was suffering from Stockholm Syndrome. The ridiculous thing about it was that the jerk parading around their station, most likely with his head held high, had caused me more damage than anyone could imagine.

"Are you sure you're okay, ma'am?"

"I promise, I'm fine." I knew I could fix this whole mess when I got to the station. Taking a deep breath, I tried to force myself to relax. "Give me a second to grab my things and I'll come with you." I gave a curt nod and headed off stage.

Alan followed me to the back dressing rooms. "Do you want me to come with you?"

I shook my head. "No, I needed to stand up to my soon-to-be *ex*-husband sooner or later." I lay my arm on his. "Keep working. I'll fix this mess and be back tomorrow."

He pulled me into a hug. "I'm glad he sent you to me. Take care of him tonight—he's going to be pissed."

"I will."

I gave him a quick kiss on the cheek and ran around to come out of the audience door instead of the stage door. The officers were still there waiting. "Let's go," I said, leading the way to the doors.

We walked out to find the place surrounded by even more cars. Members of EMS came running up to me with a stretcher.

"Are you all right, ma'am?" one of them asked, reaching out to take my hand and lead me to the ambulance.

I snatched my arm out of his reach. "I'm fine. I wasn't kidnapped, simply being tortured by my estranged husband." I looked around at all of them, standing there. "Now will someone please take me to the station so we can clear this all up?"

TRADED

"Sorry, Mrs. Tolley," one of the officers from inside said as he approached. "Please, come with me and we'll take you there."

I followed him to one of the unmarked cars. Taking my hand, he helped me in, before climbing into the driver's seat and starting the engine. The entire drive over my blood boiled, all of the things I ever wanted to say to the arrogant jerk running through my head. There would be no holding back this time. The minute the cop stopped in front of the station and opened my door, I pushed past him and took the steps two at a time. I pushed open the door and was searching for someone to talk to about getting Ashton released when *his* voice slithered over me.

"Elena, my lovely wife."

My head snapped in his direction. His words were meant for the ears of the detectives.

I knew better.

Hatred burned bright in his eyes and when he stepped in front of me and took my hands like he was making sure I was okay, I felt his fingers tighten, squeezing my hands uncomfortably, a sly smile playing at the edges of his mouth. I tried to pull out of his grasp but he was stronger and pulled me to him, keeping me close so that my front was pressed against his. His arms wrapped tightly around my waist, over my own arms, preventing me from moving, and with his chin resting on my shoulder, his mouth dropped to my ear.

"If you think for one second I'm letting you divorce me, you have another think coming. Now smile, say thank you, and get your fat ass in the fucking car."

Some of my old insecurities rose up but I pushed them back as best I could. Out of the corner of my eye, I saw Malcolm being held back by Miller. He gave me a nod and I let it fly.

Pushing free, I spoke to Dominic, my voice raised so everyone around could hear. "Get your goddamn hands off me. I'm not your *lovely* wife, as you conveniently choose to put it, considering we're surrounded by police officers. I'm your soon-to-be ex-wife because you don't know how to treat a woman." I jabbed my finger into his chest, working myself into a fine rage. "You've spent every day of the last five years tearing me down. I thought I was worthless; that no one would ever want me. You made me think that I was only worthy of being a fucktoy to you. Your problem is that I found someone else; a man who treats me better than you could ever imagine. A man who makes me come over and over again as I scream his name."

I smirked when I realized we were completely surrounded by officers. "And you have just trapped yourself by falsely accusing a man of kidnapping. A man I'm choosing to be with over you. You're an idiot. I hope you enjoy jail. I'm taking Ashton home to bed," I finished.

My knees went weak at the realization of everything that had just come out of my mouth, but, thankfully, during my rant, Miller had come up behind me and wrapped an arm around my waist. The police closed in on Dominic, who looked much more uncomfortable now than when I walked in.

"I'm proud of you, little sis," Miller said in my ear.

TRADED

"Thank you." It meant the world for him to say that to me, and the "little sis" made my heart flutter in my chest.

If only that could be true someday.

Malcolm stepped in front of me and placed his hands on my shoulders. A blush crept up my cheeks. He'd heard everything I just said. "Thank you for coming to Ashton's rescue."

"Of course I would." The thought of Ashton locked up somewhere in the building brought tears to my eyes.

"You bitch," Dominic screamed, still fighting the officer holding him even though it was obvious he had no chance of wrestling free. "No one wants to fuck an ugly whore like you. Not even to wipe out a debt. Ashton told me a few weeks ago he wants *all* of his money." Spit flew from his lips with every hateful word.

Malcolm spun around so fast he was almost a blur.

"You motherfucker," he said, advancing on Dominic. "If you don't shut your goddamn mouth, I'm going to chop your dick off and feed it to you in slices."

Miller ran around me to wrap an arm around his dad, pulling him back away from where the cops had thrown Dominic to the floor, forcing him into a set of cuffs.

The adrenaline I'd felt when confronting Dominic began to wear off, and the seat a few feet away looked extremely appealing. I walked over to it and dropped down. Both Malcolm and Miller turned their attention back to me. They shared a brief look then Miller took the seat next to mine while Malcolm stood, his neck and face red. I was having trouble controlling my emotions. The tremble of my fingers caught Malcolm's attention.

"Come on, Elena. Let's see what we can do about getting Ashton out of here."

A tall man with dark brown hair came down the hall. The fit of his gray three-piece suit made it very clear that he was not a public defender, or a detective; a suspicion only confirmed when Malcolm offered his hand.

"Arthur." Malcolm turned and gestured for me to join him. All of the hatred of a few minutes ago gone, I could feel Miller's presence close behind. Then he stepped up next to me and wrapped an arm around my shoulder for support. "Arthur Colburn, please meet Elena Tolley. Elena, this is my lawyer, Arthur."

The gentleman extended his hand toward me. "It's a pleasure to meet you."

He gestured toward one of the detectives. "Now that you're here, we'll be able to straighten this out in no time."

He led me over to the reception desk where Detective Lynch introduced himself and asked if I could answer a few questions. My hands began to sweat as I considered how much lying I might need to do to keep Ashton out of jail.

"Okay. I can do that."

He led me to an office down the hall, gesturing for me to take a seat in front of the desk. Arthur took the seat next to me. Malcolm and Miller had elected to wait out in the lobby, knowing their presence in the room wouldn't help. Detective Lynch took the seat behind the

TRADED

desk and opened the file. Pen in hand, he looked up at me.

"Now, Mrs. Tolley, you said that you were *not* kidnapped by Mr. Hawes."

"Absolutely not." I moved to get up from my seat and Arthur set his hand on my arm, signaling me to sit back down. "Ashton has done nothing but save me from being abused by my so called husband."

"I take it from the conversation a few minutes ago that your husband didn't always treat you well?" He had the grace to look somewhat embarrassed by my behavior.

"You could say that. I doubt you want all of the details—you certainly got enough earlier—but Dominic liked to put me down, make me feel terrible about myself. He isolated me from my family and friends. Ashton has done everything he can to make me see that I am worthy of being treated well. Of being loved."

"So Mr. Hawes did not trade money to have you for three months like your *husband* claims."

How close that was to reality scared me. What if I gave myself away? Trying to think about it rationally, I reasoned that, technically, Ashton didn't give any money to Dominic for me or vice versa. Using that thought to comfort and relax me, I answered. "No, he didn't."

His eyes narrowed. "Are you aware that Mr. Hawes has previously been investigated in relation to unlicensed moneylending?"

I shook my head, hoping to seem naïve to his business practices. "Ashton owns three restaurants downtown."

"What is your relationship to Mr. Hawes?"

"Ashton and I are living together." I drew little circles on the table. "When I saw Dominic last week, I told him I was filing for divorce. Apparently he decided to turn Ashton in, instead of giving me up as his *slave*."

The detective nodded with each word that left my lips. His eyes crinkled, his voice soothing. "I've seen this many times, Mrs. Tolley, although, not to the extreme your husband took it. It's not uncommon for abusive husbands to push things too far when their wife threatens to leave them, especially for another man."

"Does that mean you'll let Ashton go?"

He sat back in his seat and watched me. "While it would give me great pleasure to arrest a member of the Hawes family," his eyes darted to Arthur, who sat stoically, staring straight ahead, "this is one instance where I believe that they are innocent and have, in fact, helped someone out of a terrible situation."

I held my breath, waiting for him to continue.

"So yes, Mrs. Tolley, in this circumstance, Mr. Hawes will be released."

I wanted to jump up and wrap my arms around his neck. There were things I never told Ashton that he deserved to hear when we were alone, not over a phone, or through a glass window. With great effort, I kept myself seated and simply said, "Thank you."

The edges of his eyes crinkled with his smile. "You're welcome. I would warn you, but I think you already know more about Ashton than you're letting on."

There was a moment of silence. I could have let it go, said nothing, but I needed Detective Lynch to know.

"Ashton loves me. He makes me feel like a princess—something I've never felt before." I almost added that I didn't care what he did, but I figured that would be too much.

Detective Lynch stood. "Give me a few minutes to get all the paperwork completed, then Mr. Hawes will be released."

When the door closed behind him, I turned to Arthur. "Why didn't you say anything?"

He glanced over at me. "Because it was your story to tell. I don't need to protect you from your own story."

Fidgeting with the hem of my shirt, I asked. "Do you think they'll be long?"

He shook his head. "Not with Malcolm here. They can't stand him. They'll want him out of here sooner rather than later."

I nodded and went back to playing with anything in reach. With everything out of the way, I was nervous. Would Ashton blame me for what happened? No. Ashton wasn't like that. Arthur covered my hand and gave me a comforting smile. All of the waiting probably didn't have much of an effect on him. It was likely standard procedure.

What felt like an eternity later, the door opened.

"Mr. Hawes is free to go."

Jumping from my seat, I practically ran to the door. A hand landed on my arm and I looked up into the eyes of Detective Lynch. "I know Ashton treats you better than Dominic ever did, and you seem like a wonderful woman, just . . . please be careful."

Glancing down at his hand on my arm, I said, "I know exactly what I'm getting into." Stepping around him, I ran down the hallway toward the lobby. Ashton's blond head caught my attention. His back was turned to me as he talked to his dad and brother. Miller pointed in my direction and Ashton turned slowly, his eyes locking on mine, the green glowing behind the frames of his glasses.

For a split second I froze, waiting to see his reaction. When a slow, sexy smile curved his lips, I took off toward him.

CHAPTER 28

Ashton

Elena came bolting down the hall and right into my arms. She clutched the back of my coat like a lifeline. It felt so right to have her there; her body pressed against mine. I wrapped one arm around her waist and brought the other up to cup her face, watching her eyes as they shimmered with unshed tears.

"Elena, what's wrong?"

"I'm sorry. This is all my fault." She sniffled and buried her head against my chest.

"Elena, look at me," I demanded. Her tear-streaked face met mine. "You are *not* to blame for what one fucking idiot does."

My lips descended to hers—who the fuck cared if I was in the middle of a police station? Certainly not me.

She quickly surrendered to the kiss and her body pushed further into mine as I swiped my tongue passed her lips to deepen the kiss. I'd have taken her there and then, but the cat calls echoing around the room told me it was time to pull back. We'd have all the time in the world once we got home.

Her chest rose and fell with each labored breath. "I love you," she said.

Forgetting myself, I lifted her into my arms, her legs wrapping around my waist. "I'll call you later," I said over my shoulder to my dad and Miller. I'd been waiting to hear her say the words and now that she had, I wasn't ever letting her go.

I stepped out the doors and just like I expected, Lewis was waiting in the lot for us. When we no longer had an audience, I looked into her eyes.

"I love you so much, Elena. Stay with me." It wasn't a command, but I wasn't necessarily asking either.

"Forever. We can talk to Arthur about expediting the process."

"Later," I promised, stepping up to the car. Lewis already had the back door open. Setting her on her feet, I hurried her inside. I needed to have her home and in our bed. "Home," I told Lewis, shutting the door.

Scooping Elena into my arms, I tasted her lips, quickly losing control; by the time we reached the house, my hand had already slipped up inside her top to cup her breast. The car pulled to a stop and I sat up, adjusting her clothes. I didn't give two shits about being caught, but no one besides me was ever seeing Elena naked again.

TRADED

Taking her hand, I led her to the house and through the door. It hadn't even finished closing when I pushed her up against it, capturing her mouth roughly, tasting every inch. Need coursed through me. Simple, hot, rough sex wouldn't be enough. She was mine and it was time to show her even more.

Breaking the connection of our lips, I placed my hand on her back and guided her up the stairs to the bedroom. The toys were in the drawer, the restraints attached to the bed, but none of that would do. My body craved something more than the normal. Not that most of what I liked was "normal" by most people's standards.

We reached the bedroom and I knew exactly what I wanted. I took a seat on the bed and watched Elena, trying to decide if she was ready for what I had in mind.

Elena walked up to me, her hips sashaying gracefully with each step. She stood in front of me staring, silently. After a moment, her thigh slipped over mine until she was straddling my erection, which was straining almost painfully against my jeans.

"Are you sure you're okay?"

"Fuck yes." My voice was rough with desire. I wanted her so badly I could barely see straight.

Her body rocked against mine and I was done.

Grabbing her ass, I stood and turned to lay her on the bed. Stripping her of the skimpy tank top and shorts she had on, staring into her eyes, I asked, "Do you trust me?"

"I do," she answered without hesitation.

I reached behind me into the dresser drawer and pulled out a blindfold. Slipping it over her head, I watched her body respond. She could no longer see what I was doing. Removing one of the five senses heightens the others. Right about now she should be a mass of overwhelming feeling.

Which was exactly what I wanted.

Her thighs clenched together and she squirmed on the bed. Gently, I stroked my fingers down the inside of her calves, watching them quiver beneath my touch.

"Don't move."

A deep breath escaped her lips and she nodded. Darting down the stairs to the kitchen, I grabbed a bowl and filled it with ice cubes, before joining Elena on the bed again. I set the bowl on the nightstand, letting the glass make a sound as it touched the wood.

"Ashton?"

"Shhh." I climbed up on the bed next to her, stroking up the inside of her thigh, across her stomach, and up around her pert, pink nipples.

Reaching behind me, I grabbed a cube from the bowl, replacing my finger with it. The sound of her squeal as the ice hit her skin sent waves of fire through me. With a tight grip on the cube, I snaked it around both nipples until they stood up hard. Her breath was coming in pants. I knew I was bringing her closer and closer to the edge.

That didn't stop me from gliding the ice down the valley of her breasts onto her stomach, my tongue following behind to lick up the water. A moan slipped passed her lips when the cubed circled her naval, traveling down to her clit. Her body arced up. I placed my hand on her stomach, still stroking her with the cold ice and warned, "Be still, or I'll have to tie you up."

At the mention of restraints, a tremble traveled through her body, tightening at her core. She swallowed hard and nodded. Satisfied she'd do as she was told, I moved the cube down, stroking through her core until I found her puckered entrance. Her lower body started to come up off the bed, but she got a handle on it and dropped back, her chest rising and falling rapidly with the effort.

"That's it, gorgeous."

I took another piece of ice. Moans and whimpers permeated the air as she did her best to stay still. It didn't seem possible, but my dick continued to get harder with each and every sound and if I didn't slip into her wet heat soon, I was going to end up coming all over the bed.

One last cube.

I placed it between my lips, rubbing it lightly over hers, watching her tongue dart out to taste the water as the ice melted where it touched her heated skin. Tracing the cube down her body once again, I let my cold tongue bring her over the edge, her body convulsing in wave after wave of pleasure.

"Oh, baby, it's so hot watching you come," I groaned, crawling up her body, unable to take anymore. "And I'm going to make you come all over my dick this time."

Her head thrashed on the pillow as I slid in slowly, inch by inch.

That's where my ability for slow and steady ended.

Slipping out, I thrust back in, picking up my pace each time. The muscles tightened in my thighs. I did everything I could to hold back the orgasm, wanting her to come first, but when her body quivered and clamped down on me, it brought me over as I surged into hers. I almost blacked out when I came, over and over again.

Panting, I reached for the blindfold. "Get ready for the light."

I slipped the fabric from her face and her eyes closed tightly for a few seconds before she began to blink. Eventually, her gaze focused on me. A languorous smile formed on her lips.

"That was unbelievable."

Placing a tender kiss on her forehead, I said, "It was."

I picked up the bowl and brought it to the bathroom, dumping the leftover ice and water down the drain. When I returned to the bedroom, Elena was sound asleep. Turning out the lights, I slipped beneath the covers, pulling her close. Warmth spread through me the moment her hand landed on my chest.

She said the words.

Now I knew how my dad felt when he talked about my mom. The man was the definition of a hardass with everyone but her, and Elena did the same thing to me. She melted me in ways I never expected.

I ran over the events of the day in my head. While we'd waited on Elena and Arthur, my dad and Miller had filled me in on what had happened in the lobby: from Tolley's ridiculous accusations, to his tirade against Elena. Apparently he hadn't learned his lesson a few weeks ago when I used his face as a punching bag. They told me he'd been arrested for falsely accusing me of kidnapping, but that wouldn't keep him in jail for long. He'd either serve his days or bail himself out.

He'd be safer doing his time.

Either way, it was time for Elena to learn how to handle a small caliber gun. I'd start looking into those things tomorrow morning. I knew Elena would probably be hungry when she woke, so I forced myself out of bed, tossed on a pair of gym shorts and my glasses, and went downstairs to find something for dinner, and to call my dad.

The phone only rang twice. "Ashton."

"Dad," I said dropping down onto the couch in the living room.

"That bastard is going to pay for all this."

The mention of Tolley made my blood pressure rise. "Yeah, well until the cops release him, we're not getting our hands on him."

"You don't think I have people watching for when that fucker gets released?"

"I'm sure you do. I want to get Elena a gun and spend some time at the range."

He sighed. "I'll end that son of a bitch before he gets anywhere near her."

"You had mom take the same classes as Elena's been taking, and she didn't even have a crazy-ass ex. No harm in her knowing her way around a gun."

"You have a point. With our business the way it is, it wouldn't hurt—especially if you two are going to try and make this work. And after the display in the station today, I'm guessing that's the case."

"I told you she was moving in."

"An actual relationship?"

I rolled my eyes, knowing he couldn't see me. "Yes, I want her by my side for as long as she wants to be there."

"Good. Just don't do something fucking ridiculous, like not being honest about everything you do. She needs to know and be comfortable with *all* aspects of your life. Or you'll regret it later when she leaves you."

Dad knew what he'd been doing that night at his house.

"I'm taking her. She needs to know what she's getting into, not just remembers from that first night."

"Good."

Leaning back against the cushions, I said, "I'll make sure she keeps taking the self-defense lessons but I'll start sending Brock with her when she goes somewhere, even with Lewis. Oh, and I want to increase security around the house as well."

"I think that's a very good idea."

"Good. Now I gotta go. I need to make dinner for Elena. I'll call you tomorrow and let you know where we stand."

Dad and I said our good-byes and hung up.

Walking down the stairs to the kitchen, I wondered if attacking Tolley that night pushed him even farther over the edge. Was it my fault she was in danger? Did being with me make him even crazier?

Either way, it was too late now.

CHAPTER 29

Elena

I woke up feeling deliciously sore. After my nap, Ashton had made us dinner, which we ate without bothering to dress. Despite my hunger I was barely able to finish my meal; the sight of his hard length and muscled abs almost drove me to distraction. I did my best not to make it too obvious but I wasn't quick enough because the second Ashton noticed, he scooped me from the stool and carried me over his shoulder back to our room. After that . . . I wasn't distracted anymore.
Our room.
It felt weird to say, but if I was moving in then that's what it was.
Ours.
My life was finally on the right track. The man I was with treated me like a princess, like I was the only person in the world who mattered. I had a wonderful new career. And I was weeks

away from being free of the proverbial ball and chain that had been weighing me down.

Life was good.

Seeing as he was always looking after me, I decided to do something special for Ashton. Sneaking out of bed, I threw on the silk robe he bought me and tiptoed downstairs to start breakfast.

Once I'd started the coffee pot, I searched the pantry until I located all the necessary ingredients for my mother's famous Belgian waffles. They went perfectly with bacon.

I was just pouring the coffee when two strong arms slipped around my waist, and Ashton began nibbling on my neck as I poured the batter for the last waffle into the iron.

"You don't have to make me breakfast."

Turning, I wrapped my arms around his waist. "I know, but I wanted to. You helped me work up such an appetite last night. I was starving this morning."

I covered the waffles with strawberries, whipped cream, and powdered sugar, then took them over to the table. They smelled divine—even if I did say so myself. Ashton dived for the coffee the minute the mug touched the table.

"Mmm. This is exactly what I needed." He took his first bite and moaned. "That's absolutely delicious."

"Thank you. It's a recipe my mom used to make."

"Just saying, you can make these anytime you like."

I giggled and started on my own breakfast. That meant a lot coming from someone who owned three of his own restaurants.

A few minutes later he set his fork down, the look on his face somewhere between anxious and pensive. It was not a look I liked at any time, but especially not while he was eating my mom's special waffles. These things were like heaven on a plate so whatever was on his mind could not be good. I waited, but when he remained silent I stopped eating to see what he wanted.

"You don't have a show tonight, right?"

I shook my head. "No, we have rehearsal for a few hours this afternoon, but that's it."

"I'd like you to come to a drop with me."

"A drop?" I had a feeling I knew what he meant, but I wanted to make sure.

"A payment. I have a client meeting me at the box tonight."

The box.

It was one of the *last* places I wanted to go, and Ashton knew that. He had to. There had to be a reason he wanted me to go with him.

"Can I ask why?"

He leaned toward me taking one of my hands in his. "Last night you agreed to stay with me—to be mine. The only way I'll know if you can accept the life I lead is if you come and see exactly what it is we do."

My eyes dropped to the floor. "I've seen what you do—first hand, remember?"

A finger slid under my chin, forcing my gaze back up. "I know there are a lot of bad memories for you there, but if you hadn't been there that night, we wouldn't be together now. It's different being on the other side. Trust me."

I warred with myself, unsure of what to do. If I went, could I push away the bad memories long enough to observe objectively, or would it bother me too much?

Either way, sitting there, watching Ashton, I knew he wasn't doing this just for me. He was doing it for us. This was my opportunity to show him that I trusted him.

"Okay."

He smiled and all the tension left his body, and I knew I'd made the right call. Whether or not I would be completely cut out for this, I didn't know. But I at least owed it to Ashton to give it a try.

* * *

A little bit after breakfast, Ashton left for The Bluewater Grill. He had a lot of work to do and not a lot of time to do it in. While he was at work, I spent the day on the phone with Arthur, trying to see if we could get the paperwork for a contested divorce expedited. I knew Dominic wouldn't sign, but I guess somewhere in the back of my mind, I hoped he might make it easy on me for once.

Yeah right.

My stomach churned while I showered and got dressed for the day. From the moment I'd come to stay with Ashton, he'd taught me to be independent; to stand up for myself; to recognize that I was worth someone's love. I had a hard time equating that man with the one who collected debts, threatening people who didn't pay. I didn't want seeing him in action to cloud my opinion of him.

When it was time to leave, Brock met me out front. I very nearly blanked him, my mind still lost in this morning's conversation.

"Hey, Elena," Brock called out when I reached the car.

His voice startled me out of my thoughts. "Hi, Brock." Ashton had talked to me the night before about Brock staying with me when he wasn't able to. After the events of the day before, he was worried what else Dominic might try. If he made bail, that was.

"You all right?" He opened the car door for me.

"Yeah. Just stuck in my head today."

"Don't worry, that piece of shit won't get anywhere near you," he said through clenched teeth.

I smiled at the harsh tone in his voice. It probably should have scared me, the menace radiating from him, but it didn't. It filled me with relief. For the first time someone was willing to protect me.

"I know. It's not him. I know you and Ashton won't let him near me." For some unknown reason, I felt like opening up to someone. Brock, who didn't seem like the feeling type, happened to be the only one with me, besides Lewis, so he was my only option.

"I'm more worried about going with Ashton tonight."

"To the game?" His brow creased.

TRADED

"I've only ever seen Ashton like . . . *that* one time, and it was a day I prefer to forget."

He shrugged. "It's in the past. I know Mrs. Hawes went with Mr. Hawes one time. He swears it's the main reason they've stayed married so long."

"He did?"

Although it surprised me to hear, I could see his point.

Brock nodded once.

"Are you telling me that Ashton wants me to go so his business won't interfere with our relationship?"

"Yeah. I know he wasn't all that keen, but I'd be willing to bet Mr. Hawes or Miller talked him to it."

A warmth spread through me at Brock's reasoning, yet it wasn't enough to alleviate the queasy feeling I'd had since breakfast.

"It'll be fine," he said, as we pulled up to the theater. "Ashton talked to Alan and he's okay with me sitting in the back throughout rehearsals.

"Sounds good to me."

Brock stepped out of the car first and helped me out. "Don't worry, he's still in jail. We'll know if and when he gets out."

"Okay."

I had no idea what Dominic was capable of. He'd never put a hand on me before, but the crazed look in his eyes didn't leave me with a whole lot of comfort. It was clear that he was far from stable; especially now the three months were up and I hadn't returned home. But Brock's presence made me feel safe, and I had to trust that he would look out for me.

For the next few hours I tried to push all of it from my mind. If my performance was affected, Alan didn't mention anything. But when rehearsal ended, he pulled me aside.

"Is everything okay? I heard you and Ashton disappeared after the police let him go."

I forced a smile. "It is. I'm still getting used to the idea of living with Ashton permanently. Obviously, the last time I agreed to live with a man things didn't turn out so well."

"Ashton is nothing like that piece of shit you were married to. Besides, he needs someone like you in his life."

"Why do you say that?"

"Ashton is consumed by his work. He needs someone to remind him that life isn't all about money." He smiled.

I flung my arms around his neck and placed a quick kiss to his cheek. "Thank you. I needed to hear that today."

"You're welcome. Now get going, before Brock goes crazy."

I practically danced up the aisle, finally feeling more confident. For the first time since we'd met, I could be something more for Ashton. I was beginning to believe that we had potential, that we could make it. And not only that; other people could see it too. It was a heady feeling of content mixed with excitement. It was unfamiliar, but definitely not unwelcome.

Brock watched me prance out to the car while he walked behind me, muttering something unintelligible under his breath. But I didn't care.

TRADED

My good mood was infectious. He'd soon be smiling again.

Not that I'd ever seen Brock smile . . . not that I could recall.

When I arrived back at the house there were still a few hours before Ashton came home, so I decided on a hot bubble bath. The steam from the warm water relaxed my tired muscles as I sunk lower into the water. My eyes slid closed and I inhaled deeply, the scent of lavender washing over me. It was bliss.

A soft knock at the door brought me out of my daze. There in the doorframe stood Ashton, his heated gaze glued to the receding bubbles at my chest.

"Fuck. If we didn't need to be somewhere, I'd climb in with you." A salacious smiled curved his lips.

Swirling my fingers through the bubbles, I teased him. "Wouldn't that be fun."

"Get out of the tub, before I spank your cute little ass again."

I'd let him try that one night a few weeks ago and his words evoked a memory that made my core ache. Needless to say, I hadn't been disappointed.

Sinking my teeth into my bottom lip, I stood and stepped out of the tub, making sure every movement was slow and exaggerated. We didn't have time, I knew that, but that didn't mean I couldn't have some fun.

He groaned and took a step back. "I'll be downstairs. If I come anywhere near you, we won't be leaving the house tonight."

Ashton knew exactly how to boost a girl's courage. "In that case, I'll be down in a few," I said, batting my eyelashes. He shook his head, a smile on his lips before he headed through the door, mumbling all the way.

As soon as he left I raced to get ready, grabbing a salmon sundress from the closet and plucking matching accessories from my ever expanding closet. I had more clothes now than I'd had my entire life. Ashton really needed to stop spending money on me. But we'd talk about that later.

When I was finally ready, I went downstairs to meet Ashton, who I found in the foyer, keys in hand. He paced the floor to the point he could have worn a hole in it. The sound of my shoes hitting the floor must have caught his attention, because he turned around and froze.

"Damn. Wet and naked you were edible. That dress . . ." He blew out a long breath through pursed lips, "I could bend you over the nearest surface and fuck you until you can't walk tomorrow."

I had to squeeze my legs together to keep from running over and jumping him. He grabbed my hand and pulled me out the door. "Let's go. I only have so much control. Just know this—your body's mine when we get home."

Trying to rile him up even more, I grabbed his ass. Then, without warning, I was moving, my back up against the car, Ashton devouring my lips. Before I could even process what had just happened, he broke the connection and opened my door.

TRADED

"After you." He gestured into the car.

I stared at him for a few moments, unable to catch my breath. When he didn't move I climbed in, watching him as he shut my door and moved around to his side. After we pulled out onto the road, I turned to him.

"What was that all about?"

"That," he said with a smirk, "was to get you as riled up as me, you tease. Now I'm not the only horny one."

No doubt about it.

Shifting in my seat, I tried to ease the need pulsing between my legs, but nothing seemed to help.

"Don't worry," he whispered. "I'll take care of that when we get home."

Thoughts of him "taking care of me" distracted me the entire ride, and it wasn't until the car stopped that I noticed we'd arrived at the ballpark. Walking hand and hand with Ashton, I was confident. At least, until we reached the hallway with the bank of elevators for the club boxes.

Memories of my last walk down the hall assaulted me, taunting me, bringing back the familiar feelings of doubt and fear. I drew a deep breath in through my nose but it was no use. They still plagued me. By the time we reached the box, I was a jumbled mess of nerves. The confidence I'd built up at the house had slipped away. My stomach was in absolute knots.

"Elena, what's wrong?" Ashton was concerned, but I couldn't spoil this for him. It must have taken a lot for him to bring me here; to trust me with everything that this entailed.

Knowing what I knew, I could bring down his whole family—everything generation after generation of Haweses had worked for. It might not be legitimate, but it was still a legacy. This was a huge leap of faith on his part. I had to show him it wasn't unfounded.

"Nothing." My eyes looked everywhere and nowhere at the same time. "It just feels weird being here again."

Placing one hand on the small of my back, he guided me over to one of the chairs near the window. "Sit and watch the game while I get us drinks."

He left me but returned within minutes, handing me a glass. I smelled the white wine before I saw it and I pulled back, the drink almost dropping to the floor. His hand reached out and gripped the stem before it left my fingers.

"Elena?"

I stared wide-eyed at the window. "Too many memories."

Ashton stepped into my line of sight and knelt in front of me. "Yes, but this time is different. You're different. Now you're *mine*."

He slid his hand around the nape of my neck and guided my mouth to his. The soft caress ended the second his tongue slipped through my lips. Then his kiss took on the erotic rhythm of his body thrusting in and out of mine. If I'd thought I was needy in the car, it was nothing compared to this moment. The clearing of a throat broke us apart.

"Sorry, I didn't mean to interrupt." Brock lifted one eyebrow and crossed the room.

TRADED

My face flamed, and I had a hard time making eye contact with Brock. How did I let myself get carried away every time I was in Ashton's presence? No matter the reason, I still wanted him. I let my body cool with the realization that a little bit longer and I would have begged Ashton to take me right there in the club box. The meeting couldn't be over soon enough for me.

"It's fine," Ashton said. "We were just about to order dinner."

That was news to me, but I went along with it in an effort to distract myself. It would be a long night otherwise.

We picked our meals and Ashton called down to the kitchen. When he came back, he took the seat next to me, with Brock taking a seat on one of the chairs on the other side of me.

"Did everything go okay at rehearsal?"

I nodded. "It did. Although, I think Brock might have been a bit bored." I nudged him with my elbow and he smirked.

"Nah, it was fine."

"Good, because I want him to go with you from now on."

Brock's eyes narrowed.

"Dominic made bail this afternoon," Ashton explained, his face stoic. He was silent for a moment, letting that bit of information sink in. Then he turned to me. "What kind of moves have they taught you in your self-defense classes?"

"Mostly how to escape if someone grabs us. A knee to the crotch, a head butt. Oh, and how to knock someone off you if they have you pinned."

Ashton's fingers caressed my face. "All things I'm glad you'll know with that asshole roaming the streets."

That reminded me. Yesterday, Ashton had been arrested for kidnapping me. "Should you be doing this today? After being arrested yesterday, I mean."

He shrugged. "It goes with the territory. If we back down because the police search our businesses looking for evidence—evidence they are never going to find—then we look weak to our clients. We can't have them thinking they won't have to pay us back if the police are involved."

Brock added, "With Ashton taking the meeting tonight, it proves that they still need to pay the money back—that the police can't do a thing to stop it."

Before I could respond, there was a sharp knock at the door, and my heart leaped to my throat. The door opened slowly and a cart was wheeled in.

Our food.

I swallowed, trying to cover up just how scared I'd been. The memories of that first night were a bit fuzzy after Dominic left. My stomach started to rumble. I hadn't been in the mood to eat much throughout the day. I got about two bites into my meal when another knock sounded. That one had to be the man there to meet Ashton.

Brock stood and walked over to open the door. A small, portly man with thinning black hair walked in, a book bag on his back. He was dressed like every other guy in the stadium: shorts, jersey, and sneakers. There was nothing conspicuous about him. Had I seen him in the hallway, I would never have believed he was there to pay off a loan shark.

"Anthony."

I glanced to my left and was shocked at what I saw. The man with the smile that could melt my heart was no longer sitting next to me. In his place, was a man with a look of cold determination in his eyes.

I noticed the slight tremor to the guy's hands. He looked at me for a second but seeing Ashton's face he quickly averted his gaze.

"Mr. Hawes. I . . . umm . . . I have a problem."

"And, what would that be." Ashton's tone was cool and clipped, not what I was used to hearing.

"I . . . uh . . . only have . . . uh . . . part of the money." Anthony stuttered his response. Clearly he was terrified.

And I was about to see why.

"What? I don't think I heard you right." Ashton didn't shout, like I expected. He didn't even raise his voice. Instead his words were low, menacing, and it hit me that this kind of calm was a prelude to danger. Brock stood, his shoulders hunched, hands clenched into fists at his sides.

Brock made me feel safe in his presence, but I knew the man in front of me didn't feel the same way. And rightly so. I remembered how I'd felt the first time I saw him. Brock was an imposing individual. It'd taken me months to get used to him.

It took all of my willpower not to say or do anything. Ashton and Brock had been doing this for years. Whatever their plan, I needed to watch and see it fall into place if I were to make a fair decision about this part of his life.

"Mr. Hawes—"

Ashton put his hand up and Anthony immediately closed his mouth.

"How much?"

Anthony swallowed hard. "Seventy-five thousand."

"Twenty-five thousand short."

"Yes, sir."

Ashton steepled his fingers in front of his face and stared at Anthony. After a few more seconds, he finally spoke.

"You're lucky I'm in a good mood today." Anthony bobbed his head up and down, setting the bag down while Ashton continued speaking. "Since this is the first time you've been short, I'm going to give you another chance. You have two weeks." Anthony's shoulders relaxed, but it was too soon. "But you'll bring me forty thousand, won't you?"

"Yes, sir, Mr. Hawes. I can do that."

He wasted no time backing toward the door. When his hand closed over the handle, Ashton called out his final warning. "Just remember—you turn up light again, we won't be having a discussion like this."

"Yes, yes. Thank you Mr. Hawes."

Ashton didn't even take the time to watch the man leave. He simply picked up his knife and fork and resumed eating. And that's when it hit me—Ashton was playing a part. His audience may be smaller, his stage more informal, his performance more intimate, but that's what it was. A performance.

When the curtain went up and the spotlight was on him, he became the character he needed to be. He followed the script his father, and his father before, had written, revised, and perfected. Ashton was no different to me. And if he could accept that I changed when I was doing my job, surely I could accept the same?

I knew Ashton. He wasn't the monster they thought he was. But if I was asked to choose, I'd want him to play his part to perfection. Because Ashton's acting kept him safe.

The minute the door closed, Ashton became the relaxed, sweet man who'd stolen my heart. "What are you thinking about?" Ashton asked, searching my face for answers.

"I'll tell you later." I winked at him and watched as the tension left his shoulders and the creases around his eyes smoothed out.

"Well then, eat your dinner so we can leave. You can tell me on the ride home."

Desire coursed through me. Like water, it found its way to every part of me, and my body thrummed with anticipation. I'd wanted dessert, but the look in Ashton's eyes told me there would be something much more delicious at home.

So I ate my dinner.

Fast.

CHAPTER 30

Elena

We were halfway home when Ashton glanced over at me. "It's later."

I knew exactly what he wanted but I decided to play coy anyway. "I guess that happens when time passes."

He chuckled. "When did you become a smartass?"

"Let's just say I had a great teacher." I took a deep breath, letting my voice take on a serious tone. "I did learn something about you tonight."

His hands twisted around the steering wheel, waiting to hear what I had to say. "And that is?"

"That your *clients* are lucky to deal with you, instead of your brother or father." He glanced over like he wanted to say something, but I continued before he got the chance. "Don't get me wrong, both of them have been wonderful to me since I met them. But I know there's no way

TRADED

they would have let that man out of the box without injury for not having the money. You're willing to give people a second chance when they truly deserve one." I reached over and covered his thigh with my hand. "It may not be the ideal situation, but I understand."

A deep sigh escaped his lips and his grip loosened, the corners of his mouth turning up into a grin. "You make me sound like some kind of knight."

I giggled. "A dark, sexy knight maybe."

"You think I'm sexy?"

Déjà vu made me answer the question the same way he did what seemed like forever ago. "Fuck yes, I think you're sexy."

He groaned. "God, I love it when you curse at me."

Ashton leaned on the accelerator and my back was pushed against the seat. He seemed anxious to get home; but so was I. I could only imagine what he had in store for me when we got home.

Whatever it might be, I was more than ready.

༺༻

A week had passed and there was no sign of Dominic. The divorce papers had been served, and Arthur assured me that he'd already asked for a court date for a contested divorce in case Dominic refused to sign them. Either way, I didn't have to stay married to him.

"Elena, where are you?"

"In your room."

I was getting my things together for the day's shows. Saturdays were hectic because there was a matinee as well as an evening performance.

"How many times do I need to remind you—this is *our* bedroom, not mine."

"Sorry. I'm still trying to get used to it. It's still a little weird for me."

He smiled and wound his arms around my waist. "I wanted to tell you to break a leg tonight. I'm not happy I'm missing both shows."

I still couldn't believe he'd been to every single performance, despite being ridiculously busy with the restaurants and work for Malcolm. Somehow, he always managed to buy the same seat so I knew where to look for him. Even though I didn't mind that he had to work, it was going to be weird looking over to see someone else in "his" seat.

"I know, but missing one isn't a big deal. We still have five weeks of shows left. Besides, you need to deal with that wedding tonight."

"Doesn't mean I have to like it."

"No, it doesn't, but I'll have Brock and Lewis bring me to you when I'm done and we can go get something to eat."

"I think that's a great idea. Are you still okay with Brock and Lewis going with you?"

I nodded. "Yeah. I think Dominic might have skipped town."

"The fucker still owes me money, but losing the money is worth it if it means he stays away from you."

"Everything will be fine. Now go, before you're late. I'll see you tonight."

TRADED

Ashton gave me more than a quick peck to remember him by before leaving for the restaurant. I threw the last few pieces into my bag and headed out.

When we arrived at the theater, I told Brock and Lewis they didn't need to sit through both performances today. I'd be back stage with security. They could come back around nine, which should be a little after intermission.

"Only if you're sure," Brock said.

"I'm positive. Brock, you've been here so much, you know this show as well as I do. I'm safe here, take a break."

He watched me for a second then nodded. "Okay. We're going to grab something to eat down the street. We'll come back every so often to check on you."

"Okay." I smiled.

I wasn't trying to get rid of him—he could have stayed if he really wanted to, but this was the first time he'd have to sit through the show twice on the same day. I just couldn't do that to him. With all of the security in place to keep out the crazies I was fine, as long as I stayed back stage.

That was the thing with having two shows: there wasn't any time to get bored. Between sound checks and costume changes, lunch breaks, and shows, the day passed quickly.

The final performance over, I was in my room, changing to meet Ashton for dinner. Brock had already stopped inside and I'd told him I'd be a few. He searched the place, then told me he'd be in the car waiting. It had been our routine for the last few weeks, ever since Ashton had been arrested. Brock still scared me to a certain degree, but I was beginning to see flashes of the *real* him, and we'd built a good routine. He was a good guy, and I was pleased I had him around to keep an eye on me.

Stepping through the door, the crisp night air wrapped around me cooling my skin. Across the lot sat the Bentley. Everyone else was still inside, having a drink, celebrating the show, but I'd made my excuses, wanting to get to Ashton. It was weirder than I'd thought to not have him watch the show, and I was anxious to get to him.

Two steps toward the car a hand gripped my arm pulling me to a stop. A shudder raced down my spine when the voice spoke next to my ear.

"My dumb little wife thinks she's moved onto bigger and better things, does she?" Dominic's voice slithered across my senses.

"Get your hands off me."

"Fuck that. You're coming home with me, where you belong."

I attempted to jerk my arm out of his grasp. My gaze darted to the car and I realized that he'd pulled me out of their line of sight. Eventually they would come looking for me, but it was still early. I was going to have to deal with Dominic on my own.

"I don't belong anywhere near you. You want a slave you can emotionally destroy, not a wife."

"A wife is supposed to serve her husband in every way."

When he moved his head, I noticed the crazy glint to his eyes. He'd always been cruel to me, but now he looked as if he'd completely lost it. I clenched my fists to keep him from seeing my hands tremble.

"No, marriage is supposed to be a partnership. Ashton has shown me exactly how I deserve to be treated and it's nothing like the way you tortured me."

He growled, slapped me across the face hard enough to bring tears to my eyes and slammed me against the wall of the building. Pain reverberated down my back. With both of his hands holding my upper arms, I used the self-defense training Ashton insisted I learn, and drove my knee up into his groin as hard as I possibly could. He let go of me instantly to cup his crotch.

Run, Elena. Run!

Seeing a clear path, I started to run toward the car. Halfway there I was thrown to the ground by Dominic's weight. Spinning my body, I threw him off but I wasn't fast enough and he jumped to his feet, coming toward me, pulling a pistol out of the back of his pants.

"Now, you're going to come with me quietly, or I'm going to turn this gun on the goons in the car."

There was only one way this could end.

Throwing out my leg, I was able to knock him to the ground. The clang of metal against the concrete drew my attention to the gun that had slipped from his grip. Scrambling forward, I tried to get to the gun first. The second my hand slid around the barrel, I rolled, and pointed the gun at Dominic.

I pulled the trigger and the sound echoed through the lot.

Footsteps pounded across the pavement toward me as Dominic's eyes met mine, his hands covering the hole in his stomach. He dropped to his knees.

There was blood.

A lot of it.

Everywhere.

"Elena," Brock shouted, grabbing Dominic's shirt and pushing him away from me.

Lewis pulled his phone out of his pocket, calling first the police then Ashton. Brock sat next to me, taking the gun from my hand. "Are you okay, Elena?"

The sight of Dominic's body, oozing life, held me immobile.

"Physically she's fine." Their voices sounded like they were coming down a tunnel. "Yeah, I'm not sure she'll answer. She seems to be in shock. Of course I called the fucking police. No reason for us to clean up this mess. She was defending herself. Hold on."

A phone was pushed into my hand and raised to my ear.

"Elena?"

I couldn't speak. My voice was trapped.

"She's listening," a male voice called out. "Just talk to her."

"Elena, babe, please listen to me. I'm on my way." Horns blared in the background. "I know you didn't want to hurt him, but he left you no choice.

Sirens came closer and closer.

TRADED

"Elena, please talk to me. I love you. Please."

Something in Ashton's pleading tone snapped me out of it. "Ashton?" I whispered.

"Yeah, baby, it's good to hear your voice. I'll be there soon. Are you okay?"

Flashing lights surrounded us.

"The police are here." My tone was flat, unfeeling.

"Elena, please keep talking to me. Just listen to my voice."

Police were everywhere, yelling for us to put our hands in the air. I didn't want to lose my connection to Ashton, but I had no choice. I dropped the phone to the asphalt and held up my hands, palms out.

After determining we weren't armed, the officers separated us. They took me to a medic, who looked me over as they began to question me about what happened.

"Elena," Ashton called from behind the police tape.

They wouldn't let him through. Didn't they understand that I needed him? Ignoring the officer talking to me, I spun and ran toward Ashton. The second his arms wrapped around me I lost it, heavy sobs ripping from my body as I collapsed against him. Eventually they let Ashton through when they realized it would be the only way to get me to finish answering questions.

Somewhere in the back of my mind, I heard Brock and Lewis apologize to Ashton. I continued to answer questions. My whole body was functioning on autopilot. It was so bad, I barely noticed Ashton leading me to his car and helping me inside.

The entire drive home, I stared out the window. Dominic's lifeless body wouldn't leave my thoughts.

We pulled up outside the house and Ashton left the car at the curb, lifting me and carrying me through the front door. He set me down in the kitchen, getting a cloth and wiping at my skin, checking me over. I wasn't even sure where I was hurt at that point.

His fingers brushed over my cheek and I flinched. His hands were shaking. He clenched his fists.

"If that motherfucker wasn't already dead, I kill him myself."

Once again, my eyes filled with tears and he cursed under his breath.

"Babe, I didn't mean to upset you. I'm just so fucking angry I wasn't there to protect you."

"I . . . killed . . . a man," I cried.

Ashton pulled me to him, his hand sliding up into my hair to hold my head to his chest. "Oh, baby, I know. But you had to. You have no idea how much I wish I was the person who could have done that for you."

For long moments he held me in his arms. The scent of his cologne started to have an effect on me. I wanted him and I wanted him badly. Gazing up, I saw the same needed reflected back at me.

And then his mouth was on mine. His tongue slipped inside, caressing every inch and dancing with mine.

TRADED

"Elena, I need you so fucking bad. I need to know you're okay. If you don't want this, say now."

I ran my fingers down his face. "You can have me anytime."

The first thing to hit the floor was my shirt, then my bra, quickly followed by Ashton's shirt. Our lips reconnected, his thumb brushing over my hardened nipple and the feeling shot through me, straight to my core. I was Ashton's musical instrument and damn he was an expert at playing me.

His lips moved down my neck, stopping to suck on my pulse point, then moved lower until they closed around my nipple, almost causing my knees to buckle. Pushing me flush against the door, he held my weight up with his own.

I need more.

His hands and mouth weren't enough. My hips started grinding against his. When one of his hands slipped up underneath my skirt, pushing my panties to the side until his fingers brushed over my exposed clit, my hips bucking of their own volition.

"Please, again."

I didn't care that I was begging.

I needed to come.

I wanted him inside me.

His fingers flicked over my clit again. "Please, I don't need slow and sweet, I need you to fuck me."

His eyes widened for a moment, then lust took over and his belt was off and his pants unzipped in a matter of seconds, his cock bobbing freely in front of him. He didn't even bother taking off my skirt and panties. Lifting me by the ass, he plunged deep inside.

The feeling was exquisite.

"You feel so fucking good," he growled.

"Please, move."

I didn't need to ask twice. My body was forced against the wall, his thrusts quick and sharp until I could feel my muscles tightening, my body reaching for its peak. I knew Ashton was close. His eyes bore straight into mine and I saw dazed passion in his unfocused gaze.

As my body went down in fire quicker than I ever thought possible, I cried out, repeating his name over and over until I was hoarse. Ashton followed almost immediately, his breath coming in sharp pants.

There was a thud as his head hit the door behind me. Slowly, we regained our strength and I unhooked my legs from around his waist, allowing him to set my feet back on the floor.

Ashton stared into my eyes, lightly caressing the bruise that was most likely forming right beneath my eye. "Elena, I love you so much. You are my whole world."

Tears blurred my vision and I couldn't stop them from falling. "I love you too. Thank you for saving me."

"I didn't save you. You saved yourself."

And for the first time in my entire life, I felt at peace. I had a wonderful man who loved me and who showed me how true love should be. He taught me to stand on my own two feet and introduced me to a world of pleasure I'd never known before.

TRADED

I was pretty sure life couldn't get any better.

EPILOGUE

Ashton

Five weeks had passed since the night Elena was forced to kill her ex-husband to save her own life, and it was taking time for her mind to heal. After a thorough investigation, the police declared it self-defense, but it was hard to get Elena to see that at first. Nightmares plagued her, making her restless and tired. I did my best to wear her out each night. Exhausting her so she had no option but to sleep.

But none of it stopped her from going to the theater each night, performing her best. She proved to me that you can do anything you put your mind to.

It gave me the courage to talk to my dad about his business. Elena made me realize that it was better for me to collect the debts than Miller or my dad. Apparently, I was more sympathetic. Either way, I agreed to collect debts only. The loans had to be taken out with them.

TRADED

It was her final performance. She'd told me that, while she was sad to see it end, she was excited to keep increasing her experience in the theater world. Alan said she could work on any show he had. That brought a smile to her face so large I wanted to sponsor a show for him just to see it again.

The lights dimmed and I sat and waited for my favorite part of the play. The curtains opened and her voice took over. It was beautiful and soothing. Then she entered the stage and all thoughts of the rest of the show fled my mind.

The gorgeous vixen standing on stage was the woman of my dreams. We might have got here through some fucked up circumstances, but I wouldn't trade a moment with her. More than anything, I wanted her to be my wife. Someday she'd be ready, and when she was, I'd be there waiting to slip a ring on her finger.

Who would have guessed when I walked into the stadium that night, that I wouldn't just be trading for money, but for the rest of my life.

ACKNOWLEDGEMENTS

Writing Traded was a new experience for me. Taking on a subject like domestic abuse was harder than I expected. Not only for the difficulty of writing, but the emotional experience that comes with it. So many times I wanted to yell at Elena and I had to remind myself of all she'd been through. All of that abuse shaped her into the woman she was, but she rose above it, proving that we all deserve to be treated like a princess. Never settle for less.

Sommer and Lauren, this cover is beyond anything I ever imagined. From the beauty of the picture to the way the design represents Elena and Ashton's story. Thank you for bringing my vision to life.

Writing about something outside of my comfort zone took so much, but with a story like this research can only get you so far. Mecca, I can't thank you enough for your expertise. You helped me to understand everything Elena had gone through.

Kelley, Christine, and Miranda, thank you for all of your beta notes. Each set helps me to improve my writing bit by bit. I also must thank you for spreading the word about my books and introducing me to new readers.

TRADED

As always, Brandy, thank you for listening and letting me bounce ideas off of you. Just talking it out helps me every time I get stuck. Thank you for pushing me and helping me to get this story done.

Ryn, I've missed you. You take my words and make them pretty. Let's just say, punctuation is not my friend. You helped me to take Traded to a whole new level. Thank you so much for everything.

ALSO BY REBECCA BROOKE

Forgiven Series:
Forgiven
Redemption
Healed
Acceptance

Standalone Titles:
Letters Home
Coming Home
Beautiful Lessons
Ryder
Traded

The Folstad Prophecies:
Twin Runes

Coming Soon:
Second Chances
Binding Consequences

ABOUT THE AUTHOR

Rebecca Brooke grew up in the shore towns of South Jersey. She loves to hit the beach, but always with her kindle on hand. She is married to the most wonderful man, who puts up with all of her craziness. Together they have two beautiful children who keep her on her toes. When she isn't writing or reading (which is very rarely) she loves to bake and watch episodes of Shameless and True Blood.

Facebook
https://www.facebook.com/Rebecca-Brooke-Author

Twitter
@RebeccaBrooke6

Website
www.rebeccabrooke.com

Made in the USA
Middletown, DE
22 August 2025